Walter Lock

John Keble

Walter Lock

John Keble

ISBN/EAN: 9783337399597

Printed in Europe, USA, Canada, Australia, Japan

Cover: Foto ©Andreas Hilbeck / pixelio.de

More available books at **www.hansebooks.com**

JOHN KEBLE

A BIOGRAPHY

BY

WALTER LOCK, M.A.

FELLOW OF ST. MARY MAGDALEN COLLEGE, AND SUB-WARDEN OF
KEBLE COLLEGE, OXFORD

WITH A PORTRAIT FROM A PAINTING BY GEORGE RICHMOND, R.A.

Methuen & Co.

18, BURY STREET, LONDON, W.C.

1893

SORORI MEÆ

HAS PRIMITIAS

QUAS IPSA FOVIT, AUXIT, CASTIGAVIT,

GRATUS DEDICO.

PREFACE.

Two reasons give a special appropriateness to the publication of a memoir of Mr. Keble at the present time.

This year is the hundredth anniversary of his birth, a fact which reminds us how quickly time is flying, and in its flight bearing off those who could speak of him with first-hand knowledge.

Again, much has been published of late throwing light on the Oxford Movement; *The Oxford Movement*, by Dean Church, *The Letters and Correspondence of J. H. Newman, The Autobiography of Isaac Williams*, are books of very varied character, but they all agree in one point: they all bear a strong witness to the force, the originality, the stimulating power of that character whose humility and self-repression have often caused his real work to be undervalued.

This memoir will be found, it is hoped, more complete than any yet published. I have been allowed access to much unpublished correspondence, and have had the privilege of intercourse with personal friends of Mr. Keble, and I wish to express my warmest thanks to those who have helped me in either of these ways.

But the memoir is not complete. I have not had access to all the correspondence. There is much still to be examined and sifted and published, and I can only hope that this volume may serve for a time to revive the memory of its subject, and may then pass away before the completer account of him that ought to be given to the world. It ought to be given to the world, for there is scarcely a letter or a treatise of his through which there does not shine some glimpse of the beauty of the writer's character, from which the reader does not rise without a sense of being brought nearer to the Presence of God.

WALTER LOCK.

Feast of SS. Simon and Jude, 1892.

CONTENTS.

JOHN KEBLE.

CHAPTER I.

PREPARATION FOR THE WORK OF LIFE, 1792—1832.

> "Voice of the meekest man,
>   Now while the Church for combat arms,
> Calmly do thou confirm her awful ban,
>   Thy words to her be conquering, soothing charms.
>
>   Voice of the fearless saint!
>   Ring like a trump where gentle hearts
> Beat high for truth, but doubting lower and faint.
>   Tell them the hour is come, and they must take
>   their parts."
>   J. K., *Miscellaneous Poems*, p. 36,
>   (of R. Hooker.)

JOHN KEBLE sprang from a family which had originally come from Suffolk, but had since the sixteenth century been settled in Gloucestershire. One of his ancestors, Sir Henry Keble, grocer, had been Lord Mayor of London in 1511, and had been noted for his liberality towards the rebuilding of Aldermanbury Church and towards other charities; a descendant of his, Richard Keble, purchased the manor of East Leech Turville, in Gloucestershire, which remained in his

B

family till the beginning of the eighteenth century. At the end of that century the representative of this family was the father of the subject of this memoir, himself also the Rev. John Keble, who, after being a Scholar and Fellow of Corpus Christi College, Oxford, had married a lady of Scotch descent, Sarah Maule, the daughter of the incumbent of Ringwood in Hampshire, and had settled at Fairford in Gloucestershire, as Vicar of the neighbouring parish of Coln St. Aldwyn's. Here, on St. Mark's Day, 1792, John Keble was born, being thus eight years older than Dr. Pusey (1800), nine than Cardinal Newman (1801), ten than Isaac Williams (1802), eleven than Hurrell Froude (1803). He was privately baptized the next day, and publicly received into the Church in July. He was educated entirely by his father at home, and even if he owed to that, as he himself thought in later years, a certain desultoriness in study and a want of practical knowledge of the world, yet it was probably far the best course for one of his shy, sensitive temperament: he grew up with a fresh genuine interest in classics and mathematics, in English literature and history; with an unquestioning deference to his parent's wishes, with a warmth of affectionateness to brother and sister, in which he never failed, which affected his movements at each change in his life, and which stood him in good stead again and again, especially in the great strain of Newman's secession. In his life, as in that of St. Andrew, "Christ laid the foundations of the Church on brotherly love." [1]

The family consisted of five members, the eldest, Elizabeth (1790—1860), "his wife," as he used playfully to call her, who was nearly all her life an invalid, and,

[1] *Sermons, Occasional and Academical*, p. 275.

as such, shy and nervous at first with strangers, yet
gradually winning upon them by her sweetness and
religious spirit, and who for many years shared his
home at Hursley and his work and hopes for the
Church. "I wish you could see my father and eldest
sister," he wrote once to Coleridge; "to me they are
uniques." Then came John, born in 1792; then Thomas,
in 1793, who followed him as a scholar to Corpus Christi
College, then became Fellow and Tutor there, then acted
as curate to his father, finally settling as vicar at Bisley
in Gloucestershire. With him nearly every scheme of
action was discussed: he was a contributor to the *Tracts
for the Times,* helped John with the edition of Hooker,
the Library of the Fathers, and the *Plain Sermons;*
and was ever felt to be a steadying influence upon his
life. "I was myself inclined to eclecticism at one time
(he wrote in 1838), and had it not been for my father
and brother, where I should have been now, who can
say?" Then came Sarah (1796—1814), whose death
formed the first gap in the circle; and lastly, Mary
Anne (1799—1826), his "sweetheart," the bright, fresh,
merry-hearted one, who wanted every one to live in sun-
shine, to whom he was accustomed to talk more freely
than to any one else in the world, and who was probably
the strongest influence upon his life until the time of
her early unexpected death. Both she and Elizabeth
were highly cultured and religious, and we find them
reading Italian and French with their brother, and also
with great enjoyment Butler's *Analogy,* Hooker's *Ecclesiastical Polity,* and Strype's *Lives of the Archbishops.*
The traditions of the family were Cavalier and Non-
juring; in later years Dr. Pusey recalled to Keble the
way in which the latter's words about the Stuarts had

been one of the first things that broke through his
Liberalist tendencies. "I was thoughtlessly, or rather
I must say confidently, taking it for granted that the
Stuarts were rightly dethroned, when I heard for the
first time a hint to the contrary from you. Your
seriousness was an unintended reproof to my petulant
expression about it; so it stuck by me, though it was
some time before it took root and burst through all
the clods placed upon it." Later still, in answer to
some depreciatory opinion of Dr. Pusey's about the
Nonjurors, Keble replied, "I cannot think that the
Nonjurors' position was so very bad or useless an one.
I seem to trace our present life in good measure to it."

From such a home he came up to Oxford, "a fresh,
glad, bright, joyous boy."[1] After an unsuccessful attempt
at Magdalen College, he was elected in December 1806
to an open scholarship at Corpus Christi College, and
entered into residence at the beginning of 1807, while
still under fifteen years of age. His college life was not
eventful; he threw himself heartily into lectures, and
forty years later dedicates his volume of *Sermons* to
his tutor, the Rev. W. N. Darnell, "in ever grateful
memory of invaluable helps and warnings received
from him in early youth;" he also shared fully the
social life of his college, and his letters contain several
references to the Common Room parties held at the
end of each term, and kept with difficulty within due
limits of sobriety. "Our Common Room party was
yesterday," he writes once to his brother, "when I had
the hardest trial I have yet gone through in Oxford in
avoiding 'intostication.' However, they were on this
occasion much more sober than they have been on

---

[1] Dr. Pusey, in the *Keble College Proceedings*, 1868, p. 43.

former." He wrote frequently, but never successfully, for the prize for English Poetry; and several of his poems composed in this '*Scene of my Earliest Harpings*,' will be found in the *Miscellaneous Poems*. He calls it *Home of my Muse and of my Friends*, and it is as home of his friends that it had most influence on his after-life. The college was a small college, lending itself to close intimacies, and it contained at this time a number of striking members. There was J. T. Coleridge, elected in 1809, fresh from Eton, full of enthusiasm for the poetry of his uncle and of Wordsworth—Coleridge, who remained to the end of his life the firm friend and wise adviser whom Keble always consulted in any ecclesiastical questions which were connected with the law of the State, and who lived to be his affectionate biographer. There was Noel Ellison, "the genial, joyous, graceful Ellison," also elected in 1809, who afterwards became Tutor of Balliol, and Rector of Huntspill; John Tucker, "the single-hearted and devout," who became a missionary in India; G. J. Cornish, elected in 1810, a man of keen sensibility, of poetic taste, but quiet retiring character, who, after becoming Fellow and Tutor of his college, withdrew to parochial life, and from 1828—1849 was Vicar of Kenwyn, above Truro. He is author of the poem on the Redbreast, quoted in the *Christian Year*, and the strength of Keble's affection for him is measured by the words he wrote to a friend on his death, "My dear Dyson, do ask for me that I may meet *him* again." Then there was C. Dyson, to whom these words were written, rather senior to the other friends, perhaps the most intimate of all, the fastidious critic, the wise, cheering, cultured friend, whose influence was mainly effectual in procuring the publication of the *Christian Year*, and whom Keble seldom omitted to consult at important moments of his life. Last of all, not elected till 1811, but at once admitted into this circle, was Thomas Arnold, the eager, enthusiastic, religious Liberal, who differed from Keble in almost every point, and yet wound himself very closely round his heart. "The more I see of Arnold, the more I love him," he wrote in 1816; and in 1819, "I hardly know any one now that Dyson is gone (from Oxford), who would be so great a loss to me." To him Arnold turned when in great religious perplexity, and found comfort and peace in his advice. The line that Arnold took in later years seemed to him so "wilful and presumptuous in his way of dealing with holy things," that he felt that he could not regard him as a fellow-labourer in the same cause. This was his feeling in 1832, but the break with him had been a severe strain upon himself, and he writes in 1840, "I have had an Easter letter from Arnold, so kind and mitigated in tone that I cannot but be comforted by it, and in time I trust he may come nearer to Church views. I feel somehow that we are nearer to each other than we have been."

To these friends in college should be added one out-college friend, John Miller of Worcester College. He was some years senior, having taken his degree in 1808, and Keble always regarded him with very great reverence for his seriousness, and loved him for his genial merriment. Miller's Bampton Lectures for 1817, upon "the Divine authority of Holy Scripture from its adaptation to the Real State of Human Nature," impressed his mind very much by its cautious tone, its tender and scrupulous respect for the simple faith of the poor, and its deep reverence in the treatment of the Bible. In 1829 he called him "the most original divine of our days," and one sentence from the Bampton Lectures seems to have suggested the poem for St. Bartholomew's Day in the *Christian Year;* another sentence in one of his sermons suggested the title of the volume.

It has been worth while to dwell upon this group of friends, for with the one exception of Arnold, they were friendships for life kept up by visits and correspondence, and never without their influence upon him. But their main influence was that of the Oxford days. They did that which was all-important for the shy, sensitive, home-bred boy; they gave him confidence in himself by the unrestrained way in which they admitted him to their confidence. In many a college society such a temperament would have withered and shrunk into itself; in this kindly warmth it grew and blossomed. All the natural gaiety of heart, all the frolicsome humour which characterizes his home letters, reappears in his letters to these friends. Just as his brother and sisters have their comic nicknames, so it is with these friends. The wise Miller is "Hooker"; Arnold is "the sheep"; Cornish "the monkey"; Dyson is "Jeremiah," or "The Venerable Bede," or "Simorg"; his own brother is "Thomas Aquinas"; J. Tucker is the "Queen of Babylon," or "Bab," or "Semiramis," and is spoken of always as "she." Thus when he left Corpus Christi he carried away a stronger self-confidence; and he carried away also a wider knowledge of English literature, and a love and reverence for the memory of one of the noblest names of which the college could boast— Richard Hooker.

In the summer of 1810, when he was only a little over eighteen, he obtained the very rare distinction of a double first-class in Classics and Mathematics. As it was then common for Bachelors to reside, he continued in Corpus Christi until, on April 21, 1811, just before his nineteenth birthday, he was elected to an open Fellowship at Oriel College; Whateley, afterwards Archbishop of Dublin, being elected at the same time. In the following year he gained both the Chancellor's Essays, the English Essay on Translation from Dead Languages, the Latin on a comparison between Xenophon and Julius Cæsar as Military Historians. It was the most brilliant academical career of his time. It "invested him with a bright halo and something of awe in the eyes of an undergraduate." [1] Twelve years later the young Newman writes, "I shall only mention Keble. At eighteen he took two first classes. Soon after he gained the two Essays in one year and a Fellowship at Oriel. *He is the first man in Oxford.*" [2]

The two leading spirits in the Common Room at this time were Copleston and Davison; of these the latter became a firm and life-long friend of Keble. It was at his suggestion that the last poems of the *Christian Year* were written, and after his death Keble helped to edit his *Remains.* But he was never quite at home in the Oriel Common Room in the sense in which he had been at Corpus Christi. The tone was one of vigorous, rough-and-ready discussion of all things under heaven and earth, wanting in tenderness and reverence; he was shy of the criticism of "the Oriel wags"; among them, he seemed to Newman, "more

---

[1] I. Williams, *Autobiography*, p. 17.
[2] *Letters*, i., p. 75.

like an undergraduate than the first man in Oxford, so perfectly unaffected and unassuming in his manner;"[1] and the way in which Pusey and Newman in 1828 failed to understand Keble's character is a sufficient proof how little he had been really quite himself there.

At first he had no college work, and was busy with his own reading and with private pupils, taking reading parties in the vacation and paying visits to his friends; and many of the early poems published afterwards in the *Miscellaneous Poems* bear witness to the brightness and hopes of this time. In 1813 he refused the offer of a Sub-Librarianship at the Bodleian Library. He was Public Examiner in the Final Schools from 1814—1816; Master of the Schools in 1816; and Public Examiner again 1821—1823. One of these occasions is specially interesting; as he listened to one of his fellow-examiners assigning the class to one of the candidates, his mind wandered off to think of the future that might be in store for the Examiner himself, and the result was the poem in the *Christian Year* for St. John's Day—

> "'Lord, and what shall this man do?'
>   Ask'st thou Christian for thy friend?
> If his love for Christ be true,
>   Christ hath told thee of his end.
> This is he whom God approves,
> This is he whom Jesus loves."

His own reading during these years was very varied; we find him reading Ariosto, Chateaubriand, Madame de Staël, Blackstone's *Commentaries*, Ockley's *History of the Saracens*, Spenser, Wordsworth, Southey, Byron; but his studies were drawing more and more

---

[1] *Letters*, i., p. 72.

towards Theology. He learnt Hebrew, and wrote in
1813, "The study of Divinity grows upon me. There
are so many questions little and great, grammatical,
historical, and metaphysical, to be answered before one
can say that one thoroughly understands a verse of the
Bible, that I almost despair of reading it through on
this side of threescore." Butler's *Analogy*, more than
any other book, except perhaps Aristotle, formed the
staple of his thoughts. Butler's humility of tone, his
sense of the vastness and mystery of the Divine system,
his willingness to confess that he knew but a fringe of
a great subject, his determination not to ignore the
facts of what God has done in favour of an *à priori*
theory of what He ought to do; his strong hold upon
the analogy between nature and religion, lending itself
to Keble's poetic love of treating all material phenomena
as types of spiritual facts; his theory that the intellect
cannot carry us farther than a *probable* result in religion,
and that only faith and love can convert probability
into certainty—these fundamental positions reappear
again and again in Keble's writings; and Newman has
told us how they assumed a new power and meaning
under the influence of Keble's "creative mind"; they
rooted the Sacramental system in the eternal methods
of God's working, and won Newman himself from his
individualism.

Almost immediately after reaching his twenty-third
birthday he was ordained Deacon by the Bishop of Oxford
on Trinity Sunday, 1815, and Priest on Trinity Sunday,
1816: his Fellowship served as a title, although he also
assisted his father at Coln, riding over from Oxford for
the purpose, and in the summer of 1815 he took temporary
charge of the two neighbouring villages of East Leech

and Burthorpe. It seemed to him that "the salvation of one soul was worth more than the framing of the Magna Charta of a thousand worlds," and he approached the work with awe and trembling, and yet with unabated confidence in Christ's power to use his service. The aim that he set before him helps to explain the deep language of self-reproach and remorse which is so strongly marked in the *Christian Year* and in his correspondence. Before the ordination he wrote to Coleridge—

"Pray for me too: pray earnestly, my dear, my best friend, that He would give me His grace, that I may not be altogether unworthy of the sacred office on which I am, rashly I fear, even now entering; but that some souls hereafter may have cause to bless me. Pray that I may be free from vanity, from envy, from discontent, from impure imaginations; that I may not grow weary, nor wander in heart from God's service : that I may not be judging others uncharitably, nor vainly dreaming how they will judge me, at the very moment that I seem most religiously and most charitably employed. Without any foolish affectation of modesty, I can truly say that the nearer the time approaches, the more strongly I feel my own unfitness and unworthiness for the ministry : yet as I hope it is not such but that it may be removed in time by earnest and constant use of the means of grace, I do not think it needful to defer my Ordination, but I want all the help I can get in the awful and difficult preparation : do not therefore forget me in your prayers."

In the preceding year he had lost his sister Sarah, and perhaps this, combined with the tension of the Ordination, produced a tone of melancholy, which

oppressed him at this time and seemed to him wilful
and sinful. Much of the *Christian Year* cannot be
understood without the remembrance of this mood, and
therefore it will be well to add another extract from a
letter to Coleridge—

"Our domestic distresses have furnished me with too
good an excuse for indulging a certain humour calling
itself melancholy, but I am afraid more truly entitled
proud and fantastic, which I find very often at hand,
forbidding me to enjoy the good things and pursue the
generous studies which a kind Providence throws so
richly in my way. . . . I have long known this to be
very wrong, but I never felt the mischief of it so much
as in the midst of your happy family. I felt as if I was
saddening everybody, and thousands and thousands of
resolutions did I make that I would shake off this
selfish remembrance of past and distant calamities, that
I would enjoy myself wherever I went. I trust I shall
be able, though late, to accomplish these good resolutions, and it will be a long and steady course of
self-discipline alone, grounded upon high motives, and
assisted by the prayers, advice, and example of my
relations and friends, which will enable me by God's
blessing to do so."

His life became thus for a couple of years mainly
pastoral; his profession became "my dear delightful
profession": but at the end of 1817 he was recalled to
a more academical life, being appointed Tutor at Oriel.
In January, 1818, he writes to Coleridge that he is going
back "to lay down the laws of γὲ and δὴ to a set of
wriggling watch-consulting undergraduates." The work
was in many ways delightful to him, for tuition seemed
to him a species of Pastoral Care. His sense of a tutor's

responsibility will best be illustrated by words which he wrote years afterwards: "Considerate Catholics know well that there is practically no separating the high and comprehensive views which that name imports from any of the moral branches of education. Silence them as you may on directly theological questions, how are they to deal with ethics or poetry or history, so as not to guide their disciples by the light which the Church throws on all? And there is a yet deeper consideration: they may perhaps think that College Tuition is a branch of the Pastoral Care, at least if they are themselves ordained at God's altar; and then they will have no further alternative—they must either teach Catholicism or not teach at all." [1]

Newman has admitted how he came ultimately to see that Keble's mind was at one with his own in his conception of tutorial work, so that his description of his own tutorial aims might be transferred to Keble; there was the same willingness to spend any effort on his pupils' work (we find Keble working with them sometimes as early as six a.m.), the same attempt to cultivate relations with them not only of intimacy, but of friendship and almost of equality; in Hurrell Froude's words, "Where Keble was, donnishness and humbug would be no more in college, nor the pride of talent nor ignoble secular ambition." [2]

Keble retained this office for six years and formed many lasting intimacies, one with Sir W. Heathcote leading ultimately to his appointment as Vicar of Hursley. One who came into residence just after he

---

[1] *The Case of Catholic Subscription to the XXXIX. Articles,* 1841, p. 12.
[2] J. H. Newman, *Letters,* i., pp. 152—154.

left, and who only saw him when he applied for matricu-
lation, Sir C. Anderson, bears striking testimony, in a
letter written in 1889, to the quiet, powerful effect
which he had upon young men. "I was entered by
Keble when I went up to matriculate, a raw youth of
nineteen. Keble was then Tutor and Resident, and he
examined me, and took me to the Vice-Chancellor to
swear to the Articles, and during the two hours I was
with Keble his manner and kindness and a certain
influence, which I hardly can describe, came over me,
so that when I went to reside, and he had then left
Oxford, I found the Tutors at Oriel so wholly different
that I greatly regretted Keble's absence. I am more
than ever convinced that, had he been elected Provost,
things would have been very different at the University."

The impression which he made upon outsiders is
excellently illustrated by the following contemporaneous
account, written by a sister of his friend, George Cornish,
after a visit of Keble's to Sidmouth—

"*Sept.* 8, 1819.—Keble went away early. We are all
very sorry to lose him, as he is a person that is not to
be met with every day. I have heard a great deal of
him from George before I saw him, so that it was like
meeting an old friend. His manners are singularly
simple, shy, and unpolished, though without the least
rudeness or roughness, as he is the mildest and quietest
person I almost ever saw. He speaks very little, but
always seems interested in what is going on, and often
says the cleverest and most witty things as if he was
not the least aware of it. In his own family I should
think he must be more missed when absent than any
one else could possibly be; he seems formed for a
domestic circle and all the feelings attendant on home.

Without making any fuss about it, he seems so interested in every one, and has such a continual quiet cheerfulness about him, that I cannot imagine how his father and mother, brother and sisters, can do without him. But it is his religious character that has struck me more than anything else, as it is indeed that from which everything else proceeds. I never saw any one who came up so completely to my ideas of a religious man as Keble, and yet I never saw any one who made so little *display* of it (I use this word for want of a better at present); he seems to me a union of Hooker and George Herbert—the *humility* of one with the feeling and *love* of the other. In short, altogether he is a man whom the more you see of and know, the less you must think of yourself." [1]

During these years he was much interested by making the acquaintance of Wordsworth (1815), and of Southey and Heber (1819). His own poetic powers were reaching their maturity, and some of the freshest and most melodious poems of the *Christian Year* date from this time. In 1822—1823 he was Select Preacher before the University, and in 1823 he preached the Assize sermon; [2] but the variety of the work and the cares of discipline were trying to him; he longed for something more permanent and more pastoral. "I begin to be clear that I am out of my element here," he wrote in a moment of despondency as early as 1819; in 1821, "I have made up my mind to leave Oxford as soon as this examination affair is over;" in 1822, "I get fonder and fonder of the country and of poetry and of such things every year of my life." Finally, in 1823, he

---

[1] *Monthly Packet*, 1887, p. 189. "Diary of an Octogenarian."
[2] *Academical Sermons*, i.—iv.

accepted a college living at Coleby in Lincolnshire; but
withdrew his acceptance at the last moment.   For, on
May 11, his mother died, and he at once decided to live
in his father's neighbourhood that he might be able to
help him.   His mother's death inspired the poem on
the *Annunciation*, which appears, though in an altered
form, in the *Christian Year*.   The first draft (written
on June 1, 1823) will be found in the *Miscellaneous
Poems*.   It is in the main the same as that in the
Christian Year, but when that was published his sorrow
was still fresh, and the allusions to his mother and himself seemed too sacred for publication, and the verses
about *The Virgin Mother* were substituted.   In his own
MS. there is written by the side of the last stanza,
" May 10, 1823.   Extract from pocket-book—

> ' Eheu, eheu, vale, vale, carissima, vale, eheu, vale,
>   at veniet felicius ævum,
>   Quando iterum tecum, sim modo dignus, ero.' " [1]

On his leaving Oriel several of his pupils followed
him to his new sphere of work.   He became curate at
Southrop near Fairford, being responsible for this as well
as the other two small villages of East Leech and Burthorpe.   The home was at Southrop; here he continued
for three years, refusing, in 1824, the Archdeaconry of
Barbadoes, which was offered him by Bishop Coleridge,
and these three years are in some ways the most important of his life.   They laid the germs of the Tractarian movement.   The pupils who were with him, and
from whom he refused to receive any payment, were
men of brilliancy and promise, the first and chief being
Robert Wilberforce, afterwards Fellow and Tutor of

[1] These lines are to be found in Bishop Lowth's epitaph on his
daughter's tomb at Cuddesdon.

Oriel College; Isaac Williams, afterwards Fellow of
Trinity, and curate to Newman; and Hurrell Froude,
also Fellow and Tutor of Oriel, and the link between
Keble and Newman. In their society Keble's nature
expanded thoroughly; their intercourse was free, affectionate, joyous, playful: "there is master the greatest
boy of them all," was the gardener's comment upon it.
But under all this gaiety of heart a deep seriousness
was known to lie, and it would break out from time to
time in shy, simple ways, as when once just before Froude
was leaving, Keble took him aside and said, "Froude, you
thought Law's *Serious Call* was a *clever book;* it seemed
to me as if you had said that the Day of Judgment
was a pretty sight." [1] The moral and spiritual influence which he wielded over them was enormous.
Robert Wilberforce, when in later years he joined the
Church of Rome, is reported to have said that the
one power which had held him to the Church of England was John Keble's character and wisdom; Isaac
Williams, the Harrow cricketer and scholar of Trinity,
looked back to the day when Keble invited him to
Southrop as the era of his conversion, when he was
first roused to take a serious view of life. "It was
this short walk of a few yards and a few words spoken
that were the turning-point of my life. If a merciful
God had miraculously interposed to arrest my course, I
could not have had a stronger assurance of His Presence
than I have always had in looking back to that day." [2]
Speaking of Keble's classical tuition, he says that he can
remember in no other way to have derived so much
moral benefit and actual religious teaching as when in

[1] I. Williams, *Autobiography*, p. 28.
[2] *Ibid.* p. 16.

C

a state of tuition himself from this indirect mode of instruction in another, to whom he owes everything that renders life valuable.[1] Froude, the "bright and beautiful Froude," the most original genius of the whole; Froude, so aggressive, so restless in inquiry, so audacious, so relentless in pressing premises to their ultimate conclusions, so full of mischief, so unmeasured in speech, so keen an enemy to all that was unreal or pretentious, and yet withal so affectionate and generous and winning and imaginative, a "man fitted above all others to kindle enthusiasm,"[2] was touched and awed by the unworldly simplicity of his tutor, and put himself unreservedly under his intellectual and spiritual guidance. It was like a high-bred horse responding at once to a master's touch. The effect upon these pupils will be best illustrated by Dean Church's account of it in his description of Isaac Williams : "He had before him in John Keble a spectacle which was absolutely new to him. Ambitious as a rising and successful scholar at college, he saw a man looked up to and wondered at by every one, absolutely without pride and without ambition. He saw the most distinguished academic of his day, to whom every prospect was open, retiring from Oxford in the height of his fame to busy himself with a few hundreds of Gloucestershire peasants in a miserable curacy. He saw this man caring for and respecting the ignorant and poor as much as others respected the great and learned. He saw this man, who had made what the world would call so great a sacrifice—apparently unconscious that he had made any sacrifice at all—gay,

[1] *The Christian Scholar*, Preface, p. liv. Cf. *Thoughts in Past Years :* "Others admire in thee a poet's fire" (written about Keble).

[2] J. H. N., *Correspondence*, ii., p. 241.

unceremonious, bright, full of play as a boy, ready with his pupils for any exercise, mental or muscular—for a hard ride, or a crabbed bit of Æschylus, or a logic fence with disputatious and paradoxical undergraduates, giving and taking on even ground. These pupils saw one, the breadth of whose religion none could doubt, 'always endeavouring to do them good, as it were, unknown to themselves and in secret, and ever avoiding that his kindness should be felt and acknowledged'; showing in the whole course of daily life the purity of Christian love, and taking the utmost pains to make no profession or show of it." [1]

But the influence was not wholly from him upon them; they too, and especially Froude, reacted upon him. His ecclesiastical principles became more clear cut; on the one hand, there had been growing upon him an intense distrust of the Evangelicalism of the day, which seemed to depend entirely upon feeling, to neglect the sense of duty and the cultivation of character; it seemed to him so often unreal, and he was fond of quoting William Law's warning to Wesley, "Remember that a man may deceive himself as easily by the phrase 'justification by faith,' as by any other combination of syllables." On the other hand, he loathed even more strongly the cold Deism of the last century with its modern Erastianism, which would reduce the Church to a mere creation of the State, and would ultimately deny the supernatural. The "Anglo-Hanoverian" Church tone of the eighteenth century repelled him with its utilitarian *cui bono* principles, its presumptions in favour of liberty and against self-denying faith, its preference for external evidences of

[1] *The Oxford Movement*, p. 59.

religion, its excessive and easy-going toleration, its want of a charitable austerity.[1] It neglected the feelings as Evangelicalism neglected the character, and his mind craved for a religion which should affect the whole man, and keep both feelings and intellect under the control of the will. To enforce this he fell back upon the conception of the Church which he had inherited, as of a body independent of the State, founded by the Lord Himself, perpetuated by direct succession from the Apostles, one in continuous history and in doctrine with the Primitive Church, filled with a supernatural and sacramental life, witnessing to a high moral standard before the world. Such a conception fired him with indignation at State encroachments, at neglect of discipline and doctrine, at the prevailing worldliness of tone; it made him doubt the wisdom of much that the Reformers had done. In 1824 he wrote to Coleridge that he doubted Davison's application of the apostasy to the Church of Rome, and adds, " My impression for a long time has been that we have as much to do with it as they."

Such a noble conception of the Church naturally laid hold of the imaginations of his pupils, and through them passed as a power into Oxford. To make that conception a reality he devoted his whole life with a Quixotic chivalry which nothing could daunt: for that he sent forth his pupils as a band of missionaries. Not that any immediate result was yet produced: the train was laid, but the circumstances were not yet favourable for firing it, nor was the genius yet with them who was to apply the light.

---

[1] Cf. his Review of "'The Unpublished Papers of Bishop Warburton." *Occasional Papers and Reviews*, p. 108.

This intercourse with pupils ceased in the year 1825, when Keble became curate in sole charge of Hursley, near Winchester, under Archdeacon Heathcote. The Archdeacon, who lived in Winchester, was responsible for the charge both of Otterbourne and of Hursley, and was obliged to depute the latter entirely to his curate; and as this was a widely-scattered parish of more than a thousand inhabitants, the new curate had no time to devote to tuition. He passed a year of great happiness in this new work, receiving visits from his father and sisters and many of his college friends, including Arnold. But the brightness was clouded and stopped by the most unexpected and perhaps the deepest sorrow of his life. In September, 1826, his favourite sister, Mary Anne, was taken suddenly ill at Fairford, and died within a few days. In answer to a letter of sympathy from Froude he wrote—

"I knew you would be very sorry when you heard of what has come upon us, and I feel that I can write freely to you about it; but I cannot half describe to you the depth and intensity, at least as it seemed to me, of my thoughts and feelings during Mary Anne's illness and for some time since. Certainly no loss could be so great, humanly speaking, to Elizabeth and my father, but they are both such sort of people that I have long been used to consider everything that happens to them as a certain good; and there was nothing bitter in my grief as far as they were concerned, much less in thinking of Mary Anne herself; but the real bitterness was when I thought of many things in which I have been far less kind to her than I ought to have been. Somehow or other I have for years been accustomed to talk to her far more freely

than to anybody else in the world, though of course
there were two or three whom I loved quite as well.
But it has so happened that whenever I was moody or
fretful she has had to bear with me more than any one,
and if I chose I could sit down and torment myself by
the hour with the thought of it. This is the only
feeling of real bitterness that I have on the subject,
but I know it is wrong to indulge it, and I trust soon
to get over it entirely; indeed, I seem to have done so
already, only I feel one cannot in any way depend upon
one's self. I am certain no person who believes in the
Atonement ought to indulge in bitter remorse, and
therefore, by God's blessing, I don't mean to be uncomfortable if I can help it, even in the thought of my
past faults. I have been so too much already, and it
only seems to make one lazy and weaken one's own
hands and one's friends. If you please, therefore, don't
let us encourage one another in melancholy any more;
but let us always resolutely look to the bright side of
things, and among other helps to be quiet, let us always
talk as freely to one another as we do now, for nothing
relieves one so much as making a clean breast." [1]

To this occasion we owe the short *Fragment on his
sister Mary Anne's death*,[2] and the simple unrhymed
poem on *The Burial of the Dead*, which was intended
for the *Christian Year*. He shrank, however, from
publishing it so soon, but later it appeared in the
Lyra Apostolica, No. 50.[3] This loss changed Keble's
plans once more; his father and sister needed some
companion, and he returned to Fairford and acted as
curate there until his father's death in 1835, refusing

[1] *Letters of Spiritual Counsel*, p. i.
[2] *Miscellaneous Poems*, p. 236.   [3] *Ibid.* p. 15.

the living of Hursley when offered him by Sir W. Heathcote in 1829, and that of Paignton, which was offered to him, "as to the most eminently good man in the Church," by the Bishop of Exeter in 1831.

He still remained a Fellow of Oriel, but his friends there were not content that he should only appear at the rare intervals of college meetings, and on more than one occasion they attempted to revive his connection with Oxford. At the end of 1827 the Provostship of Oriel became vacant by the appointment of Dr. Copleston to be Bishop of Llandaff and Dean of St. Paul's. There was no doubt that the choice would fall either on Keble or on Hawkins. On December 8th, Hawkins wrote to Keble what the latter describes as a "kind little letter," apparently asking whether he would be a candidate; to which he replied on December 9th, postponing his answer, but adding, "I am in great hopes that by not caring too much for things we shall be enabled to turn what might have been unpleasant into a time of comfortable recollection as long as we live. You and I agreed to remember one another at a trying time for both a little more than a twelvemonth ago; if you please, we will do the same now."

Meanwhile, Keble's old pupils were strongly in his favour and urged him to stand. He was quite willing to do so, feeling that it was not so very much more difficult a trust than any other pastoral employment, and conscious that he had some qualifications for it; but he had left Oxford, and was not intimately known by many of the Fellows. Hawkins was a resident tutor in full work; he too had gained a double first-class, having taken his degree a year after Keble, and he was a man of shrewd practical wisdom and intellectual

keenness, though devoid of any deep power of sympathy.
By a strange irony the balance was decided against
Keble by Newman and Pusey. Neither of them knew
Keble at all intimately, Newman having been elected
in 1822, Pusey in 1823, just as Keble was leaving
Oxford. Pusey wrote to him on December 14th, saying
that he had decided to vote for Hawkins, " yet should
the choice of the majority finally fall upon you, I should
anticipate from your promotion high and extensive
benefits to the college. It is difficult on the subject
not to say too much or too little ; I will therefore only
add that it is not upon any comparison of the individuals, but in relation to a practical office that I have
formed my decision." Newman wrote on December
19th, a letter marked by delicate consideration, and yet,
as experience proved, showing an extraordinary want
of insight into the relative sympathy of Keble and
Hawkins with his own conceptions of College and
University reform. On December 27th, Keble wrote to
Froude withdrawing his candidature, and putting it
with thoughtful unselfishness on selfish reasons; he
doubted whether he would be comfortable there ; he
had calls elsewhere ; he was afraid of the Oxford
epidemic of intellectualism. On December 28th, he
wrote to the same effect to Hawkins, and the contest
was ended.

Whether the result would have been less disastrous
to the College and the University if Keble had been
elected is an idle speculation. Newman never regretted
his vote, for it seemed to him afterwards that, had Keble
been elected, he himself would have still retained his
tutorship, and so would have had no leisure for the
Tractarian movement. Pusey regretted it deeply :

"Unhappily, some of us who loved him did not know the power of his deep sympathy with the young heart, and thought another more practical. He could not bear division, and so withdrew. The whole of the later history of the Church might have been changed had we been wiser; but God, through our ignorance, withdrew him, and it must have been well with him, since God so over-ruled it. To us it became the sorrow of our lives." [1] Yet the whole correspondence gives such an impression of considerateness, of thoughtfulness, of sincerity, of perfect freedom from self-seeking, from jealousy, from bitterness on all sides, that it is refreshing to read. And Keble, who had written years before on the occasion of Hawkins' election to a Fellowship, "Everything was conducted on so liberal a plan that it does my heart good to belong to such a society as Oriel," felt this still, and went back to his pastoral work with no trace of embittered feeling, but with a deeper devotion to his duties, as though God had more clearly put them as a sacred trust into his hand. It may well be that the way in which he accepted this disappointment may have gained him the power which he wielded over Newman and Pusey in later years; it may well be that the life at a distance from Oxford, amid the realities of pastoral work, gave him coolness and self-control and wisdom which would scarcely have been generated in the heart of the conflict; and thus his very rejection may have gone to make him "an unseen silent influence, moving hearts at will." [2]

But though absent his voice was still heard in any-

---

[1] Sermon at Keble College, St. Mark's Day, 1876, p. 27.
[2] J. H. N., *Essays*, ii., p. 446. For the best account of the election see the *Guardian* for January 30, 1889.

thing which stirred the University; in 1829 Mr. Peel, having suddenly changed his mind and passed the Roman Catholic Emancipation Act, offered himself for re-election at Oxford, but many Churchmen there felt that they could not change their opinions thus readily; the independence of the Church and of Oxford seemed to them at stake, and Mr. Peel was rejected. Keble (who afterwards dated the conflict between Church and State from this time) threw himself heartily into the opposition, and published with his signature a short set of queries addressed to the electors, ending with one, very characteristic—"Whether, on occasions like this, we are not bound to look forward and consider not only how our academical interests may be affected at present, but how our conduct will appear in the pages of future history ? "

When the election was over he wrote a humble and affectionate letter to Pusey, asking pardon of all Mr. Peel's friends, and especially, through Pusey, of the Bishop of Oxford, "if anything in which I have had a part may have given him a moment's pain, or if I have seemed unworthily suspicious of one for whom he must be deeply interested."

For a few years his letters give the impression that he was casting about for some adequate life's work. The *Christian Year* was now published, and he had no pupils. We find him examining for the Ireland Scholarship in 1828; for the India House in 1830 and 1831; he composes the Index to Cardwell's edition of Aristotle's *Ethics* (1830)[1]; he is working at his translation of the

---

[1] Cf. the Preface : "Indicem toti operi amico cuidam acceptum referimus, digniori sane qui ipse Aristotelem illustrandum suscipieret, nobis vicissim suas partes traditurus."

Psalter into English verse; he is interested in the conditions of the poor and studying Malthus, and anxious to promote emigration on a large scale in order to relieve the distress.   At one time, when there were agrarian riots in the neighbourhood, he rode out fearlessly and good-naturedly with the mob, arguing with them and trying to keep them from mischief.   In 1831 he published anonymously a pamphlet entitled *A Hint from Bristol*, in which he took advantage of the Bristol riots to plead against Reform, and to exhort honest men to have true courage to set themselves calmly and resolutely against the "evil spirit which is abroad teaching this nation all kinds of irreverence."   In this year, however, two different events supplied him with the work which he desired; at the beginning of the year he undertook for the Clarendon Press a complete edition of the works of his favourite, Richard Hooker; and in the winter he was elected Professor of Poetry.   His friends had been anxious that he should be a candidate for the chair in 1821, but he then refused to oppose Milman. By this time, however, the *Christian Year* had established his poetic reputation, and he was elected without any opposition.   This office had the advantage that it brought him up to Oxford once a term for his terminal lecture, and also required his presence at Commemoration in alternate years to deliver the Creweian oration in commemoration of the Benefactors of the University.

Thus through the most eventful years of the Tractarian movement, he was in constant touch with its leaders, while the preparation for these two important works made the next few years some of the busiest of his life.   One of his own poems will best show the spirit with which he was setting himself to his task.

THE CHURCHMAN TO HIS LAMP.

"Come, twinkle in my lonely room,
Companion true in hours of gloom ;
Come, light me on a little space,
The heavenly vision to retrace,
By saints and Angels loved so well,—
My mother's glories ere she fell.

There was a time, my friendly Lamp,
When, far and wide, in Jesus' camp,
Oft as the foe dark inroads made,
They watch'd and fasted, wept and pray'd ;
But now, they feast and slumber on,
And say, ' Why pine o'er evil done ?'

Then hours of Prayer, in welcome round,
Far-severed hearts together bound ;
Seven times a day, on bended knee,
They to their Saviour cried ; and we—
One hour we find in seven long days,
Before our God to *sit* and gaze !

Then, lowly Lamp, a ray like thine
Waked half the world to hymns divine ;
Now it is much if here and there
The dreamer, by the genial glare,
Trace the dim Past, and slowly climb
The steep of Faith's triumphant prime.

Yet by His grace whose breathing gives
Life to the faintest spark that lives,
I trim thee, precious Lamp, once more,
Our Father's armoury to explore,
And sort and number wistfully
A few bright weapons, bathed on high.

And may thy guidance ever tend
Where gentle thoughts and courage blend ;
Thy pure and steady gleaming rest
On pages with the Cross imprest ;
Till, touch'd with lightning of calm zeal,
Our Father's very heart we feel."

CHAPTER II.

THE PROFESSOR OF POETRY.

"ῥῆμα δ' ἐργμάτων χρονιώτερον βιοτεύει
ὅ τι γε σὺν χαρίτων τύχᾳ
γλῶσσα Φρένος ἐξέλοι βαθέιας."

PINDAR, *Nem.,* iv. 11.

IN dealing with Keble as a poet, we start with the
great advantage of having not only his poems themselves, but also his critical theory of Poetry. Although
the fullest statement of this is subsequent to the
publication of the *Christian Year*, whether in the Latin
lectures as Professor of Poetry (1832—1841), or in a
shorter English form in his review of the *Life of Sir
Walter Scott* (*British Critic*, 1838); yet it had already
been sketched in outline in a review of Copleston's
Prælectiones Academicæ (*British Critic*, 1814); and in
an article on "Sacred Poetry" (*Quarterly Review*, 1825):[1]
hence it will, both logically and chronologically, be
the true order if we discuss the theory first, and the
application of it to his own poems afterwards.

Keble never professes to give a full definition or

---

[1] These three reviews are reprinted in the *Occasional Papers
and Reviews;* the references will be to that volume.

description of Poetry, but only to describe and illustrate one function which it serves; and this he approaches from the point of view of the poet, and only incidentally from that of the reader.

The title *De Poeticæ Vi Medica* points to the kernel of his theory. Poetry is essentially for him a relief to the poet, a relief for overcharged emotion. It is the utterance of feelings which struggle for expression, but which are too deep for perfect expression at all, much more for expression in the language of daily life.

Feeling of any kind, he points out, is always seeking some form of expression for itself; the infant can find it only in cries, in gestures, in expression of the features; the grown-up man finds it mainly in the power of speech. "My heart was hot within me, and while I was thus musing the fire kindled, and at last I spake with my tongue" (Ps. xxxix. 3),—this verse is quoted by him as expressing the secret of all poetry. This is true of all feelings, but most true of the deepest feelings, which are stirred either by the sight of external nature or by the facts of human life. Nature appeals to the feelings either by its mystery and vastness, stirring man's wonder, his questioning, his awe; or by its tranquil beauty and calm, soothing his wearied spirit. Human life appeals to them either by its happiness suggesting a perfection which lies beyond it, through the finite stirring the passion for the infinite; or by its sadness, suggesting the contrast between what it is, and what it might be, and so stirring tenderness and pity and melancholy. In either case the feelings are stirred by the sense of higher spiritual truths which underlie the visible phenomena. But it follows naturally from this that the deeper the feeling, the less adequately will it be

able to be expressed; language fails it; the prose
language of daily life is felt at once to be inadequate;
and further, the feeling itself shrinks from publicity, it
is too sacred to be cast before every one; true love and
true grief alike shun the light of day and the sight of
men. Hence there is a necessary reserve and modesty
about the expression of it; metrical language serves
both to conceal as well as to reveal the truth; again,
the poet hides his passion under allegory and simile, or
description of some event in the heroic past which is
sufficiently akin to the present to relieve his feeling
while it does not betray his secret. Hence expression
will be more poetical in proportion as it gives the sense
of struggling with an ideal truth.

Yet another distinction must be noticed. The facts
of life affect people differently according to their
temperament. With one class the feelings are passionate, tumultuous, headstrong, bursting out into lyric
utterance on the spot and then passing away. With
another they are quiet, strong, permanent; they feed
themselves on their object; they persist throughout life;
they work themselves out in longer and more sustained
efforts of epic or dramatic poems. Of these two classes
Keble unhesitatingly gives the preference to the second.
"In quietness and calm will always be found the true
praise of poetry, whether you seek for sweetness or for
majesty."[1] The permanence of the feeling is a test of
its reality; the self-control is the proof that the poet
feels himself overmastered by a Higher Power.

From this distinction springs his classification of
poets.

Primary poets are those who sing because they must,

[1] *Prœl. Acad.*, p. 608.

who have some one strong, consistent, permanent
feeling, which reappears again and again; secondary
poets are either those who are stirred genuinely by a
passing emotion, or those who are little more than
clever literary imitators, writing for pleasure or for
interest. The form of the poetry is never taken as the
dividing line, though it is used at times as a clue to
guide the reader to the truest and most genuine feeling
in the poet, on the ground that truth of feeling feels
after truth of form. The more trustworthy tests are
modesty, reserve, the absence of paradox and display,
and above all, consistency; that poet is the highest poet
who,

> ". . . . when brought
> Among the tasks of real life, hath wrought
> Upon the plan that pleased his childish thought."

Taking these tests as his standard, Keble in his
lectures examines all the chief Greek and Latin poets,
not without a touch of humour here and there, as
though he were a Public Examiner once more, as where
he stops to wonder whether Sophocles' love of Attic
scenery may not earn him a first-class, but ultimately
decides to place him in the second; there are also many
interesting illustrations from modern poets and digressions on points where poetry touches on the borderland
of religion. As the lectures have never been translated,
we venture to give an outline of his argument, with a
fuller account of one or two details which he has touched
with a loving fullness himself.

Homer comes first, and is classed at once as a primary
poet. His overmastering feeling is a sad regret for
the heroic age, with its common national feeling, its
reverence for its leaders, its faith in the interposition of

Gods. The *Iliad* is the glorification of heroic warfare; it represents the feelings of the veteran soldier delighting in his past campaigns. Hence it is not merely "the wrath of Achilles:" it is an Iliad, a story of a successful warfare, exhibiting every kind of fighting, singing the praises of every warrior, whether Greek or Trojan; dwelling on the incidents of camp life, of the feasts, the games, the armour, the horses, the hunting, the peasant life around, the scenes of Nature, and the wealth of Troy. We see Agamemnon, the proud aristocrat, caring for his country much but for his dignity more; Diomed the ambitious; Ajax the rough, brusque, simple, obedient soldier; Hector the lovable, brave, domestic, human hero; but above them all, the type of an almost superhuman consecration, Achilles, the eager, noble warrior, who knows that death awaits him and yet has gone forth to the war, self-consecrate, preferring a glorious death to inglorious inactivity; full of affectionate remembrance for his parents, devoted to his friend, honouring old age, recognizing excellence in friend or foe, and, for all these reasons, dear to heaven.

The *Odyssey* is the work of the same writer, though in his old age. It is the work of the veteran soldier with his warrior instincts still alive in him, recording the love of exploration which marked the heroic era. As Alexander the Great combined in his own person the warrior and the explorer, so Homer in his poems. The type is now Ulysses, the explorer, wise, shrewd, full of expedients, self-trustful; longing for home with a strength of feeling which is proof against all seductions and all perils; but he is essentially a king; the *Odyssey* is not merely the return of a traveller, it is the triumphal victory of a king, who comes to enjoy his own

D

again and to right his country. The influence of the
Gods is over all: they protect Ulysses and punish the
suitors; their presence is seen only by their favourites;
yet sinners are warned against their doom; there is
nothing like fatalism in the story. The suitors are the
type of the arrogant, irreligious democrats, who neither
respect guests, nor honour the dead, nor reverence the
Gods, but measure all things by the standard of their
own enjoyment; and so the poet is against them; for
true poets are almost bound to oppose the popular
party, because of its utilitarian standard, which is never
carried away by any lofty enthusiasm, and because of
its absence of true reverence and self-restraint. It
would have everything open and public. It was this
want of self-restraint which caused the popularity, and
was a fatal flaw in the real poetic power of Byron.

Two other interesting observations lead to comparisons
with modern poets. Homer's frequent references to
simple peasant life, his description of beggars, the dignity
with which he invests slaves, show that, like Burns, he
was a poor man, in sympathy with poverty. But Homer
tries to soothe the lot of the poor; he looks with a
simple peasant's admiration on wealth, he treats it as
the gift of heaven; but he never rails against riches,
nor is indignant at the injustice of Providence. On the
other hand, Burns, with the same love of peasant life
and simple nature, is unable to treat the rich with
courteous gentleness; his undisciplined love of pleasure
leads to anxiety, indignation, querulousness; he chafes
against fortune and rails against the rich. Unlike
Homer, he cannot be

"A wise good man, contented to be poor."

Again, a subtle examination of the treatment of

Nature in the *Iliad* and *Odyssey* leads Keble to think that the *Iliad* was written before, and the *Odyssey* after, the blindness of Homer. The *Iliad* is full of similes which are drawn from the passing phases of Nature, the gambols of animals, the changes in the sky, the quick movements of men, and are such as give evidence of a keen sight. The *Odyssey* has few such, but more complete descriptions of places, cities, harbours and rivers, such as a poet could recall and dwell upon in memory. If this is true, how much more striking still becomes the uniform spirit of bravery in the face of fortune, of happy contentment with the ways of heaven; it lifts him to a level above Milton, the other great blind poet, who even in that poem of endurance and chastened religious spirit, the sonnet on his blindness, wants the full charm of Homeric content, and shows that in political life he would not side with Homer but rather with the restless popular cause.

The examination of Homer is followed by an interesting discussion, in which it is hard not to believe that Keble is referring to his own poetical history. The question is raised whether a great example in literature is likely to deter or to stimulate other poets. On the one side it is urged that young poets might think that all was done that could be done in poetry; and that the more sensitive a poet was, the more would he be discouraged from placing his poetry into competition with his great predecessor. On the other side,—and it is this with which Keble sympathizes,—contact with a true poet kindles and inspires the timid; the strong and sanguine are stirred by emulation; and the inexperienced are at least helped in the *form* of expression. No doubt thus a danger arises of the growth of a school

of servile imitators. Servile imitation, however, only
affects the *form*, and the danger of it can be avoided by
writing in a different kind of poetry. The conclusion
is that a great example stimulates far more than it
depresses. This was the case with Homer's example:
for nearly all the poets of early Greece bear traces
of his influence, and yet they have their own overmastering impulse, growing naturally out of and meeting
the needs of their own days. The Minor Poets, Alcæus,
Sappho, Archilochus, Simonides, short as their extant
fragments are, were all clearly primary poets, each of
them striking out new metres to express their feelings.
Such conspicuously was the case with Æschylus, who
receives a fuller treatment than any poet. The whole
of the lectures about him are marked by loving and
keen insight; the treatment of the *Oresteia* is excellent
and will repay dwelling on at some length.

The dominant feelings in Æschylus are twofold: (1)
a hearty love of fighting, whether by land or sea; (2)
the sense of the mystery which hangs over human life,
passing into a belief in an overruling Providence. No
doubt the *Prometheus Vinctus* gives a contradictory
impression; Zeus seems there to be treated as an arbitrary tyrant, angry at benefits conferred on mankind;
but this is only one play of an incomplete trilogy, and
even in this there is a glimpse of a future deliverance
for Prometheus, the friend of mankind. It is in the
Oresteia that the religious tone and teaching of Æschylus
find full expression; it might be even regarded as a
palinode for the *Prometheus*. It is a great vindication
of the ways of God to man, for the fortunes of the family
of Pelops are not the real centre on which the interest
turns, but rather the triumph of Zeus. Zeus appears as

a righteous God, sternly inflicting punishment for sin;
but he is also a kindly God, who teaches mankind
by their sufferings. Throughout the *Agamemnon* there
runs a sense of awed expectation at the coming
judgment. The half-comic rustic homely wit of the
warder at the opening of the play is like the calm
before a storm. Like the humour of Shakspere, it
heightens the contrast with the tragedy to come; it is
so true to life, with its grotesque touches in the midst
of sorrow. The sense of doom is intensified in the
Chorus by the omens, given by birds and animals,
which so often seem to share the secrets of heaven: the
destruction of Troy was the act of Zeus taking vengeance for violated hospitality; there are hints of other
doom yet in store for Agamemnon, and even in the
beautiful picture of the sacrifice of Iphigenia, the
interest is centred on Agamemnon as he shelters the
weakness of his will under the plea that the sacrifice is
an act of necessity. Clytemnestra tempts him to his
fate, by forcing him by her taunts to walk on the purple
tapestries; her words are full of double meaning; yet
in her pretence of love, in her defence of the murder, in
her appeal to the genius of the house, in her sacrifices
to the Gods, she seems to bear witness to the stings of
conscience, to the power of an innate fear of God.
Cassandra appears as the type of prophecy, the witness
for a present God though pointing to a future event.
In the presence of the hypocrisy of Clytemnestra she
is silent. When that is withdrawn, she bursts forth
into inarticulate cries; as she finds sympathy in the
Chorus, her prophecies become clearer and clearer.
She is the most touching of all prophets on the Greek
stage; tender-hearted, full of pity for the sorrows of

men, ever mindful of parents and of country and of the love of Phœbus, she pours forth her prophecy, unfeed, unforced, not summoned from afar as an outsider, but herself sharing in the events. Her inspiration comes from no omens or auguries, but direct from the God himself; she is a standing witness that they who increase knowledge increase sorrow for themselves; that the sharer of the secrets of heaven shares them to her own ruin; she has well-nigh the dignity of a martyr for the truth. Thus, though unrighteousness triumphs for the time, through the clouds and darkness is seen a hope of retribution: over all is felt a sense that no chance or fatalism is guiding events, but a wise and kindly providence.

In the *Choephoræ* this is more marked still. Instead of brooding expectation there is only serene confidence in the justice of God. The whole play is like a great liturgy; it opens with prayer; the action is carried on before the father's tomb; the death of Clytemnestra is raised above all suspicion of personal vindictiveness into an act of righteous vengeance; prayers recur again and again; the Chorus recalls past instances of Divine Justice; Orestes is like a priest offering the victims upon the altar; over all stands supreme the command of heaven, and the sense of the presence of the murdered dead. The terrible character of the act is softened in the case of Orestes by the fact that he is acting against his natural instincts at the bidding of duty; in the case of Electra by her gentleness for her mother and fondness for Orestes. The plot, however, grows more complicated. The murderess is punished, but a fresh deed of murder has been committed, and once more the murderer is punished.

What is to be the solution? This is given in the *Eumenides*. There we see the reconciliation of mercy with strict justice, effected by an appeal to Zeus. Orestes is pursued to the very shrine of Apollo; so near is he to destruction. The *Eumenides* represent the common idea of strict justice insisting on punishment: Apollo represents forgiving mercy; Orestes says little, he is confident in his cause, but humbly and reverently leaves it to Apollo. The final appeal is to the decision of Zeus, given—to please Attic pride— through the Areiopagus. Mercy triumphs, but the representatives of Justice are only just outvoted, and are ultimately reconciled and welcomed to dwell among men; lest any should think himself pious and good without godly and reverent fear.

This trilogy is described in much greater detail than any other poem, and we have lingered over it as a piece of true criticism, which is of permanent value for the real appreciation of the plays. Probably no such sympathetic reading of the character of Cassandra is to be found elsewhere.

The other Greek tragedians are treated slightly. But scant justice is done to Sophocles. His strongest claim to be regarded as a primary poet is based upon his love of home and the places associated with early life; but this is not expressed often enough to put a permanent stamp upon his poetry. There is, apart from this, no *one* dominant feeling; he does not draw direct from Nature; his wonderful descriptions of pain are rather those of the bystander than of the sufferer; the comic element of life is absent; his minor characters are featureless: whole situations recur in different plays; he is too even-tempered (εὔκολος) to sympathize with strong feeling. His very excellences, the finished style, the over-elaborate plots, the scenic effects, make against his claim; so he is ranked among the secondary poets, though first among them.

About Euripides, on the other hand, Keble's opinion had changed with the deeper study required for these lectures. He ranks him now as a primary poet. His faults are, no doubt, obvious—the rhetorical and frigid sententiousness; the too frequent political allusions; the separation of his choral songs from the subject of the plot; yet he has a dominant passion in the love of human life in its domestic and simple forms. As Socrates brought philosophy into daily life, so Euripides brought poetry; slaves are treated with dignity; the feelings of his heroines are common to women of all classes; he is no misogynist at heart, as the portraits of Antigone and Polyxena show; he has no unbelieving hatred of the Gods, for nowhere are to be found more religious portraits than those of Hippolytus the chaste, of Ion, the dedicated servant of the Delphic temple, of the Bacchæ, the stewards of divine mysteries.

Pindar meets with an even fuller and more enthusiastic treatment. He is undoubtedly a primary poet, for through all his elaborate metres, through his many digressions, through the variety of his themes, there is seen a genuine love for the old heroic age and for the great national games of Greece. This may seem a trivial point; but as Scott's poetry had sprung from his love of hunting and of country life, so to a Greek the national games were a training-field for warfare, a rallying-centre for all his fellow-countrymen; they were that which in Pindar's days most nearly reproduced the heroic age. So he lavishes his praise on everything connected with them, the prizes, the banquets, the processions, the beauty of the victors, the liberality and virtues of the kings. He is a thorough aristocrat, but his own belief in an after-world, and the sanctity then allowed to poets, make him bold to rebuke and to advise both aristocrats and tyrants; he combines the courage and self-confidence of youth with the cheerfulness of old age : he is true to his childish thought throughout his life; fond of children, fond of flowers, fond of his country and its scenery. He is like the lark, that lyric bird with its free, joyous, unceasing song; which starts from some simple nest in the barest field, and soars up with joy and song into the highest heavens, with no care to be uniform, but changing its note with each new thought in wondrous harmony.

Pastoral poetry is discussed next, the poetry of the quieter spirits. This has always developed later than the poetry of action; there was none in Greece proper in spite of the Greek love of Nature; it began in Sicily and was developed at Rome : and this is partly because Nature is the natural solace of those who are wearied, wearied either with the life of action, like Virgil, or with the life of thought, like Lucretius. Theocritus is the real inventor of such poetry, and he is inspired by a genuine love of the country; but yet he is not to be ranked as more than a secondary poet. The love of the country disappears in his later poems; it was not a lifelong, overmastering feeling; his style is diffuse and luxuriant; he is coarse and wants reserve. On the other hand, Lucretius and Virgil are both primary poets. The dominant feeling in Lucretius is his sense of the sadness of human life and the infinite mystery of Nature. He is always in earnest about his theme; he dwells mainly on the infinity of the universe, the swiftness of its movements, the strength of its hidden forces, the brightness of the heaven, the quick changes of the clouds, the density of the forests. It is true that he denies the existence of the Gods; yet we may pardon one who lived before the fuller revelation had come, and whose mind was touched with madness; and his very love of the infinite is a witness to a striving after God. "It may even happen that while the main theme of a poem is the open denial of the existence of the Gods, yet its tenor and tone is on the side of believers."[1] So it was with Lucretius; this love of the infinite, his unwilling acknowledgment of a Providence that guides the world; his sense of the evils of human life, of the emptiness of earthly pleasure; his praise of quiet thought and philosophy; his reverence for the dead; the very roughness of his style, preferring truth to eloquence, and oppressed by the inadequacy of his native language to express the truth, are signs alike of a poetic and religious spirit.

Virgil again is a primary poet—but not as the poet of action, not as the writer of the *Æneid*. His heart is not in the battle fray; he neither loves nor makes us love his hero; neither Æneas nor the lesser heroes are real, living characters; war is "terrible war," breaking up the operations of peace. Whereas in Homer Nature is always subordinate to the action, in Virgil, as in a painting of Claude Lorraine's, action is subordinate to the natural beauty. The *Æneid* was written only to please Augustus; if there were any feeling of his own in it, it was the feeling of gratitude to Augustus for having secured him the enjoyment of the country life he

[1] *Præl. Acad.*, p. 685.

loved. There all his heart is; he loves the country-folk; he reproduces their quaint phrases and their homely proverbs; he loves their flocks and their bees, like the true peasant, who treats them not as mere means of gain, but as friends and companions, and is alive to all their wants, anxieties, and comforts. The very vines are half personified; their training is like the education of the young; and the country itself appeals to him as strongly, though quite differently, as it did to Lucretius. Lucretius dwells on its infinite mysteries; Virgil on its tranquil beauty: Lucretius scarcely ever mentions any particular place, unless it is necessary for his argument; Virgil is constantly introducing local allusions, whether to places known in his childhood, or visited in travel, or consecrated by some religious association: Lucretius never mentions his childhood at all; · Virgil dwells affectionately on his: Lucretius emphasizes the evils of life; Virgil faces them as an optimist, and sees in them a stimulus for action and a ground of hope. His admiration for Lucretius did not make him an Epicurean; rather his belief in the universal spirit, infused into all life and guiding all history, his frequent mention of Gods, Nymphs, and Manes; his faith in omens; his sense of the sympathy of Nature with man; his reverence in speaking of the dead—mark him as a Platonist. Thus he—the last primary poet among the Latins (for Horace with all his charm has no one overmastering impulse)—in many ways prepared the way for Christian Truth, and becoming the text-book of education and the inspirer of Dante, has remained an influence to the present day.

The examination of the classical poets ends with

Virgil, in the lectures on Poetry. In the course of them there are several interesting illustrations from English poetry, and some of these are more fully worked out in the *Reviews*. Thus Shakspere "gave play to the real sympathy which he seems to have felt towards all natural and common affections, in a degree hardly conceivable by ordinary men."[1] Spenser is ranked higher than Milton as a sacred poet, because of the reserve which led him to throw his poem in the form of an allegory, and by that means and by his allusive style to veil the depth of his thought in the *Faërie Queen*, which is "a continual, deliberate endeavour to enlist the restless intellect and chivalrous feeling of an enquiring and romantic age on the side of goodness and faith, of purity and justice."[2] Milton was of a cast of mind originally austere and rigorous. He made a noble effort to rescue religion from the Puritan's degradation of it, by choosing a theme of universal and eternal importance; but he was too out-spoken, too much marred by intellectual and spiritual pride; hence his undervaluing of woman's character, his half-attractive portraiture of Satan, his want of purity and spirituality in his conception of heaven, are serious blemishes, though they do not affect his claim to be considered "the very lodestar and pattern of that class of sacred poets in England."[3] The inspiration of Scott is drawn from the passionate love of Scotch chivalry which was associated with the scenes of his childhood. His lameness, his profession, his domestic sorrows prevented any active indulgence of such love, and threw back his feelings upon themselves, until at last they found

---

[1] *Life of Sir W. Scott*, p. 23.　　　[2] *Sacred Poetry*, p. 98.
[3] *Ibid.*, pp. 102—104.

expression in his poetry. "His theme is 'a romantic idealization of Scottish aristocracy'; but his romance is not like Homer's, who rejoiced in describing the present, and investing it with a supernatural light; it is not like Tasso's, told with solemnity and reverence, as though in fulfilment of a religious vow; nor like Spenser's, the form and garb in which the visions of an ideal world and longings for supernatural perfection are clothed. It is more like that of Pindar, starting from the present and working back into past ages; yet the association with his childhood marks him off from all these poets, and gives his poetry a colouring of simplicity short only of that which would have resulted from actual truth."[1]

The theory of poetry here advanced rests mainly upon the *Poetics* of Aristotle. "Expression by metrical words" is Keble's translation of μίμησις; the refusal to test poetry merely by its form is common to both. The distinction of primary and secondary poets corresponds in some measure to that of the enthusiastic and versatile temperaments to which Aristotle traces poetry; the medical effect of poetry is akin to the "purgation" which Aristotle attributes to tragedy. But Aristotle writes as a critic, and is thinking of the effect upon the readers; Keble, as a poet, dwells primarily on the effect upon the poet, and secondarily on that upon the readers. He is independent too of his master, and ventures to criticize him on several points, such as the importance which he assigns to the action in a tragedy. He draws from a much wider store of knowledge than Aristotle, and takes as his final guide the poems of the Old Testament, "that sacred volume which corrects so

[1] *Life of Sir W. Scott*, p. 50.

many of our erring anticipations."[1] "From their perfect parallelism they are the most artificial of all compositions, yet none ever so apt to relieve the deepest and most overflowing minds; exhibiting therefore by their very form, as compared with their matter, the perfection of that self-control which must itself be the perfection of a mixed creature like man; thoughts that breathe and words that burn, exactly obeying a certain high law and shaped by it into perfect order."[2]

To some such a theory may seem too much to deny the value of spontaneity, too much dominated by a religious mood, too relative to a dogmatic standard. But it must be remembered that Keble does not profess to explain every function or source of poetry; he is only seeking for a standard that shall guide us to the *best* poets; he does admit of a different standard in judging heathen writers; and he believes that the truest spontaneity is that which is controlled by the sense of dependence on a higher Power. "The worshippers of Baal may be rude and frantic in their cries and gestures, but the true prophet speaking to or of the true God is all dignity and calmness."[3] The canon for which he contends is this, that the best poets are those who have felt throughout their life the deepest feelings about Nature, about man, and about God which were possible at their time.

Such a theory at least adds the highest dignity to the function of the poet. Keble approaches the subject with something of religious awe. Although in his review of Copleston's lectures he had condemned the practice of lecturing in Latin, he defends and even

---

[1] *Sacred Poetry*, p. 95.   [2] *Life of Sir W. Scott*, p. 19.
[3] *Sacred Poetry*, p. 91.

welcomes it for himself, as it enforces deeper thought and makes the lecturer consider what is true, not what is taking or eloquent. His task is "most serious, well-nigh sacred." Poetry is treated by him as akin to philosophy; they both seek truth, though philosophy begins with Nature as apparently the more abstruse theme, and comes back to human life when the problems of existence become more difficult; poetry begins with human life, and takes refuge from its perplexities in Nature. More closely still is poetry akin to religion. Providence has watched over it, ordering even the developments of its various styles. As among the Jews the poetic writings of the prophets prepared the way for the Messiah, so among the Gentiles the best literature, whether philosophical or poetical, played the same part. Hence it is that Christians can still read the Pagan poets with a religious interest; they can afford to judge such a poet as Lucretius more tolerantly than Cicero could, as they view him relatively to his times. But he fancies he hears the Puritan objection that the study of such Pagan literature is unnecessary now that we have a fuller Revelation. No, he answers, far from it. It is true that in the early Christian Church some writers denounced Pagan literature, but even they used it, and were only anxious that it should not stand as a rival to the absolute Truth. It is true, too, that the early Christian Church had few poets of its own; but they had as solace for their overburdened feelings the Hebrew poetry, the grandeur of the early Liturgies, and the whole Sacramental system.[1] We who have so little hold on this may well be thankful to God for the poets

---

[1] *Prœl. Acad.*, xxxi.

who soothe our feelings and stir our aspirations. Even if Pagan poets seem unnecessary, yet Nature is ever liberal of its gifts; it showers them on man with no utilitarian hand; and poetry, such as that of Virgil or Lucretius, is one of its greatest gifts, with its constant witness that neither action nor thought are adequate to satisfy the human spirit. When Christian poets did arise, they prepared the way for improvements in Religion, just as Shakspere and Spenser led the way to the Caroline revival, or Scott revived the interest in the past in our own times. For in essence Poetry and Religion are at one, and they demand one and the same temper of mind. Each is an attempt to express man's strongest feelings and to lay hold of the highest truths. Poetry lends its wealth of symbol and simile to the service of Religion, and Religion returns them glorified. Poetry takes to itself "all subjects which can anyhow take entire hold of the imagination and cause it to seek relief by indirect expression."[1] "The poet of the Church will find neither feeling nor condition in human life or in the works of God beyond his reach or without his province."[2] Yet Poetry, like Religion, hides its deepest truths and reveals them only to the pure in heart, to those who love them enough to press into their secrets. Thus Poetry rises almost to the dignity of a Sacrament, with its outward visible words and inward spiritual truth. As the poet himself needs, no less than the religious man, to choose his object of love worthily, to praise it sincerely, to commit himself heartily to it, to be courageously and consistently loyal to it, so the reader has to approach the poem as a worshipper would a Sacrament, with

[1] *Life of Sir W. Scott*, p. 15. [2] *Ibid.*, p. 79.

reverence and a determination to press inward to its heart. "A good deal is to be gained from the mere habit of looking at things with a view to something beyond their qualities merely sensible; to their sacred and moral meaning and to the high associations they were intended to create in us. Neither the works nor the word of God, neither poetry nor theology, can be duly comprehended without constant mental exercise of this kind. Without something of this sort, poetry and all the other arts would be relaxing to the tone of the mind." [1] The instrument which the poet uses is the imagination; all poetic pleasure is referred to the awakening of some moral or religious feeling, not by direct instruction but by way of association; hence there must be some elasticity in the reader's mind, else it will not vibrate to the touch of the artist. "Wherever, from the beauty of the thing imitated or from the skill of the imitator, the mind is excited to fill up the picture for itself, there is poetical pleasure, not however produced by the perception of likeness, but by the workings of the imagination." [2]

This outline fails to do justice to a volume which Dean Church has called "the most original and memorable course ever delivered from the Chair of Poetry in Oxford;" [3] and Bishop Moberley, in even stronger praise, "One of the most charming and valuable volumes of classical criticism that ever issued from the press." [4] But it may serve to draw the attention of a later generation to it and may suggest the advisability of an English translation.

---

[1] *Sacred Poetry*, p. 100.   [2] *Review of Copleston*, p. 156.
[3] *The Oxford Movement*, p. 273.
[4] Preface to J. K.'s *Miscellaneous Poems*, p. xxi.

CHAPTER III.

THE *CHRISTIAN YEAR.*

"Thy book I love because thyself art there."—I. WILLIAMS.

EVER since his undergraduate days poetic expression had been a relief to Keble in his deepest moods, and at least as early as 1819 he had begun the poems which now appear in the *Christian Year*, and by 1820 had formed the idea of a complete collection to illustrate the Sundays and Holy Days of the year. The conception was probably original with him, although of course it is in a line with much of Christian Poetry. The *Peristephanon* and *Cathemerinon* of Prudentius are exactly parallel, not being hymns for public worship, but poetic meditations on the Martyrs' festivals and the daily hours. There is, too, something akin to it in English poetry in *The Hymns and Songs of the Church* by G. Wither (1623), and an even closer analogy is to be found in Eaton's *Holy Calendar* of 1661.[1] This is a small and interesting volume, consisting of a treble series of epigrams written to illustrate all the chief

---

[1] The *Holy Calendar*, by N. Eaton, Doctor of Philosophy and Medicine, and Vicar of Bishop's Castle, Salop, 1661 ; reprinted by J. Tasker, Shrewsbury, 1888.

festivals and saints' days of the Church of England. It
is written by a strong Cavalier and Churchman. As
is natural at such a moment, the epigrams are fulsome
in their adulation of the King, and quaint and fanciful
in conceit; yet there is much of real beauty and true
feeling in them, and they are a striking witness to the
continuity of the doctrine of the Church of England;
there is as strong a reverence for the saints and
especially for the Blessed Virgin, as clear a statement
of the doctrine of the Real Presence of the Lord in
His Sacrament, as would be found in any Tractarian
writings. It will therefore be excused if I quote two
specimens of this book. The first is a good instance of
the writer's simple sweetness of thought.

NEW YEAR'S DAY. (Epigr. 1.)

" 'Tis custome, Lord, this day to send
  A gift to every vulgar freind,
  And shall I find no gift for Thee,
  That art the best of freinds to me ?
  There's nothing which my thoughts survey,
  My life, my soul, the light, the day ;
  But they are all Thy gifts to me,
  And shall I find no gift for Thee ?
  Yea, Lord, behold I hear conferr
  My life, my soul, and whatsome're
  Thy liberal hand hath given to me,
  Back as a new-year's gift on Thee.
  Say'd I a gift ? Ah ! 'tis not so,
  Alas both men and Angels know
  That all these things Thy Christ hath bought,
  And therefore I can give Thee naught."

The second will serve to illustrate the writer's
interpretation of the doctrine of the Church of
England—

ASCENSION DAY. (Epigr. 2.)

" Look in what sense the Son of Man was said
  To be in Heaven whilst yet on earth He stayd.

In the same sense we grant His body, though
In Heaven, may still be say'd to be below.
He is ascended all agree, that same
Material flesh and blood of His that came
From the pure Virgin's Womb, Heavens now retain,
And until all things be restor'd again,
Must still retain it ; yet it is confest,
That when the holy Elements are blest
By the Priest's powerful lips, though nothing there
To outward sense but Bread and Wine appear,
Yet doth there under those dark formes reside
The body of the Son of Man that dy'd :
This, what bold tongue soever doth deny,
Gives in effect even Christ Himself the ly.
Yet this whoe're too grossly doth maintain,
Pulls his ascended Lord from Heaven again.
A middle course 'twixt these two rocks to steer,
Is that becomes the Christian Mariner.
So to beleeve the Ascension as to grant
His Real Presence in the Sacrament ;
Yet so His Real Presence there to own
As not to make void His Ascension."

There is no evidence that Keble knew this work, although his article on *Sacred Poetry* shows a wide acquaintance with previous religious poets. His favourite poets were Shakspere ; [1] Spenser, whose allegorical form seemed to him to suit the true reserve which a poet ought to feel; George Herbert, with his deep penitence and chastened love for his Master; Wordsworth, with his religious sympathy with Nature; Scott, with his enthusiasm for the days of chivalry and loyalty; and, though in a less and lessening degree, Southey. Yet his poems cannot be said to bear the trace of any direct influence upon their form. The interesting discussion in the *Prælectiones* on the influence of Homer perhaps suggests that the writer himself was conscious of having been kindled by some

[1] Froude (*Remains*, i., p. 209), in a letter to J. K., speaks of " Your favourite play, *Measure for Measure*."

one great poet; if so, was it Homer? Certainly the
language of Homer has inspired some of the best
poems of the *Christian Year.*[1] Or was it Scott, to
whom he goes back so frequently in the *Prælectiones,*
and of whom he speaks so lovingly in his review of
Lockhart's life? Certainly either Homer with his
idealization of the heroic age, or Scott with that of
the age of chivalry, would kindle his own love of the
recollections of childhood or the glories of the early
Church, though the very sense of such dependence
would keep him on his guard against direct imitation
of their form. In the earlier poems, indeed, Southey's
influence of form and thought is perceptible, and in a
less degree that of Scott and Wordsworth, but he had
shaken himself free and has a style that is independent and entirely his own in the *Christian Year.* It is
marred from time to time by want of smoothness of
metre, by obscurity in the connection of the thought
between verse and verse, but on the whole it is spon-
taneous, melodious, and clear.

It was while he was Tutor at Oriel that the collection
of poems began to grow, but it was the time of his
curacies in Gloucestershire and Hampshire which was
most prolific. This was a period when his feelings
were deeply stirred, both by his mother's death in
1823, and by that of his favourite sister in 1826. In
1825 a long attachment on which he had set his heart
ended in a refusal, and some of the sweetest efforts
after resignation in the poems date from this year; and
it was, too, a period which supplied him with the tranquillity which transfuses emotion into poetry. He had

---

[1] Cf. *The Holy Innocents; Sixth Sunday after Epiphany;
Monday before Easter.*

no idea of publication; he would have preferred that
the poems should appear after his death, but they were
shown among his friends. Arnold wrote as early as
1823, "It is my firm opinion that nothing equal to
them exists in our language; the wonderful knowledge
of Scripture, the purity of heart, and the richness of
poetry, which they exhibit, I never saw paralleled."
Froude was more critical, thinking that they were
addressed too much to matter-of-fact good people, and
that they did not do enough to sober down into practical
piety those whose feelings were acute, and who were
inclined to indulge in a dreamy, visionary existence.
He was afraid that people would take the writer of
them for a Methodist.[1] Dyson pressed him to publish;
Davison suggested that he should add the poems for
the Occasional Services; his own father was anxious
to see the work published before his death, and this
was a pressure which he could never resist. Accordingly
many poems were retouched to meet the criticism of
obscurity, the last poems were written in the spring
of 1827, and on May 30th the Preface was composed.
The draft of this, which is preserved in the Library of
Keble College, is written, like so many of his poems, on
the back of an old letter, and consists of two paragraphs.
In the first copy the paragraph which now stands
second came first, but on writing it out he seems to have
thought it better to state first the true spirit of the
Church of England, and then the way in which this
book attempted to conform to it. The whole object of it
was to promote a *sober* standard of feeling in matters of
practical religion and to illustrate the *soothing* tendency
of the Prayer-book. It may be interesting to notice

---

[1] *Remains*, i., p. 184.

two changes which were made at the last moment. In
the MS. of the *Morning Hymn* there is found after the
fourth stanza a fifth which has not been published—

> " Hence the poor sinner still has found
> Life but one dull unvarying round ;
> And mourned ere half his course was run,
> That nought is new beneath the sun."

This appears in the proof of the first edition, but it
must have been struck out at the last moment, perhaps
from a feeling that the sad side of life had already been
sufficiently dwelt on in a morning hymn which was to
open the volume. Again, in the poem for Christmas
Day, after stanza v. was inserted—

> " The heart imbued with earth
> Is but a place of guests,
> Where foul-winged thoughts of lowly birth
> Successive make their nests ;
> Each in his twilight gloom with cheerless moan,
> Fluttering a little while, and then for ever gone."

It will be seen that this gives fresh point to the
contrast in stanza vi. of the pure thoughts which dwell
where Christ is; but again the writer has not cared to
emphasize the dark side of the picture.

The volume was a success at once : Newman writes
on June 10th, " Keble's hymns seem quite exquisite."
His sister says, " The commendation of them from all
the choicest people is so great as to satisfy even our
voracious appetite for praise." A second edition was
called for within the year, and edition has succeeded
edition with almost unparalleled quickness ever since.

Nowhere in the Preface is there any reference to
himself, and the book (in two volumes of small 8vo.)
was published anonymously; nor did he add his name
in subsequent editions. In the third edition in 1828

the last six poems were added, including the poem on November 5th, which was entitled, *An Address to Converts from Popery.* Beyond this no further alterations were made, save that on his deathbed he sanctioned the change in the thirteenth stanza of this poem. This had run—

> "O come to our Communion Feast!
> There, present in the heart,
> *Not* in the hands, the eternal Priest
> Will his true self impart."

Probably he would not himself have written this line in later life, for he stated in 1845 that when he wrote the *Christian Year* he did not fully understand the doctrine of the Holy Eucharist, but he frequently refused to alter it. Froude had criticized it as early as 1835 (*Remains*, i. p. 403); Dr. Pusey had discussed it with him in 1855, and he had then half playfully said, "I suppose that the real correction would be to put 'As' instead of 'Not';" but it seemed to him valuable as a protection against a notion of a gross carnal Presence (*Euch. Ador.* Pref. p. xiii, note, 1859); and he argued that on the analogy of such passages as "I will have mercy and not sacrifice," it might be legitimately interpreted as meaning "not in the hands only."[1] But on February 9th, 1866, Bishop Jeune had quoted the lines in Convocation as expressing Mr. Keble's opinion against a real objective Presence; and this weighed upon his mind so much that he decided to make the alteration which he had previously suggested, and it was carried out after his death by his executor.

[1] In one copy of the Original Poems he has written "There, *treasured* in the heart." It seems a pity that this was not preserved.

He never liked to speak of the volume or hear it spoken of. Why was it that he shrunk from this? The answer shall be given in the words of an old parishioner of Hursley, whose husband had been in Keble's service, and who said twenty-four years after his death, while her honest face glowed with pleasure as she spoke of him—"Father and I do read the *Christian Year* every Sunday, and *it do bring him out to us* more than we knew even when he was alive." It laid bare all his deepest feelings of love and penitence; it had been written purely for his own relief, and it seemed to be wanting in due reserve to publish it. He had frequently treated poetry as well-nigh sacramental, as the outward and visible sign of an inward and spiritual truth ; and this seemed almost like exposing a Sacrament to be gazed at. There was too the humbler feeling that he had such a slight hold upon that inward and spiritual truth; that he might have misrepresented it; that as far as he had truly represented it, it had only flashed from time to time upon his sight, and that if people could only come and gaze into his heart, they might find it so very different from the ideal which he had tried to portray. This will appear even more clearly if we judge him by his own test. He has said that every true poet has some one permanent overmastering emotion which breaks out again and again and clamours for utterance. Would it not be true to say that with him it was "the love of *innocence*"? There is deep down in his heart the belief that man can answer to the love of God; that sin is an outside element which need not be with us; that innocence is possible; that if it has been forfeited, still the grace of the Lord Jesus Christ can restore it. It is the passion for purity

which made him so very gentle to children; it is this
which inspired the *Lyra Innocentium;* it is "the
innocent brightness of an infant's face "[1] which drew him
to them, which made him bend over the children whom
he baptized with such loving tenderness as they recalled
the sense of what he might have been, and what Christ
yet might make him; it was "the bliss of childlike
innocence" that seemed to him to give such insight
to the old age of a true Christian; it was this which
made him love the fifty-first Psalm so much, because
it told of that free spirit blest

> "Who to the contrite can dispense
> The princely heart of innocence."[2]

It was this which turned his thoughts so often to
the type of purity, the Virgin Mother "so pure and
sweet," and prompted that which seems to have been
the earliest poem of the volume,

> "Bless'd are the pure in heart,
> For they shall see our God ;
> The secret of the Lord is theirs,
> Their soul is Christ's abode."

But this was not simply a personal individual feeling.
M. Renan has said of St. Paul that he felt for his
churches the same affection which ordinarily people
feel for the dearest objects of their love. That is true
of Keble's feeling for the Church of England : he is
jealous for her innocence, her good name, her purity,
her freedom. As he had chosen for his favourite poets
those whose overmastering emotion was for the glories
of the past, so his own enthusiasm was kindled by the

[1] *The Holy Innocents,* stanza iv.
[2] *Sixth Sunday after Trinity.*

glories of the early Church, and the bright spots in her
subsequent history. In his own words, " the *Christian
Year* always supposes the Church to be in a state of
decay," and he cannot acquiesce in a Church so sluggish,
so worldly, so utilitarian, because of the purity of his
ideal. But he cannot despair : he recalls the student
Jerome "cheering his sickening heart with his own
native air," in the worst days of error ; the mailed
monarch St. Louis, through court and camp holding
his heavenward course serene ; the calm and sweet of
Isaac Walton's life amidst the age of light, light
without love ;[1] and all these memories are meant to
awaken the slumbering, to inspire fresh hope, to lead
the Church to be true to its first eager life of purity
and truth. The whole volume is a dirge over the
lost glory of the Church ; but it is much more than
that ; it is a trumpet-call to Christians to be true to the
life which is in them, even though they may have to
face the martyr's death. Christian brothers must draw
closer together to bear witness to the value of each
soul and to knit firmly the bond of brotherhood. It
seemed to him that it was the true function of poetry
to rise above the marks of sin and woe and to recreate
the ideal before men, and he rouses poets to their
task in these stirring words—

> "Ye whose hearts are beating high
> With the pulse of Poesy,
> Heirs of more than royal race,
> Fram'd by Heaven's peculiar grace,
> God's own work to do on earth
> (If the word be not too bold),
> Giving virtue a new birth,·
> And a life that ne'er grows old—

---

[1] *First Sunday in Advent.*

> Sovereign masters of all hearts !
> Know ye who hath set your parts ?
> He who gave you breath to sing,
> By whose strength ye sweep the string ;
> He hath chosen you, to lead
>   His Hosannas here below ;—
> Mount, and claim your glorious meed ;
>   Linger not with sin and woe."

It was the thought of this ideal which saddened him so much that poets like Byron and Shelley—" Lips that might half heaven reveal "—should linger over passion and vice and be scaled in thankless silence towards God.

Taking then this love of innocence as our keynote, we will examine the *Christian Year* rather more in detail. Some of its most beautiful poems are drawn forth by the love of Nature: there is little wealth of description; the voices of the mountain and of the sea are but little heard in it; in the main he depicts the quiet woodland scenery of the neighbourhood of Fairford. In his own words about his poems—

> "their cherished haunt hath been
> By streamlet, violet bank, and orchard green,
> Mid lowly views and scenes of common earth."

The soft green willow that teaches him "contentment's power" grew on the road from Fairford to Coln St. Aldwyn. The spot where, near to each other, rise the Thames and a small tributary of the Severn, suggested the poem for the Monday in Easter week; a small island in the river Test that for the next day.[1] Or again, he dwells on the features of the Holy Land as known to him from travellers' descriptions; but in both alike he touches with a delicate accuracy the

[1] Miss Yonge, *Musings on the Christian Year*, pp. 47, 129, 131.

characteristic feature and makes it live before our eyes.
His poems have been compared to a woodland scene
by Gainsborough for their freshness, their absence of
exaggeration, their indescribable charm. Sometimes he
describes Nature for the sake of her own beauty; he is
the poet of the fresh sunrise, of the rainbow pride of
summer days, but—how characteristically—more of the
sunset's beauty and the glory of decaying autumn. As
he watches it, a life seems to pervade the universe;
nay, it seems to throb to the stirrings of love.

> " The clouds that wrap the setting sun
>   When autumn's softest gleams are ending,
> Where all bright hues together run
>   In sweet confusion blending :—
> Why, as we watch their floating wreath
> Seem they the breath of life to breathe ?
> To fancy's eye their motions prove
> They mantle round the sun for love.

> " When up some woodland dale we catch
>   The many-twinkling smile of Ocean,
> Or with pleas'd ear bewildered watch
>   His chime of restless motion ;
> Still as the surging waves retire
> They seem to gasp with strong desire ;
> Such signs of love old Ocean gives,
> We cannot choose but think he lives."

But it is seldom that Nature is described for her own
sake : his mind hurries on to catch her lesson for man,
and to draw out her influence upon him, to interpret

> " The *secret lore* of rural things,
> The *moral* of each fleeting cloud and gale,
> The whispers from above that haunt the twilight vale."

The joyous praise of Nature, as she does her work, " all
true, all faultless, all in tune," as she pays her " tribute
to the genial heaven," as,

> "True to her trust, tree, herb, or reed,
>   She renders for each scattered seed,"

is a type of true, innocent service; as she passes away
in quiet decay, losing her life though pure from sin and
stain, yet all unmurmuring, she is a type of the good
man sinking peacefully to his end.

> "How quiet shows the woodland scene!
>   Each flower and tree, its duty done,
> Reposing in decay serene,
>   Like weary men when age is won,
> Such calm old age as conscience pure
> And self-commanding hearts ensure,
> Waiting their summons to the sky,
> Content to live, but not afraid to die."

More often a sad contrast is drawn; Nature is ever
"reproving thankless man"; her obedience stands over
against his "rebel works and will"; her gratitude against
his "thankless joyless sight"; her "trust entire and cease-
less praise" against his sadness, whether it be that man
only forgets God and yields nought in return for his
lavish gifts, or whether it be that the sinner is borne
down by the sense of remorse and penitence, and cannot
rise to the true joyousness of forgiveness, but idly
"dreams of blessings gone,"

> "Or wakes the spectral forms of woe and crime,
>   When Nature sings of joy and hope alone,
> Reading her cheerful lesson in her own sweet time."

But Nature is no cruel censor of man; her lesson is
cheerful; her nurslings are companions gay in childhood, soothing in the sorrows of older years; she can
even lend of her own stores of innocence to man, and
will lend ungrudgingly.

" Ye dwell beside our paths and homes,
    Our paths of sin, our homes of sorrow,
And guilty man, where'er he roams,
    Your innocent mirth may borrow.
The birds of air before us fleet,
They cannot brook our shame to meet—
But we may taste your solace sweet,
    And come again to-morrow." [1]

But there is a deeper truth still ; the whole of Nature is rich with symbolic meaning, and full of teaching about the things of God. " My book," said St. Antony, " is Nature, and it is always by me if I want to read the works of God." This is the very spirit of the three great poems on Nature in the *Christian Year,* those for Septuagesima Sunday, and for the Fourth Sunday after Trinity, and for the Fourth Sunday in Advent. It is brought out in logical argument in Tract No. 89, with which we shall deal later : here it is expressed in lyrical beauty. All Nature is the work of God's hand, laid out by him for man to read. It is, in a word, sacramental, it is an external, visible sign, through which we ought to read a spiritual truth;

" The colouring may be of this earth,
    The lustre comes of heavenly birth."

Even Pagan seers and poets had a faint consciousness of this deep meaning of earthly things, but for Christians all is made clear. Now that the earth has been made the scene of the Incarnation,

" Henceforth, to eyes of high desire,
    The meanest things below,
As with a seraph's robe of fire
    Invested, burn and glow."

---

[1] *Fifteenth Sunday after Trinity.*

Christ's death and resurrection have given earth a newer meaning—

> " And the base world, now Christ has died,
> Ennobled is and glorified."

So the eyes of his high desire are keen to trace these analogies: his Love to offer of her best. The sky is like the Maker's Love; the sun is like the Light of the World; the moon like the Church which reflects its rays; the stars are the saints above; the trees the saints below; the dew is the grace of heaven; the fire and the wind tell of the Spirit; the oleanders on the shores of the Lake of Gennesaret are like hermits watching around the sacred hill where the Saviour had prayed; the Paschal moon is like a saint left alone with Christ; the morning sun shining on each dew-brightened blade of grass, and giving it a new lustre, speaks of the value of each soul; or again, as it scatters the darkness of the night and the mists of the morning and lights up the whole city with its glow, it is a symbol of the Gospel message reaching and kindling Mammon's gloomiest cells, and fills us with the certain hope that

> " No mist that man may raise shall hide the eye of Heaven." [1]

Some of these illustrations may seem fanciful, but the analogy underlies all our Lord's teaching by parables, and if we do not take Nature as the *adequate* type of man with his free will, it must be true. But even in tracing these analogies the thought of sin breaks in; we may interpret these analogies wrongly; we may be entirely deafened to their message; we may only cast

---

[1] In every summer night "Heaven is teaching earth to comfort man." *Miscellaneous Poems*, p. 242.

wistful looks at the bright things in earth and sky; but
the fault lies with us, not with them, and not with Him
who made them—

> " Two worlds *are ours;* 'tis only sin
> Forbids us to descry
> The mystic heaven and earth within,
> Plain as the sea and sky."

The passion for innocence is equally marked in the
treatment of human life. Each soul is of infinite value
in Christ's sight: each Christian has received special
privileges, and cannot ever be as the heathen, ever be
as though he had not received them. Hence the true
attitude even of sinless human life is that of grateful
dependence upon God, and while true to that, each
human virtue is strong and beautiful. The son's and
mother's love is of all the most sacred, because that
was Christ's own; the love of brother for brother lasts
unimpaired although they part in life; a comrade's
song bids the lonely watcher to be bold and strong;
married life seems to have a glory above that of this
earth—

> " And there are souls which seem to dwell
> Above this earth—so rich a spell
> Floats round their steps, where'er they move,
> From hopes fulfilled and mutual love."

Nowhere could we have a more exact description of
all that makes the Englishman's idea of a true home
than in the lines—

> "Sweet is the smile of home ; the mutual look
> When hearts are of each other sure ;
> Sweet all the joys that crowd the household nook,
> The haunt of all affections pure."

And though none need leave the world for cloistered
cell, yet in a sense the " hermits blest and holy maids "

F

are the nearest heaven on earth; for this earth has
but shadows which we may not rest in; no help save
Him who made it is meet for the soul, and all earthly
love must be foregone at His dear call.

Thus much would be true had man never sinned;
but, in fact, he is "a sinner in a life of care"; even
joy has its dangers,

> "There is an awe in mortal's joy,
> A deep mysterious fear."

Praise is a peril to him; his tears of penitence may
be self-deceiving; there must be discipline, self-denial,
sobriety, reserve, "clean hands and a self-ruling mind."
Each Christian has to learn "the lowly lesson of content"; his voice must take "somewhat of Resignation's
tone"; he must be

> "Ready to give thanks and live
> On the *least* that Heaven may give,"

for "to be tranquil and be blest" is the path of safety,
and the lesson of sweet peace is "rather to be resigned
than blest." Those who live such lives, who spend with
Christ their happy days, are sure to know Him by proof,
and are able to tell of Him to their brethren, till they
too see the Saviour plain. And yet we may not have
any sense of assurance such as will . let us for one
moment relinquish effort or lose the sense of dependence. "The gray-haired saint may fail at last":
nothing but death can bind us fast to the shore of love.
This is a part of our probation, and the thought recurs
again and again in the poems, as we shall find it later
in the arguments about the Roman controversy. It is
found in the most strong of all the outpourings of

personal affection for the Saviour, in one of his earliest poems—

> "Then, fainting soul, arise and sing,
> Mount, but be sober on the wing ;
> Mount up, for heaven is won by prayer,
> Be sober, for thou art not there ;
> Till Death the weary spirit free,
> Thy God hath said, 'Tis good for thee
> To walk by faith and not by sight ;
> Take it on trust a little while ;
> Soon shalt thou read the mystery right
> In the full sunshine of His smile."

It is found equally strong four years later—

> "There are who, darkling and alone,
> Would wish the weary night were gone,
> Though dawning morn should only shew
> The secret of their unknown woe :
> Who pray for sharpest throbs of pain
> To ease them of doubt's galling chain :
> 'Only disperse the cloud,' they cry,
> 'And if our fate be death, give light and let us die.'

> "Unwise I deem them, Lord, unmeet
> To profit by Thy chastenings sweet,
> For Thou wouldst have us linger still
> Upon the verge of good or ill,
> That on Thy guiding hand unseen
> Our undivided hearts may lean,
> And this our frail and foundering bark
> Glide in the narrow wake of Thy belovèd ark."

Sorrow and disappointment are treated as God's blessings in disguise, because they make us see that this is to be no world of rest for us. We may not wish them away, we can only pray for a thankful heart, and feel that we are never so safe as when

> ". . . . our will
> Yields undiscerned by all but God."

But what of the sorrow of sin, of remorse, of the secret

memories of evil, which weigh us down? That too is
God smiling on us in wrath : but we may not give way
to melancholy ; we may not nurse even thoughts of
remorse : we must confess our sins ; but then we must
look away from self to Christ's atoning work—

> ". . ... by the judge within
> Absolved, in thankful sacrifice to part
> For ever with thy sullen heart,
> Nor on remorseful thoughts to brood, and stain
> The glory of the Cross, forgiven and cheer'd in vain."

Here, where he is speaking of each worshipper taking
part in the Commination Service, the language is only
of the judge within : elsewhere he speaks of the comfort of human aid—

> "How sweet, in that dark hour, to fall
> On bosoms waiting to receive
> Our sighs, and gently whisper all !
> They love us—will not God forgive ? "

For through humanity man passes up to God. On the
one hand he who fails in human love will be unable to
respond to the Divine—

> "The heart that scorn'd a father's care,
> How can it rise in filial prayer ?
> How an all-seeing Guardian bear ?
>
> Or how shall envious brethren own
> A Brother on th' eternal throne,
> Their Father's joy, their hope alone ?
>
> How shall Thy Spirit's gracious wile
> The sullen brow of gloom beguile,
> That frowns on sweet Affection's smile ? "

On the other hand, Christ's pastors have to teach
" first filial love and then Divine " ; the love of human
friends is an assurance that God, who loves us better
than He knows, will forgive ; for His love will not

fail, even if father and mother forsake ; Christ will ever perform a brother's part.

Principal Shairp has singled it out as one of the special characteristics of Keble that, combined with devout reverence for the Person of our Lord, there is in him, first perhaps of his contemporaries, a closer, more personal love to Him as a living Friend. Again, Dean Church has said that one result of Tractarianism was the increased care for the Gospels and study of them as compared with other parts of the Bible.[1] Is there any connection between these two facts, and is this another part of the debt which Tractarianism owes to Keble ? Certainly the Gospel scenes are dwelt on with loving details ; certainly the Lord is ever present as the abiding Friend, as the Saviour. The doctrine of the Atonement is indeed dear to the writer ; it is only when "sprinkled with His atoning blood" that Christians can stand before their God ; but (to adapt Dean Church's words) the great Name stands no longer for an abstract symbol of doctrine, but for a living Master, who can teach as well as save. He is the Friend who can abide with us from morn till eve ; He is dearer than father or mother, than brother or husband ; caring for each of His followers " as if beside nor man nor angel lived in heaven or earth." What language could tell of trustful personal love more directly than this ?

> "My Saviour, can it ever be
> That I should gain by losing Thee ?
> The watchful mother tarries nigh
> Though sleep have closed her infant's eye,
> For should he wake and find her gone,
> She knows she could not bear his moan.

---

[1] *Oxford Movement*, p. 167.

> But I am weaker than a child,
>   And Thou art more than mother dear ;
> Without Thee heaven were but a wild :
>   How can I live without Thee here ?"

This personal love of God is ever round us; in Nature, in the Gospel, in the Church are His gifts and His appeals to man ; and if man refuse to listen to this appeal, then the same love has "wrath that can relent no more." The voice that promised eternal bliss has also threatened eternal woe; that warning may not be neglected; God's truth and justice may not be sacrificed. If it were,

> " Where is then the stay of contrite hearts ?
>   Of old they lean'd on Thy eternal word,
> But with the sinner's fear their hope departs,
>   Fast link'd as Thy great Name to Thee, O Lord."

As we shall see throughout his life, no false tenderness can keep back the stern side of the Gospel ; and though it is perhaps an accident, it is not an insignificant accident that the last word of the completed volume is a word of fear—

> " And oh, when worn and tired they sigh
>   With that more fearful war within,
> When Passion's storms are loud and high,
>   And brooding o'er remembered sin
>
> The heart dies down—O mightiest then,
>   Come ever true, come ever near,
> And wake their slumbering love again,
>   Spirit of God's most holy *Fear !*"

Yet with all its sternness, the one really descriptive epithet of the book is "*soothing.*" Its object was to illustrate " the *soothing* tendency of the Prayer-book." " I woo the soothing art " was the writer's professed aim ; it speaks of the " soothing " power of Nature ; of the " soothing charm " of the Holy Communion service ; of the awful "soothing" calm which alights on mourners. " It was the most soothing, tranquillizing, subduing work of the day; if poems can be found to enliven in dejection, and to comfort in anxiety, to cool the over-sanguine, to refresh the weary, and to awe the worldly; to instil resignation into the impatient and calmness into the fearful and agitated—they are these." [1]

Its most permanent value lies in this power to soothe; but perhaps at the time its power to stir was of even greater weight. In it will be found nearly all the truths and the tone which came to the front in Tractarianism. Dean Church has said that the Oxford Movement had two great sides, the one theological, the other resolutely practical. Theologically it forced an answer to the questions—" What is the Church ?   Is it a reality, or a mode of speech ?   On what grounds does it rest ?   How may it be known ?   Is it among us ? How is it to be discriminated from its rivals or counter-feits ?   What is its essential constitution ?   What does it teach ?   What are its shortcomings ?   Does it need reform ? "   On the other hand, its ethical tendency was shown in its increased care for the Gospels and study of them ; and in the increased sense of the necessity of self-discipline.   " Seriousness, reverence, the fear of insincere words and unsound professions, were essential in the character which alone it would tolerate in those who made common cause with it."

Both these sides are characteristic of the *Christian Year*, written before the movement and confessedly contributing to it. The detailed questions about the Church are indeed absent; its notes, its relation to,

[1] J. H. Newman : *Essays*, ii., p. 441.

other bodies—these were forced to the front in later days; but every reader must have been brought face to face with the question of its reality and of its claims upon his own life; he must have been drawn closer to the Gospels, and braced to self-discipline and the pursuit of holiness.

The poems awe and stir and soothe alike, because they are so real; they have so vivid a sense of the spiritual world, with all its terrors as well as its beauty and grace. He is the prophet of the fear of God no less than the poet of His love. For the success of the Christian lyrist it is "essential that what he sets before us must be true in substance, and in manner marked by a noble simplicity and confidence in that truth, by a sincere attachment to it and entire familiarity with it."[1] That was his own ideal, and one who knew him well has said, "If there is one quality which more than any other may be said to mark ;his writings, it is their intense and absolute veracity. Never for a moment is the very truth sacrificed to effect. I will venture to say with confidence that there is not a sentiment to be found elevated or amplified beyond what he really felt, nor, I would add, even an epithet that goes beyond his actual and true thought. What he was in life and character, that he was transparently in every line he wrote—entirely, always, reverentially true."[2]

The result upon others is best summed up in the words of Hurrell Froude: "Your poems are the best helps to conceiving that we really are the people for whom such great and wonderful things have been done,"[3] and the secret of this in the words of Dr. Pusey:

[1] *Occasional Papers and Reviews,* p. 91.
[2] Bp. Moberley: Preface to *Miscellaneous Poems,* p. xvii.
[3] *Remains,* i., p. 210.

" It taught, because his own soul was moved so deeply ;
the stream burst forth, because the heart which poured
it out was full; it was fresh, deep, tender, loving,
because himself was such ; it disclosed to souls secrets
which they knew not, but could not fail to own when
known, because he was so true and thought aloud ; and
conscience everywhere responded to the voice of
conscience." [1]

[1] Sermon at Keble College, 1876, p. 26.

CHAPTER IV.

THE STRUGGLE. 1833—1841.

" What if to the trumpet's sound
Voices few come answering round?
Scarce a votary swell the burst
When the anthem peals at first?
God hath sown and He will reap.
Growth is slow when roots are deep."
                    J. K. : *Lyra Apostolica*, clxviii.

WE must turn back from poetry to the prose and
struggle of life, or shall we say from Lyric Pastoral to
Tragedy? While Keble was thus working at his lectures,
Fortune seemed to be turning more and more against
the Church. The Reform Bill had flushed the demo-
cratic spirit; everything was to be brought under the
control of the people and tested by a narrow, utilitarian
standard. The Church could be no exception to this;
and as Convocation had been virtually suppressed, she
had no voice by which to speak, and the State pro-
ceeded to set her in order through a Parliament which
was no longer essentially a Parliament of Churchmen.

But " when the tale of bricks is doubled, Moses is at
hand." The spirit of Churchmanship was rising in
rebellion against this treatment in many quarters. In
1814, Bishop Jebb of Limerick had foretold such a

crisis, and the way in which it would be met. "Perhaps we may live to see our Dodwells and Hickeses and Colliers divested of the old peculiarities, shorn of some excrescences, and enlarged by a philosophic apprehension of the Scripture. Perhaps, too, a little of persecution, or of somewhat resembling persecution, may be providentially permitted to train up men with an attachment to the Church as a hierarchy, as distinct from the State, and as dignified only by its intrinsic excellence, by its venerable antiquity, and by its apostolical institution." [1] In 1833, as the events drew nearer, an even more detailed prophecy is to be found in the striking words of one of the old-fashioned High Church leaders, Mr. Sikes, of Guilsborough. Noticing that the great want in the teaching of the time was that no account was taken of the Holy Catholic Church, he foretold that the neglect of so important an article of the Faith must have its reprisals. "When it is brought forward it will swallow up the rest. . . . Our present confusion is chiefly owing to the want of it, and there will be yet more confusion attending its revival. The effects of it I even dread to contemplate, especially if it comes suddenly, and woe betide those, whoever they are, who shall in the course of Providence have to bring it forward. . . . They will be endlessly misunderstood and misinterpreted. There will be one great outcry of Popery from one end of the country to the other. It will be thrust upon minds unprepared and upon an uncatechized Church. Some will take it up as a beautiful theory unrealized; others will be frightened and scandalized and reject it, and all will want a guidance which one hardly knows where they

[1] Quoted in Perry: *Student's English Church History*, iii., p. 180.

shall find. . . . How the doctrine may be first thrown
forward we know not, but the powers of the world may
any day turn their backs upon us, and this probably
will lead to those effects I have described."[1] This is
exactly what was happening; the powers of the world
were turning their backs upon the Church; but its
champions were being prepared. In London an active
body of Churchmen, with Joshua Watson as their centre,
had done and were doing much to carry Church
principles into active work. The National Society
had been founded in 1811; the Christian Knowledge
Society had been reorganized; King's College had been
founded in 1829; the bishoprics of Calcutta (1814),
Jamaica, and Barbadoes (1824) had been founded and
endowed by the State. At Cambridge, Hugh James
Rose, "the most accomplished divine and teacher in
the English Church,"[2] was, as Christian Advocate in
the University pulpit, and, after 1832, as editor of the
British Magazine, bidding "us, when hearts were failing,
stir up the gift that was in us, and betake ourselves
to our own true mother."[3]

But it is with Oxford that we are primarily concerned. There Oriel had become the centre of Churchmanship. Newman had entirely emancipated himself
from Whateley's influence, and had accepted Keble's
principles. This had been Froude's doing, and he boasts
of it as the one good work of his life, that he had brought
Keble and Newman to understand each other; and

---

[1] From a conversation with Rev. W. J. Copeland, preserved in
Mr. Copeland's handwriting in his copy of Sikes' *Parochial Communion*, and printed in J. H. Newman's *Letters and Correspondence*, ii., Appendix, p. 483.

[2] R. W. Church, *The Oxford Movement*, p. 86.

[3] J. H. N. : Dedication to *Parochial Sermons*, vol. iv.

Keble was the link between Newman and his Fairford and Bisley friends. In 1831 he had invited Newman to Fairford with the words, "I want some of your criticism, for somehow I can't get it out of my head that you are a real honest man"; in 1832 he wrote : "My brother wants to see you, and I want you to see him." Isaac Williams, who had been curate to T. Keble at Bisley, was now curate to Newman at St. Mary's, and formed another link with the older Churchman. Dr. Pusey also was drawing closer to Newman and his friends, though he had not yet definitely committed himself to them. In this group Newman was coming clearly to the front as leader in Oxford ; for since 1830 he had ceased to be tutor, and only held the Vicarage of St. Mary's, a post which gave him leisure for study, and made him known as a preacher ; one writer has even traced the start of the movement to his sermon on "Personal Influence the means of Propagating Truth," preached in 1832.[1] Finally, his Mediterranean holiday with Froude in the winter of the same year enabled them both to stand by for a while, to look at the conditions of the struggle on which they were entering from the outside, to take its measure, and to prepare their weapons, while the recovery from his serious illness in Sicily seemed to Newman a Divine sanction to the inner conviction that he had a work to do for the Church.

But Newman, as well as the others, still looked to Keble as "the true and primary author" of the movement ;[2] he writes of himself that while lying on his sick-bed at Syracuse, "I began to think of all my

---

[1] *The Times* : Obituary Notice, August 12, 1890.
[2] *Apologia*, p. 75.

professed principles, and felt that they were mere intellectual deductions from one or two admitted truths.
I compared myself with Keble, and felt that I was
merely developing his, not my, convictions."[1]   While
on the journey he had written : "We are in good
spirits about the prospects of the Church. We find
Keble is at length roused, and (if once up) he will
prove a second Ambrose."[2]   As a matter of fact, the
signal for concerted action did come from Keble. In
spring of 1833, the difficulty of collecting tithes in
Ireland induced the Government to propose a bill
abolishing the Church cess, one of the most obnoxious
forms of payment, and in order to raise money to meet
the deficiency so produced it was proposed to suppress
ten Irish bishoprics and appropriate their revenues for
the purpose.   Bishop Blomfield supported the bill, but
Archbishop Howley opposed it, and to the mass of
bishops and clergy it seemed an act of spoliation. The
grievance was that "bishopricks may be suppressed to
any extent by the sovereign at the request of a body
of laymen, any number of whom may be heretics, contrary to the express protest of the Episcopal body."[3]
The time had come when it seemed to Keble that
"scoundrels must be called scoundrels."   The spirit
which stirred him found vent once more in poetry—in
the poems of the *Lyra Apostolica*—how different from
those of the *Christian Year!* Rugged, austere, wanting
the old melody, yet with a ring of the battle trumpet
through them, they breathe defiance

> ". . . . against the ruffian band,
> Come to reform where ne'er they came to pray."

---

[1] *Letters*, i., p. 416.   [2] *Ibid.*, p. 377.
[3] J. K. : *The State in its Relations to the Church*, p. 42.

Jeremiah is the model; Nadab and Abihu, Korah, Dathan, and Abiram, the messengers of Ahaziah, the fall of Tyre, the fall of Babylon, these are the themes. When the Irish Church Bill was brought in he wrote—

> ". . . . then welcome whirlwind, anger, woe,
> Welcome the flash that wakes the slumbering fold
> Th' Almighty Pastor's arm and eye to know,
> And turn their dreamy talk to holy Fear's stern glow."

While the bill was still under discussion, an opportunity for speaking out presented itself, he being nominated to preach the Assize Sermon before the University on July 14th.

Taking for his text the words of Samuel, when the people rejected him and demanded a king: "As for me, God forbid that I should sin against the Lord in ceasing to pray for you : but I will teach you the good and the right way" (1 Sam. xii. 23), he cautiously yet clearly applied the scene to modern times. It was possible that a Christian state might in the same way repudiate its duty to God; it might wish " to be as the heathen," like the nations around it ; perhaps external danger or grievances in the government of the Church might be the pretext, but the real reason would be decay of faith. Much was pointing to such a danger: the tendency to a shallow indifferentism, as though one form of opinion was as good as another ; the unwillingness to submit to religious restraints ; the disrespect towards the successors of the Apostles—all tended one way, and might issue in apostasy. What then would be the duty of Churchmen at such a moment ? It would be to imitate Samuel, whose combination of sweetness with firmness, of consideration with energy, constituted the temper of a perfect public man. Their

first duty would be intercession, which would secure
candour, respectfulness, guarded language in their dealing with their opponents, and also hopefulness in their
cause. Then there must be remonstrance, calm, distinct,
persevering; also loyal patriotic submission to the State
within its own sphere; and above all, each Churchman
would need to be careful of his own spiritual life, of the
daily duties of piety, purity, charity, justice, lest his
behaviour should disparage the name of his Church,
or lest public concerns should prove ruinous to himself,
by occupying all his care and thoughts to the undervaluing of ordinary duties, more especially those of a
devotional kind. With such precautions, however, it
was impossible to devote oneself too entirely to the
cause of the Apostolical Church, and that with a
certainty of success in the end.

"I have ever considered and kept this day as the
start of the religious movement of 1833," wrote Newman
thirty-one years afterwards.[1] Within the following week
the bill was passed, whereupon Keble published the
sermon under the title *National Apostasy*, with a preface
dated July 22nd, calling on Churchmen to consider
what was their duty in the face of this usurpation by
the State; for if they were to submit to such profane
intrusion, they must at least record their full conviction
that it was intrusion. The result was immediate combination and action. Froude, who had returned to
Oxford before Newman, had secured the co-operation
of Isaac Williams and William Palmer, Fellow of
Worcester College, a learned Irishman, whose work on
Origines Liturgicæ, and whose papers on Dissent in the
British Magazine had shown his Church sympathies.

[1] *Apologia*, p. 100.

Even before the sermon was preached Rose had summoned a few friends to meet at his parsonage at Had-
leigh, and the meeting took place from July 25th to
29th. Palmer, Froude, and the Hon. A. P. Perceval—
he, too, a pupil of Keble in former times—were present;
but Keble was prevented by home ties from coming,
and Newman also was absent.

The meeting did not produce any immediate results,
but the friends were practically agreed in their principles. Feeling that it was necessary to make Churchmen realize the essential bonds of Churchmanship, as
opposed to the artificial and temporary dependence
upon the State, they aimed at asserting the reality of
the Church as a spiritual body perpetuated by the
Apostolical Succession, and conveying life through its
Sacraments—this as against the individualism of the
Evangelicals and the Erastianism of politicians; the
authoritative dogmatic character of its formulæ—this
as against the liberalism of Whateley and Arnold and
Hampden : and more subordinately its independence
of Rome. But in all this there was no thought of
innovation; the one conception was that they were
reviving neglected truth and "principles of action which
had been in the minds of our predecessors of the seventeenth century." "Stir up the gift of God that is in
you," was their motto. Long lists of previous writers
were soon added to the *Tracts* as more or less upholding
or elucidating the doctrines found in them. Of Keble
himself it has been said that the highest praise which
he seemed able to give to any theological statement
was, "It seems to me just what my father taught me."[1]

The conferences were continued in Oxford, and

[1] His pseudonym in the *British Magazine* was μισονεολόγος.

G

had two main results. Palmer and Perceval formed
a more conservative group. They aimed first at form-
ing a great association of Churchmen, and an appeal
on which such might be based was put forth, but
this proposal came to nothing. Instead of it an address
to the Archbishop, thanking him for the firmness
and discretion which he had shown, and assuring
him of their devoted .adherence to the Apostolical
Doctrine and Polity of the Church, was signed by
more than 7000 clergy, and presented in February,
1834. A similar lay address was promoted by Joshua
Watson in London, and received the signatures of
230,000 heads of families, and was presented to the
Archbishop in May. The more uncompromising Oriel
group led by Keble, Froude, and Newman were quite in
sympathy with these addresses, Keble characteristically
pleading that poor people might be allowed to sign or
put their mark, and he formed one of the deputation
to Lambeth.

But this group were not content with mere addresses;
they were rather afraid of associations; they were
anxious for writing, and anxious that each writer should
be unchecked by any committee. The following basis
of action was ultimately agreed upon : considering that
the only way of salvation is the partaking of the Body
and Blood of our sacrificed Redeemer, that the means of
this is the holy Sacrament of His Supper, and the
security for the due application of this is the Apostolical
commission, and that there is peculiar danger of this
being slighted and disavowed, " we pledge ourselves
one to another, reserving our canonical obedience, to be
on our watch for all opportunities of inculcating a due
sense of this inestimable privilege; to provide and

circulate books and tracts to familiarize the imaginations of men with the idea; to attempt to revive among Churchmen the practice of daily common prayer, and more frequent participation of the Lord's Supper; to resist any attempt to alter the Liturgy on any insufficient authority, and to explain any points in discipline or worship which might be liable to be misunderstood." The form of this agreement was due to Keble, and the result was the publication of the *Tracts*. These were short papers—price 1*d.* or 2*d.*—dealing with points of spiritual life or doctrine, attempts to force the world to realize what the Church meant. No less than forty-six were issued in the course of 1833-34, in addition to eighteen short extracts from Patristic writers. Rose took no part in them at all; Palmer partly contributed to one; Froude was out of England nearly the whole year. They were all published anonymously, except that Dr. Pusey insisted on attaching his initials to his tract on Fasting—a fact from which perhaps the name of Puseyite grew to be attached to the party. Perceval, J. Keble, T. Keble, J. W. Bowden also contributed, but nearly a third of the first volume was from Newman himself. To the second volume, which appeared in November 1835, Keble contributed four tracts (Nos. 52, 54, 57, 60), and as these are closely connected in thought with those in the first volume, and quite different from his only other contribution (No. 89), it will be well to deal with all his earlier tracts at once.

The keynote of these is given in the title of No. 4, "Adherence to the Apostolical Succession the safest Course." The clergy are urged to take a higher view of their privilege as Christ's ordained ministers, whose duty it is to convey the blessings of the Holy Feast.

What if the doctrine is not absolutely certain? it is at
least probable; there are sufficient indications in the
New Testament that it was Christ's will, and that is
sufficient for loyal followers who are content to be
guided by the "Lord's eye," without definite command.
No. 13 stands apart by itself: it is a plea against any
change in the lectionary, based upon a subtle but rather
over-strained attempt to trace the principle which
originally guided the selection of Lessons. It is interesting as showing his great knowledge of the
underlying principles of the Old Testament; and is
one of the earliest expressions of his favourite principle
that God's dealing with Israel as a nation was a type
of His dealing with Christians as individuals; but the
changes in the lectionary have deprived it of present
interest for us. No. 40 is a bright, interesting
dialogue on the importance of Holy Baptism, and the
duty of Churchmen in avoiding marriage with Dissenters. In No. 52 he returns to the importance of
the Apostolic Ministry as conveying the reality of the
Eucharist; in No. 54 the Ministry is shown in a clear
historical statement to have been the guarantee of
Apostolical Doctrine in the second and third centuries;
while No. 57 is an historical argument to prove the
converse of the last, that those Churches which have
surrendered the Apostolic Ministry — whether in
ancient or in modern times—have also failed to hold
Apostolic doctrine; even the Roman Church, which
has minimized the doctine of Apostolical succession in
order to exalt the Papacy, having suffered in this way.
No. 62 is a more general argument, illustrated by
historical instances, that mere personal devotion is
inadequate for the Christian life, apart from true

doctrine: the only safe way is to take God's will exactly as we find it declared to us in His Word, as interpreted by His Church.

All these tracts are written freshly and vigorously, with happy and sometimes humorous illustrations. They show a great knowledge of the Bible, and love of its mystical interpretation. The writer has a deep sense of the corruption of human nature; for instance, the very repugnance which people feel to the warnings of the Athanasian Creed or of certain chapters of the Bible is to him only a proof of how much they are needed. For the same reason he dwells upon the need of caution and reserve in communicating religious truth, and upon the importance of considering truth from many sides; because the intellect alone can not attain to it; the feeling and temper of mind must be right; and we must be humble enough to be content with probability. Perhaps the characteristic note of these Tracts is "safety"; it is the *safest* course to adhere to the Apostolical Succession; it is a word that will recur again and again in his writings, notably in his argument about the Roman Church; and it is a word which jars upon us at first, for it seems to speak of a cold calculating prudence. But this would do Keble a great injustice, for by a safe course he means that which is most likely to satisfy all sides of our nature, and to make surest response to the obligations which we owe to others. Safety is that which secures piety and reverence. It had been the safest course for him to withdraw from the contest for the Provostship of Oriel and to stay at home with his father and sister, and if now he urges a belief in the Apostolical Succession as the safest course, he means the course which is most likely to make the most demands upon men's faith and life.

The year 1835 was the most eventful in Keble's private life. On January 24th his father died in his ninetieth year, and the home at Fairford was broken up, his sister retiring to Bisley, and he himself coming to Oxford for a while to work at his edition of Hooker. But in the summer the vicarage of Hursley again became vacant, and it was offered to him at once by Sir W. Heathcote, and gladly accepted by him. This added much to his work, as it was a large scattered parish, being conjoined with Otterbourne and Ampfield; but while he was there much was done to relieve the vicar. Mainly at his own expense a new church and parsonage-house were erected at Otterbourne; the same was done for Ampfield by Sir W. Heathcote, and both these became separate parishes. But if Hursley added to his work, it also gave him all the peace and rest of a fixed home; for before moving into it he married a lady —the younger sister of Mrs. Thomas Keble—who was often indeed an invalid, but through her sweetness and cultured intellect a strength to him, thoroughly able to enter into all his hopes for the Church, and to help him in his work. She was sweet-looking, with beautiful brown eyes and hair, a very delicate complexion like porcelain, and an air of extreme refinement. "My conscience, my memory, and my common sense" is his own description of her, after nearly thirty years of married life. Her very delicacy was in some ways a blessing to him, as it rendered necessary changes of air and scenery, and led to visits to Wales, Scotland, Ireland, the Isle of Man, and Switzerland. Whately is said to have remarked that Keble was now "a caged eagle"; it was no true prophecy, but it is a striking tribute to one side of his character that has often escaped notice, the eager, impetuous, soaring keenness which his strong will was ever holding in check. Other friends, including Newman, with whom celibacy was gaining a religious halo, felt a touch of disappointment; but to Keble it was rest, soothing, and safety. Hursley also gave him the friendship of Dr. Moberley, who was appointed head-master of Winchester in the same year, and for thirty years he proved Keble's dearest and most trusted friend in the neighbourhood.

His Oxford friends soon found that the eagle was not yet caged. Before the end of the year Newman, who saw the need that the *Tracts* should deal with the Roman claims, pressed Keble to undertake the editorship; but his hands were too full of work, and he did not feel himself competent to deal with the subject. In the beginning of 1836, another attempt was made to bring him to Oxford. Dr. Burton, the Regius Professor of Divinity, died; and Keble's name, with those of Newman, Pusey, and others, was submitted to the Prime Minister. Newman wrote at once to press Keble to accept the professorship, if it should be offered him; and he wrote to Froude to induce him to use his influence for the same end, urging that "Keble is a light too spiritual and subtle to be seen unless put upon a candlestick." [1] The Archbishop is said to have pressed Keble's appointment, but it was one which could not have been expected from a Liberal Government. But neither was the appointment that was made expected. Lord Melbourne nominated Dr. Hampden; a nomin-

[1] *Letters,* ii., p. 163.

ation which stirred up vehement opposition among
Churchmen at Oxford, spreading far beyond the group
of Tract writers.   Dr. Hampden had preached in 1832
a set of Bampton Lectures embodying the indi-
vidualistic principles, against which the whole movement was directed, and practically undermining Church
authority; in 1834 he had published a pamphlet
advocating the abolition of subscription to the
Thirty-nine Articles, which was required from all
who entered the university, his object being to throw
it open to Dissenters.   A proposal, founded on this, to
abolish the subscription had been submitted to Convocation by the Heads of Houses in May, 1835, and
rejected by a majority of five to one.   This majority
therefore naturally resented the appointment within a
few months of the champion of this cause to the chief
post of religious teaching in their midst.   An attempt
to induce the Prime Minister to withdraw the nomination
failed, but a proposal to deprive the new Regius Professor of his vote in the nomination of Select Preachers
was carried by an enormous majority (474 to 94).
Throughout this controversy, though the whole mass of
Churchmen were in sympathy, the active workers, who
wrote the pamphlets and conducted the campaign, were
Newman and Pusey.   Keble was in thorough sympathy,
but he was too busy to render much active co-operation.
During this year, however, he supplied two considerable
contributions to the work of the movement, the edition of
Hooker and the sermon on Primitive Tradition.   The
former was published in the spring ; it had been a labour
of love, and we may well fancy how Hooker's " resolution
to make the best of things as they were, and to censure
as rarely and as tenderly as possible what he found

established by authority," had come home to him and deepened the tendencies of his own character. It is a thorough piece of work, and gives proof of the editor's critical insight. The text was collated with the MSS. at Corpus Christi and at Dublin; it was split up into paragraphs, and accompanied by a running paraphrase; the allusions to Holy Scripture and the Fathers were verified: the references to Cartwright and other contemporary Puritan writers supplied, and some interesting MS. notes by Hooker himself in answer to early Puritan criticisms on the book were reprinted from the Corpus Christi MS. It is in dealing with the last three books that his critical acumen found scope. Here he discovered that the sixth book, though by Hooker himself, is not a proper part of the original work, but had been substituted, whether intentionally or by accident, for a discussion of Lay-Eldership, which is now lost. The genuineness of the seventh book was established, though it was shown to be imperfect. From the eighth book one whole section was excluded, as being an extraneous sermon inserted by mistake, and two sermons on St. Jude were rejected, as being far removed from "the sedate majesty which reigns in all Hooker's known compositions."

But further, though it always went to his heart to criticize the great and good man,[1] the Preface prefixed to the edition shows a masterly power of rising above Hooker's position, and seeing at once its strength and its limitations. The two points which he examines fully are Hooker's conceptions of Church authority and of the relation of the Church to the State. At the time of the Reformation there were three rival views:

---

[1] *Spiritual Letters*, cxxi.

the Papal, centring all authority in the Pope, and
making the civil government the instrument to exe-
cute his decrees; the Erastian, held by the prerogative
lawyers in France and Henry VIII. in England in their
desire to strengthen the local governments, and putting
Church laws and constitution at the mercy of the civil
Government; and the Presbyterian, a strong ecclesiastical view, placing the authority in the elders of the
Church, receiving their commission by positive enact-
ment of Holy Scripture: this was the view of Calvin
and Beza. The Church of England had clearly broken
with the first view; Cranmer had inclined to the
second, but in the reign of Elizabeth many causes—the
reaction against Queen Mary, the sympathy with the
Protestants abroad and in Scotland, the patriotic
resentment against the bull of Pope Pius—all were
tending to strengthen the Presbyterian view. In order
to meet it, Jewel, Whitgift, and others held that the
authority centred in the Church, which had for
practical convenience centred it in the Bishops; they
only pleaded that Episcopacy was ancient and allowable;
but as the fear of Rome grew less strong and the
Church felt its own ground firmer under it, Bancroft,
Saravia, Sutcliffe, the author of the *Querimonia
Ecclesiœ*, and Bishop Bilson had taken up the wiser
and bolder position, that Episcopal authority rested on
Divine appointment. Hooker, although the bias of
his education had been Presbyterian, practically joined
this side, using the strongest language to assert that
" the first institution of bishops was from heaven, was
even of God "; yet the exigencies of his time compelled
him to make qualifications which were seen to be
impossible after the fuller vindication of the Ignatian

epistles by Archbishop Ussher, and which would not
have been admitted by Laud ; for he allowed of non-
Episcopal ordination in cases of a supernatural call, or
in the absence of a bishop. So again he identified
Church and State too absolutely, giving the monarch
the power of dominion over the bishops, with power
to overrule them in matters of jurisdiction and legislation as well as in nomination to offices. This could
be only tolerable when the monarch was a Christian,
exerting his sovereignty through a Christian Parliament; yet, even so, the theory had proved inadequate,
and made the Church a slave to the civil power. With
a Parliament not Christian the theory was impossible.
The true theory is that of a co-ordinate authority of
Church and State, somewhat on the analogy of the
co-ordinate authority of the Sovereign and the Houses
of Parliament. "If their veto on acts of civil legislation did not impeach the King's temporal sovereignty,
why should the Church's veto impeach the same
sovereignty in case a way should be found to giving
her a power over any proposed act of ecclesiastical
legislation ? "[1] (p. lxxx). He wrote to Froude—" I am
more and more satisfied that Richard was in most
things a middle term between Laud and Cranmer, but

---

[1] The fullest statement of Keble's views on Church and State
is in his review (*British Critic*, Oct. 1839) of Mr. Gladstone's treatise,
The State in relation to the Church. He insists on the
essential distinctiveness and superiority of the Church ; on the
duty of the State to guard her interests as " a nursing father " ;
but at the same time to impose no terms which will imply
sacrifice of principle by the Church. There is danger that the
Reformation settlement, as worked by a Parliament not confined
to Churchmen, may impose such terms, and therefore it is
essential that the Church should be allowed free exercise of
moral discipline over her members, a voice in the appointment
of bishops, and a legislative power in her own internal concerns.

nearer the former; and also that he was in a transition
state when he was taken from us, and there is no
saying how much nearer he might have got to Laud,
if he had lived twenty years longer." Yet with all
these limitations, Hooker—with his reverent treatment
of the deepest doctrines, his faith in the reality of
Sacramental grace, his sense of the quasi-sacramental
value of all Church usages, his treatment of fast and
festival and of Church property as all being expressions
of man's sacrifice to God—seemed to him God's chief
instrument for saving the Church from Rationalism in
the sixteenth century; and "bold must he be who
should affirm that, great as was then her need of a
defender, it at all exceeded her peril from the same
quarter at the present moment. Should these volumes
prove at all instrumental in awakening any of her
children to a sense of that danger, and in directing
their attention to the primitive Apostolical Church as
the ark of refuge divinely appointed for the faithful,
such an effect will amply repay the editor"[1] (p. cviii).
The suggestion of this part of the Preface was due to
Newman, and we find Bowden writing to the latter on
June 30, 1836—"Keble's Preface is most glorious."

In the autumn of the same year, Keble was
nominated to preach the sermon at the Archdeacon's
Visitation in Winchester Cathedral, and took the
occasion to deliver his "masterly exposition of the
meaning of Tradition."[2] He begins with a statement
of the perplexity of the time: this, it is interesting to
note, he regards as spread over the last seven years, *i. e.*
he dates it from the Roman Catholic Emancipation

---

[1] J. H. N., *Letters*, ii., p. 198.
[2] R. W. Church, *The Oxford Movement*, p. 246.

Act of 1829 ; during that time the foundations of the Church have been laid bare; the defenders of the Church have been obliged to consider the limits of the civil power in ecclesiastical matters, the vindication of the Anglican Church against the exorbitant claims of Rome, and the reconciliation of voluntary combination of Churchmen with due loyalty to episcopal prerogative. It is impossible to stand aside and avoid responsibility any longer. Now one guide in this perplexity is Tradition, not as overriding the sole and paramount claim of Holy Scripture as a rule of Faith, but as supplementing it. Such Tradition has its analogy in unwritten civil law; its existence is recognized in Scripture itself, and was constantly appealed to in the early centuries; it served even as a test for Apostolical writings until the Canon was formed, which in its turn served as a check upon Tradition. To it we owe the systematic arrangement of the Articles of the Faith in the Creed, the preservation of the typical method of the interpretation of Scripture, and many practical points of Church discipline, such as the observance of Sunday, the method of consecrating the Eucharist, &c. The security that we still possess the Tradition is guaranteed by the Apostolical Succession. We cannot afford as loyal churchmen to neglect this aid. Of the two tests, Tradition and Holy Scripture, either suffers if the other is neglected; and in our present day we need to be guarded against the desire for novelty, against the danger of an empty Nominalism, which resolves the mysteries of the faith into mere externals and methods of speech with no real counterpart in the nature of things; and against Erastianism, which would surrender ecclesiastical government to the State.

The sermon met with a good deal of criticism, to which Keble replied in an elaborate postscript, showing the hearty recognition of Tradition in Anglican writers, and elaborating at great detail the part which Tradition had borne in the formulation of the Nicene Creed.

During the same year Pusey, Newman, and Keble as joint editors started the Library of the Fathers; the proposal was welcomed by the Archbishop, who pressed the advisability of translating whole treatises instead of mere selections, and the series was dedicated to him. To this Keble contributed a translation of St. Irenæus, a work on which he was engaged from this time onwards, though it was not published till after his death; he also did much work as editor, revising the translations of some of the volumes of St. Augustine and St. Chrysostom.

In the spring of 1837, Pusey writes, asking—" What are *you* doing, our father in the faith, perhaps Newman's elder brother only now?" The answer is that he was working at his translation, and was with Newman preparing Froude's *Remains* for publication. Froude had died in 1836, and it had been like the loss of a younger brother to Keble. Both he and Newman were conscious how much they had owed to Froude, and when they came to examine his journal, and understood, as never before, the strength and severity of his self-discipline, as well as the logical boldness with which he faced the results of the movement, they determined that the world should know what he had been, and decided to publish extracts from his journal and correspondence as well as his fragmentary writings. It was a bold step, for Froude was fearlessly out-spoken in his attacks on Rationalism and on the Reformers, and the book was sure to swell the cry of Popery against the Tractarians. They determined, however, to face the cry, and the first two volumes appeared in 1838, with a joint preface, in which Keble justified the publication of matter so private, and Newman showed that Froude could not be legitimately charged with Romanism, in the sense of preferring the actual system of the Church of Rome to the English Church, because he had been equally outspoken in denunciation of that Church. At the same time they boldly claim that ministers of the Established Church owe no sort of allegiance to any enactments by which the State has fettered her freedom of action, but at the outside only such a literal acquiescence as the law requires. "Their loyalty is already engaged to the Church Catholic, and they cannot enter into the drift and intentions of her oppressors without betraying her. For example, they cannot do more than submit to the statute of Præmunire ; they cannot defend or concur in the present suspension, in every form, of the Church's synodal powers and her power of excommunication ; nor can they sympathize in the provision which hinders their celebrating five out of the daily services which are their patrimony equally with Romanists." [1]

The outcry raised against the book was bitter and loud ; to Dr. Arnold the predominant character of the volume seemed to be extraordinary impudence in its language about the Reformers. But the editors were not daunted. Two further volumes were published in 1839, with a preface almost entirely due to Keble, and quite unflinching in statement. He recalls the tone of Church feeling a few years before ; he

[1] Preface, p. xv.

shows how Froude's sagacity had anticipated all the
improvements which had occurred since then; only
in some such startling way was it possible to make
a protest heard. All that Froude had done was to
carry out uncompromisingly, in points both of doctrine
and feeling, the appeal to antiquity; that appeal was
the only ground on which the English Church could
maintain its existence against Rome, and therefore he
was quite justified in denouncing all that was inconsistent with it in the dominant tone of theological thought.
Further, the same principle justified him in denouncing
any rationalistic or irreverent or Erastian temper in the
Reformers; no doubt natural piety and gratitude for our
debt to the Reformation would make us wish not to
find fault with them, but this was impossible; they
were not as a party to be trusted on ecclesiastical and
theological questions. The true plan was to emphasize
the fact that the Church was not to be identified with
the Reformers, and to claim the right and duty of taking
her formulæ as we find them, and interpreting them
as, God be thanked, they may be always interpreted in
all essentials, conformably to the doctrine and ritual
of the Church Universal. Providence has wonderfully
over-ruled the Reformation from expressly contradicting
antiquity, so that, "as a mark of decay and deserved
anger, our Church seems to have been left an inadequate image of antiquity; as a token to encourage hope
and penitence and labour, it was not, however, an
untrue image." Thus, whatever they may think of the
Reformers, people need not be driven to Rome; there is
the ancient Church waiting to receive them, and the
Prayer-book and Anglican Divines of the seventeenth
century ready to cover their retreat. This condemna-

tion of the Reformers was clinched by a catena of quotations from the works of Bishop Jewel, to show the low doctrine which he held on points such as the Apostolical Succession and Sacramental Grace.

Such language naturally did little to allay any feeling of bitterness; but before we dwell on the effect produced, it may be well to mention two other works on which Keble was engaged. In May 1839, he published anonymously his translation of the *Psalter*. He himself confesses that it was really impossible to represent the Hebrew rhythm by metres, but as metrical versions of the Psalms were in use, and as he was impressed with the want of reverence of Tate and Brady's version, he made an attempt to represent them as faithfully as possible, each Hebrew clause being represented by one line, and the metre varied, even within the same Psalm. No attempt was made to express a Christian meaning, that he might be true to the working of God's Holy Spirit, accustomed "to keep himself to the generality under a veil of reserve, through which the eyes of men might see just so much and so clearly as they were purged by Faith and Purity and Obedience." The whole work was revised by Dr. Pusey, and consequently it is valuable as a commentary upon the original. Dr. Cheyne, in the Preface to his own translation of the Book of Psalms, speaks of Keble's too little known metrical version as the production of a poetical student, and acknowledges his indebtedness to it now and again for a felicitous phrase. Keble had hoped that the Bishops of Winchester and Oxford would formally license it for use; but though the latter accepted the dedication of the book, neither was willing to do this; and, in truth, it is little fitted for congre-

H

gatioual worship, the attempt to be literal having hampered his freedom too much.

At the same time he had been interested in tracing out the Patristic method of the mystical interpretation of Holy Scripture. On his visits to Oxford as Professor, he had read more than one paper on it at the gatherings for theological study, which Dr. Pusey had instituted at his own house. These were thrown together in a completed form, and appeared in 1841 as Tract No. 89. It extends to nearly two hundred pages—so completely had Dr. Pusey's influence altered the character of the tracts and converted them into treatises —and even so is unfinished. He proposes at the outset to deal with four points, with regard to which the vague and ambiguous charge of mysticism was urged to discredit the Fathers, viz. their figurative interpretation of Holy Scripture, their fanciful application of Nature to spiritual realities, their readiness to see providential interferences in the events of history, and their counsels of perfection in favour of a monastic and contemplative life; but it is only with the first two of these that the Tract deals. After a large catena of illustrations of this mystical interpretation it is urged that this method has the sanction of the New Testament, that it cannot be exactly formulated or regulated, but is the result of a happy sagacity inwrought into the thoughts and language of the Church, and independent of critical questions. Yet it was never put forward as the exclusive meaning; it was never allowed to evacuate the literal truth, nor did it interfere with moral judgments upon acts of doubtful character. In dealing with such points the Fathers, while they always upheld the doctrine of a permanent standard of morality, yet were doubtless far more lenient in judgment than modern writers, and far less willing to condemn any of the saints of the Old Testament. They were content to point to a Divine command without justifying it, or simply to see the typical value in the action; suggesting excuses and shrinking from censure if possible. Such leniency of judgment was due to two principles; on the one hand it sprang from a deep sense of the communion of saints; they felt a real bond of union with the Old Testament saints, their fathers in faith, in a sense their brethren in grace; and a natural piety made them shrink from criticizing: they would rather pass no judgment than a verdict of guilty upon members of their own family. On the other hand, they had also a deep and reverential sense of God's peculiar presence in Jewish history. The whole Jewish kingdom was to them "a great prophet, because he is great who was the subject of their prophecy,"[1] and so they had a trembling consciousness that they were near the invisible line which separates God's agency from that of His rational creatures, and such a thought will make a religious man slow to censure, lest he may be found blaming his Maker's work unawares.

The similar mystical treatment of the New Testament is shown to rest upon a belief in the Divinity of the Lord; "the words and doings of our Blessed Saviour, being, as they are, the words and doings of God, it cannot be but they must mean far more than meets the ear or the eye, they cannot but be full charged with heavenly and mysterious meaning."

Finally, in dealing with Nature, it is shown that the

---

[1] S. Aug. c. Faustum xx. 24; totum illud regnum gentis Hebræorum magnum quemdam, quia et magni cujusdam, fuisse prophetam.

Fathers discourage the mere scientific study of it; they are always piercing through to a mystical sense. This is analogous to the poet's use of illustrations from Nature; but it runs deeper than this, and it is so common that it cannot be traced to any one Father's influence. It is the poetry of the Lord Himself, "a set of holy and divine associations and meanings wherewith it is His will to invest material things"; the works of God are so many visible words, tokens from the Almighty to assure us of some spiritual fact or other, which it concerns us to know; in St. Augustine's words, "All beauty in Thy creatures is but so many beckonings of Thine." [1] Sun, moon, stars, plants, animals, all are treated as symbols of spiritual realities; the body of a man is a symbol of his soul, and his soul a type even of God Himself. All are reflections, types, embodiments of Him who is the Reality, the True Light, the True Vine, the True Bread. If our own words seem often full of a deeper meaning than we intended, if the same words produce upon us quite a different effect at different times, it is natural that we should be constantly able to find new meanings in Divine language, and that it should speak a different language to those whose hearts are prepared to receive it.

Such is the general argument, which is worked out with great wealth of illustration. But it was an "inopportune Tract." [2] Why was this? It was a treatise which at any time would have provoked opposition and would have required a nature of delicate insight and ready sympathy to appreciate its merits. There is no compromise in his attack on the tendencies of modern theology; he is ready to throw it entirely overboard in

---

[1] *De Libero Arbitrio*, ii., p. 43: "Nutus tui sunt omne creaturarum decus.

[2] R. W. Church, *Oxford Movement*, pp. 229, 230.

contrast to ancient methods; while he urges that the
taste of modern writers may be imperfect, he forgets
that that may be equally true of the ancient. He makes
no attempt to screen fanciful uses of the method, but
selects the examples most likely to startle and scandalize
the modern reader: he goes near to shocking the moral
sense by his unwillingness to condemn immoral actions
in the Bible; and throughout the whole there is too
great an effort to formulate too exactly a method
which is essentially poetical and imaginative. Yet,
when all these deductions have been made, it is a
beautiful specimen of the true reverence with which the
Bible should be handled, and all who care for poetry or
spiritual life will value it highly. For it is a poet's
protest against a prosaic age, pleading for the beauty
and fullness of life. Material things are treated as not
only material, but as able to express the spiritual; words,
especially Divine words, are seen to represent realities
greater than they are adequate to express: they are not
to be narrowed down to a dead level of utilitarian
literalism; they are legitimately capable of the meanings
we can find in them, and therefore Origen, with his
threefold interpretation, was so far superior to the mere
literalist that he had three Bibles to the other's one.
It is the protest again of the religious man against
excluding God from His world. He is there in material
things which are a revelation of Himself. He has been
present at every moment of history, so that there are
"as many different manifestations of the Word, as many
Christs as there are believers." Therefore what He did
then has a lasting value for us, and we are one with the
saints of old and must look to find God in every detail
of our lives. "People little know what they do, when

they deal contemptuously with anything, be it in Scripture or in common life, under the notion that it is too slight, too insignificant for the ordering of the Most High" (p. 22). Lastly, it is a protest of the heart against the intellect, a plea that the pure in heart shall see God, that the love of Him will open our eyes to see deeper meanings in His words. As the lover sees likenesses of his mistress in many a face, and loves them for her sake, so the lover of Christ's Cross will find symbols and anticipations of it in trifling details of the Old Testament, which get a new value for its sake. Such suggestions cannot be tied down to exact details, nor the mystical method restrained by certain limits, but this was part of the charm of it to Keble. To him it seemed "one of the tokens of true theology to acknowledge doubtfulness and perplexity, more or less, in every subject, for the doubtfulness of many things has this advantage, that it lessens the apparent difference between the scenes of Scripture and common life; lessens the temptation to forget how near God is with us; helps us to feel our true condition as full of supernatural wonders, could we but realize them, as ever was that of the Jews and Patriarchs of old."

It would have been difficult for these views to win ready acceptance at any time, most of all in Oxford in the beginning of 1841. A nightingale might as soon have expected to be listened to on a field of battle. Keble might be willing to remain in doubt and perplexity; others were not: neither friend nor foe were in that frame of mind. For a change had come over the movement in Oxford, to understand which we must go back over the last few years.

CHAPTER V.

THE STRUGGLE (*continued*). 1841—1845.

"The second Temple could not reach the first ;
And the late Reformation never durst
Compare with ancient times and purer years ;
But in the Jews and us deserveth tears."—G. HERBERT.

" ἀμηχανῶ φροντίδος στερηθεὶς
εὐπαλάμων μεριμνᾶν
ὅπᾳ τράπωμαι, πίτνοντος οἴκου.
δέδοικα δ' ὄμβρου κτύπον δομοσφαλῆ
τὸν αἱματηρόν. Ψεκὰς δὲ λήγει."

ÆSCH. *Agam.*, 1531-6.

WE have seen that one of the objects, though but a
subordinate object, of the movement, had been to resist
the claims of the Roman Church. But the Hampden
controversy in 1836 had produced an apparent change.
The stress laid upon the dogmatic character of Catholic
truth, and the importance attached to Church authority,
lent themselves to the charge, which the friends of
Hampden knew well how to use, that the movement
was really Romanizing, that its principles must end in
secession. Nor was this a wholly unfounded suspicion.
The appeal to antiquity, the doctrine of Apostolical
succession, the sense of continuity, all were equally
valid for Rome as for England. The sense of this

came home with a strange shock and reversal of opinion
to men who had been accustomed to think of the Pope
as Antichrist; and when once this prejudice was
shaken, the Roman Church, with its wide-spread
organization, its developed life of self-sacrifice in
brotherhoods and sisterhoods, its elaborate system of
dogma and of canon law, offered a more attractive
picture to the imagination than an insular provincial
Church, struggling to preserve a Catholic creed in the
spirit of compromise, and obscuring its witness for self-
sacrifice in what was too often an atmosphere of self-
satisfied worldliness. Were there, then, no counter-
balancing facts? or, if not, was the Church of England
to surrender its position? To this problem Newman
addressed himself in his lectures on the Prophetical
Office of the Church, in 1837. Discarding, as indeed
Keble had done as early as 1824, the theory which
identified the Pope with Antichrist, he urged that
we are bound to recognize heartily all that is good in
Rome, that both Rome and England are branches of
the Catholic Church, that Rome has preserved sides of
truth which we have lost, and bears more clearly the
note of Catholicity; but that on the other hand it bears
less clearly than we the note of Apostolicity; its
witness to the Truth is less clear, less true to Tradition;
its doctrine of Infallibility is not borne out by history,
and it claims for the human mind a greater certainty
than man has a right to claim.

But the suspicions were not allayed. In 1838, the
Bishop of Oxford, in a Charge which was not unsympathetic, yet spoke cautiously and warningly of the
movement; there was "a cloud from Cuddesdon," but
a cloud that soon blew over. Newman's first inclina-

tion had been to cease the Tracts, but Keble was strongly for continuing them. "No one has encouraged me but you," Newman writes to him. But the more conservative Bisley group of Tractarians had taken fright at a proposal to translate the Breviary for the use of English Churchmen; and again Keble was the mediating and soothing influence. Yet, "unpleasant tendencies to split were developing themselves on all sides";[1] for there was a new factor in the problem, a contingent of allies who were destined to have a great influence on the issue of the campaign. The excitement of battle, the deep spiritual appeal of Newman's sermons, the intellectual subtlety of his lectures, drew round him a band of young Oxford men, full of enthusiasm, ready for self-sacrifice, but untrained in any historic sense of Churchmanship, and therefore liable to be carried away by the conception of an ideal Church presented for the first time to their minds. The leader of these was W. G. Ward, a man of strong logical power, with a passion for dialectic, with a longing for personal sanctity, who had been converted from a follower of Arnold to that of Newman, but one who had no knowledge of history, no real care for it, and little consideration for the feelings of others; one who in some ways was the Hurrell Froude of the later part of the movement, but Hurrell Froude such as he was untamed and unsoftened by the influence of Keble.

Such were the "tendencies to split developing themselves on all sides" at the beginning of 1839, nor did they grow less during that year. The publication of Froude's *Remains,* with his outspoken language in

---

[1] J. H. N. : *Letters,* ii., p. 272.

condemnation of the Reformers, and his praise of many
points in the Roman system, unbalanced by the qualifications which his love of truth would have supplied
had he been reviewing the whole question, or had he
been writing in the face of the circumstances of the time,
tended to widen the split and to increase the violence
of the Romanizing party: "It delighted me more than
any book of the kind I ever read," wrote Ward to Dr.
Pusey.[1] The counter-move of the Oxford residents to
erect the Martyrs' Memorial drove the cleavage further.
Newman would not subscribe to it; Keble would have
preferred some memorial of the Reformation without
mention of the Reformers, and was unwilling to express
a public dissent from Froude in his opinions of the
Reformers as a party; Pusey was willing to recognize
that we owe to the Reformers our position of adherents
to Catholic antiquity; but all three ultimately refused
to subscribe.

In the course of the same year Newman himself
received the first shocks to his own allegiance to
Anglicanism : in the study of the Monophysite heresy,
a suspicion crossed his mind that the position of the
Anglican Church was similar to that of the Monophy-
sites ; in the study of the Donatist heresy the principle
on which St. Augustine decided against them, " securus
judicat orbis Terrarum," seemed to favour Rome rather
than England. But Newman's doubts were known to
few ; indeed they seemed to pass from his own mind ;
he wrote in the *British Critic* of January, 1840, an
article on the Catholicity of the English Church, still
upholding the theory that both Churches were true
branches of the Catholic Church, and should be neutral

---

[1] *W. G. Ward and the Oxford Movement*, p. 84.

in their judgments of each other. He was, however, very apprehensive of lapses on the part of the younger writers, who urged that while both Churches were Catholic, the Roman was the nearer to the ideal, that it had retained the most valuable truths, and that English Churchmen were at liberty to revive and restore everything in doctrine and practice which they found there. The tone of their articles in the *British Critic* was already giving offence to Keble, who was fearful lest people "should speak in a light, lawless tone of the Church of England and her authorities in their greater veneration for the Church of the Fathers." The position of Newman was intensely difficult. He craved for quiet and time for thought. He resigned his editorship of the *British Critic* to his brother-in-law, T. Mozley; he prepared to leave his rooms in Oriel and live entirely at Littlemore; he even consulted Keble on the duty of resigning the Vicarage of St. Mary's. He urged that he did not really influence those who were his *bonâ fide* parishioners, that on the other hand he did influence the undergraduates, for whom he was not responsible, in a way which the Heads of Houses resented, and again that he found that he excited sympathies in favour of Rome stronger than the arguments which he used against it. Keble replied shortly on the first two points, that we may not measure our influence by what we see, and that the Heads of Houses had no authority over the Vicar of St. Mary's; on the third point he was more explicit: he did not see how the resignation of St. Mary's would mend matters as long as he continued exercising influence by his writing. No doubt the Tractarian position lent itself to such risks, but his presence in

Oxford helped to minimize the risk ; no one had yet joined the Church of Rome, and his retirement might cause equal scandal and distress. His advice was, then, clearly against retirement, unless Newman could see some way to obviate the scandals which might ensue.

Newman followed this advice and remained, but the pressure from the Romanizing party was still upon him ; and early in 1841 he wrote Tract 90, with the object of showing that the Articles had been composed as articles of peace between the two opposing parties at the time of the Reformation, that they could not have been intended to contradict the teaching of the Council of Trent, which was formulated after the Articles, but were only aimed at the current popular Romanism, and consequently that they were capable of a Catholic interpretation, for they were intended to keep the Catholic party in the Church : " Though the offspring of an uncatholic age, they are, through God's good providence, to say the least, not uncatholic, and may be subscribed by those who aim at being Catholic in heart and doctrine." This was proved by a careful and legal examination of their language. The Tract before publication was sent to Keble, who read it through with his curate and strongly recommended its publication. The tone of it, in its desire to keep men loyal to the Church in England and yet to recognize thoroughly that Church's shortcomings, the call to repentance and confession and prayer for unity, and meanwhile the exhortation to submit to imperfections as a punishment, to go on teaching, if only "with the stammering lips of ambiguous formularies and inconsistent precedents and principles partially developed "—these exactly fell

in with Keble's own patient humility, and, in fact, the
Tract did not in its position advance an inch beyond
the ground which he had taken in common with Newman in the Preface to Froude's *Remains*. But the
atmosphere was more charged now with elements of
disturbance. Everywhere were feelings of distrust,
doubt, panic; and panic begat injustice.

On February 27th the Tract was published, but,
like all the other Tracts except Dr. Pusey's, published
anonymously. On March 8th, four tutors, alarmed at
the tendency of it, printed a joint memorial to Newman, as editor of the series, asking that the name of
the writer should be revealed. Newman began at
once to prepare a defence of the Tract, showing how
the tutors had misunderstood him; but, meanwhile,
the Hebdomadal Board, though no appeal had been
made to them, took cognizance of the matter. On
March 10th the Vice-Chancellor laid the Tract before
the Board; on the 12th it was decided to condemn
it, and a Committee was appointed to draw up the
resolution. In vain Newman wrote, pleading for
delay till his answer to the four tutors should be
printed; in vain Dr. Pusey wrote privately to the Vice-
Chancellor to bear witness to the loyalty of the writer
of the Tract, and to his desire to keep back anxious
minds from Rome by writing it; in vain Keble wrote,
taking upon himself the responsibility for the publication. On the 15th a resolution was passed by the
Board, which repudiated the whole series of Tracts as
being in no way sanctioned by the University itself,
and passed judgment on this particular Tract on the
ground that the modes of interpretation suggested in
it, evading rather than explaining the sense of the

Thirty-nine Articles, and reconciling subscription to them with the adoption of errors which they were designed to counteract, defeat the object and are inconsistent with the due observance of the statutes which require subscription to the Articles. On the 16th Newman's answer was published; this was still anonymous, but on the publication of the decision of the Board he wrote to the Vice-Chancellor to acknowledge the authorship, and to take the sole responsibility upon himself. The injustice of the decision, and the touching humility with which Newman received it, drew Churchmen closer together; the more conservative element of the party rallied round him; the extremer party, through the mouth of Ward, were equally enthusiastic, but damaged his cause by pressing the argument further than Tract 90 had done, and claiming the right to hold all Roman doctrines. A shower of pamphlets followed; but it is only with one that we need concern ourselves. On April 2nd Keble addressed a letter to Judge Coleridge, pointing out the dangers involved in the course proposed by the Board—a letter which was privately circulated at the time, and not published till 1865. In it he pleaded for patient reflection and enquiry before any irretrievable step was taken; for the danger was that a liberty of interpretation which had always been allowed in the Church should now be barred. A resolution of the Board was not authoritative; but it would be a serious matter if the whole Convocation of the University were to condemn authoritatively such an interpretation; it would be difficult for any tutor who believed the interpretation to be true to hold his office; nay, it would be a question whether Masters of Arts who had subscribed the Articles when this interpretation was left open, could remain members of the University. Such an act of Convocation would really be the adoption of a new test. The matter was even more serious if applied to clerical subscription; if the Catholic interpretation of the Articles was barred, what were the clergy who believe it to do ? It was true that only a Synodical act of the whole Church could make such a change, and such a Synod was not likely to meet; yet if all the bishops, or a majority of them, were to pronounce separately against the interpretation, if even one's own bishop were officially to denounce it, the duty of the consistent Churchman would be very difficult; he must either continue his work under protest from his bishop to the Metropolitan or to a Synod, or he must retire into another diocese or into lay communion. "Farther than it, we could not even appear to separate from that which we believe to be the manifestation of the Holy Catholic Church in our country. We could not be driven into schism against our will. We could only wait patiently at the Church door, wishing and praying that our bonds might be taken off, and pleading our cause as we best might from reason and Scripture and Church precedents." The letter ended with an appeal to those who did not sympathize with him, not to force on extreme measures which would weaken the Church's position as against Rome, which would drive many from taking Holy Orders, and be the cause of schism and controversy.

The extracts quoted above show how much Keble feared the possibility of some secessions to Rome, and tried to meet the danger, even as Newman's words in Tract 90, "Every change in religion carries with it its own condemnation, which is not attended by deep re-

pentance," betray the same fear, and a desire to secure
that, at any rate, a change should not be made with a
light heart. But, for the moment, the danger passed.
When, on St. Andrew's Day, Keble, who was appointed
to preach before the University, prepared a sermon
against secession, Newman dissuaded him from preaching it; he thought there was no one in Oxford in any
immediate danger of such an act. Moreover, the
Heads took no further steps against him. He was
waiting quietly to see what would happen outside
Oxford; whether the bishops would acquiesce in or
denounce the Catholic interpretation. The Church
seemed to him on her trial.

In the course of the year two things occurred, each of
which seemed of bad omen. The Archbishop of Canterbury agreed to a plan suggested by M. Bunsen, for
appointing a Protestant Bishop at Jerusalem, to exercise jurisdiction over the German and English residents.
To Newman this was naturally abhorrent, as it showed
that the English Church was ready to ally itself in
common action with Lutherans and Calvinists, and to
admit them to communion without any renunciation of
their errors. "The Archbishop is doing all he can to
unchurch us," he wrote to his sister, and he liberated
his own soul by a formal protest which he forwarded to
the Bishop of Oxford. Keble had been doubtful of the
wisdom of this protest; it seemed to him rather wanting in reverence towards those whom he censured, and
the fact of a presbyter protesting against an act of his
Metropolitan seemed to require some very commanding
call of duty to justify it.

The other matter touched Keble more closely. In
July the Bishop of Winchester refused to give Priest's

Orders to his curate, the Rev. Peter Young, on the ground of his statements about the Real Presence in the Eucharist, and in September spoke severely of Tractarianism in his Charge. For the moment Keble was inclined to resign, or at least to challenge the Bishop to bring the matter to a legal issue; but he was dissuaded by Pusey and Newman, and ultimately contented himself with a formal protest against the Bishop's action, addressed to his Metropolitan. The Archbishop's answer was kind, but rather vague and unsatisfactory, and it produced no result. Mr. Young remained in Deacon's Orders, a faithful, affectionate, trustworthy, and trusted curate at Hursley, till 1857, when he removed to the Exeter diocese, and was ordained for the Bishop of Exeter by the Bishop of Oxford at Cuddesdon.

Meanwhile the anti-Tractarian party grew more aggressive, and there was a quick succession of sharp struggles. On October 19, 1841, Keble delivered his last lecture as Professor of Poetry, and it became necessary to elect his successor. Isaac Williams was the most obvious candidate, and was at once proposed by his friends. But he was a Tractarian, the author of Tract 80 on "Reserve in communicating Religious Knowledge," and on that ground unacceptable to many. Mr. Garbett of Brasenose was entered as a rival candidate. Owing, partly, to a kindly but ill-judged letter of Dr. Pusey's, the election was treated as a party question; and on a comparison of promises it was found that Mr. Garbett could command 921, as compared with 632 given to Mr. Williams, and the latter withdrew.

In June 1842 further ill-will was caused in connection with Dr. Hampden. An attempt made by his friends to rescind the censure passed upon him

I

in 1836 was rejected by 334 to 219; in the autumn of the same year Dr. Hampden himself attempted to crush out the Tractarian teaching by making the theses which were written by candidates for the B.D. degree into a test of orthodoxy. This was a new departure, and beyond the actual power allowed him by the statutes; hence Mr. Macmullen, whose degree Dr. Hampden refused, appealed against it, and when the Vice-Chancellor vetoed the degree, his veto was appealed against and ultimately overthrown. Keble, who felt the injustice of the treatment, was inclined to throw himself into the breach. "I suppose it would be a bravado," he wrote to Dr. Pusey, "if I came up and took my B.D. degree myself, and so got them to try it out in my case rather than his."

In the next year the opponents essayed a higher flight. On May 24th Dr. Pusey preached a sermon before the University on "The Holy Eucharist a Comfort to the Penitent." This was delated to the Vice-Chancellor by Dr. Faussett; the Vice-Chancellor at once sent for the sermon, appointed six doctors, including Dr. Faussett, to examine it; they, refusing a hearing to Dr. Pusey, passed their condemnation upon it as contrary to the doctrine of the Church of England, and the Vice-Chancellor suspended Dr. Pusey from preaching for the space of two years. A request, signed by sixty members of Convocation, that he would make known the grounds of the decision, and state what parts of the sermon were contrary to the teaching of the Church, was refused by the Vice-Chancellor.

It was a Cadmean victory. The humility with which Dr. Pusey accepted the sentence won sympathy for his cause; he refused to have its legality challenged, bore his silence with patience, and on resuming his turn as preacher after the suspension, resumed the subject as though nothing had happened. And further, the effect of the conduct of the opponents was this. They had silenced the voices of the two people at Oxford who by the weight of their character and of their learning could have controlled and guided the younger spirits. Pusey was suspended from preaching; Newman, wincing under censure, had withdrawn from Oriel and was living in quiet and retirement at Littlemore, feeling that one condemned by the Hebdomadal Board had no right to take active part in academical politics. Meanwhile, the younger members of the movement were unchecked. In the pages of the *British Critic*, Ward and Oakeley were pressing their views to extremes. The Articles were treated by them as essentially Puritan, and therefore needing to be explained away in what Ward afterwards called a " non-natural " sense; the ideal notes of the Church were enumerated, and it was argued that the English Church not only failed to reach that ideal, but fell far short of the point reached by the Church of Rome : the Roman teaching was accepted as the right development of primitive truth. The failures of Rome, the positive excellences of England in teaching and in practice, were alike thrown into the background. Both Pusey and Keble were anxious about the tone of these articles, and Palmer wrote his *Narrative of Events connected with the Tracts for the Times*, in order to protest against this tendency to Romanism. The result was that the *British Critic* was discontinued, but Ward prepared an answer to Palmer, which appeared in June, 1844, entitled *The Ideal of a Christian Church*, reiterating and developing the superiority of the Roman

Church, and claiming the right to hold the whole cycle of Roman doctrine. This, naturally enough, gave the signal for another great struggle in Oxford. The Hebdomadal Board took up the matter in the Michaelmas Term, and in December gave notice that in the Hilary Term they should propose to condemn Mr. Ward's book, and to deprive him of his degrees. Six passages were quoted in full, and were charged with being inconsistent with the Articles and with Mr. Ward's good faith in subscribing them. But the Board went further than the immediate danger, and proposed to guard against a recurrence of it by enacting that every one who subscribed the Articles henceforth should make a declaration that he did so in the sense in which they were both first published and were now imposed by the University.

The outcry against this third resolution was so great that it was withdrawn on January 23rd; but yielding to a largely-signed petition, the Board substituted for it an equally unwise proposal, to pass upon Tract No. 90 the censure which they themselves had passed upon it when it first appeared. The outcry against this was as great as against their previous resolution; pamphlets were written, legal opinions circulated on both sides. On a cold, snowy day in February nearly 1200 members of Convocation came to vote. Feeling had turned somewhat in Ward's favour, but his speech was absolutely uncompromising and unconciliatory. The proposal to condemn the book was carried by 777 to 391; that to degrade the writer by 569 to 511; while the censure on Tract No. 90 was vetoed by the two Proctors, Mr. Guillemard and Mr. Church. An expression of thanks which was circulated by Mr. Charles Marriott and signed by 543 members of Convocation, showed that the Proctors had rightly interpreted the feeling of the University. Keble was in the minority on each vote. Early in the controversy, on January 16th, he had written from Hursley a short paper entitled, *Heads of Consideration on the Case of Mr. Ward,* "the most weighty of all the protests on Mr. Ward's behalf."[1] He was not personally acquainted with Mr. Ward. He was repelled by his off-handness. He admits that he feels serious disagreement with some of his principles; but he was attracted by his thoroughness and earnestness. He felt grateful for much that Mr. Ward had written, and was especially fired by the injustice which meted out to Romanizing exaggerations a measure so different from that meted to ultra-Protestant or even Sabellian teaching. The two points on which he lays stress are the inexpediency and probable illegality of the act. It was inexpedient for a deliberative body, like Convocation, ever to perform a judicial act. It was specially inexpedient in this case, because there was no necessity for it, as so few people agreed with Mr. Ward; because there was no security for impartiality where it was notorious that more flagrant inconsistencies with the truth passed unpunished; and because it impugned the *good faith* of Mr. Ward, whereas every one, who knew his character, knew that that at least was untrue. It was probably illegal because it was doubtful whether Convocation could degrade a Master of Arts except for offences for which this penalty was imposed by the statutes. When the degradation had passed, it is said that Keble refused, for a whole year, to wear his own

[1] Wilfrid Ward, in *William George Ward and the Oxford Movement.*

Master's hood, so keenly did he feel the unfairness of the judgment.

Such was the drama being enacted before the world —a drama serious enough, though Ward, with his rollicking humour, with his comic songs, with the sudden surprise of his engagement to be married at the moment when he was upholding the celibacy of the priesthood, contrived to mystify the spectators, and make them think that it was a comedy which was being played. But behind the scenes it was a real tragedy which was being enacted. Newman had retired from his Oriel rooms, and settled at Littlemore in February, 1842; in his retirement there, the charges of the Bishops, repudiating the principles of Tract 90, seemed to him to show that the Church of England would refuse to accept her Catholic heritage. In February, 1843, he retracted the hard things which he had said about Rome; in August of the same year, Lockhart, one of the inmates of his house at Littlemore, who had come there perplexed about the claims of the Roman Church, and who had promised to give three years to the consideration of the question, broke his promise and joined the Church of Rome before one year had elapsed. In September, Newman resigned the Vicarage at St. Mary's, this time with Keble's acquiescence. In 1845, the theory of development seemed to open a way to Newman by which he could explain honestly the divergences between Primitive and Roman doctrines. On October 6th he resigned his Fellowship at Oriel, and within two days was received into the Church of Rome. They were years of spiritual and physical tension, painful alike to the sufferer and to those who knew what was passing. The scene might be compared to that of Prometheus chained to the rock; and meanwhile, from time to time, there came from Hursley voices of sympathy, of encouragement, of hope, of delicate suggestion, of respectful tenderness for the mystery that was passing in the recesses of another's soul, like the utterances of a chorus, one in heart and in years with the Protagonist.

Thus, in answer to Newman's request for advice about resigning St. Mary's, Keble writes, on May 14, 1843—

." Believe me, my very dear Newman, that any thought of wilful insincerity in you can find no place in my mind. You have been and are in a most difficult position, and I seem to myself in some degree able to enter into your difficulties; and although one sees of course how an enemy might misrepresent your continuing in the English Priesthood with such an impression on your mind, I have no thought but of love and esteem and regard and gratitude for you in this as in everything in this way. But I can only just say what I feel, perfectly unequal as I know myself on every account to give you advice on this awful matter. My feeling is that your withdrawing from the English Ministry under the present circumstances will be a very perilous step, not so much in itself, but because of its bringing you, as I fear it would, in every respect nearer what I must call the temptation of going over. (2) That this latter would indeed be a grievous event, considering that for what is wrong without our fault in the place where God's providence has set us we are not ourselves answerable, but we are for what may be wrong in the position we choose for ourselves. (3) That this difference in point of responsibility ought in a matter

of practice to outweigh the difference you feel on the
other side in the evidence for the claims of Rome and
against her additions to the Creed, and especially as
(4) you seem to ground your impression chiefly on
points of historical evidence; you speak of it as a
'hideous dream' from which you would gladly awake;
it does not overpower you with a sort of intrinsical
lustre, as many Divine truths I suppose might.
(5) You speak in one part of your letter of our
Church showing no sign of repentance, no yearning
after Catholicity; but is not the time too short for any
one to be acting on this impression? Certainly there
is a great yearning even after Rome in many parts of
the Church, which seems to be accompanied with so
much good that one hopes if it be right it will be
allowed to gain strength. But from Bishops one could
hardly look at present for more than toleration; and
that I consider even myself to have from my Diocesan,
much more you from yours. Are you sure that some
of your feeling on this head is not owing to a natural
reaction from having had too eager expectations at
some time? (6) I am not sure how far it is right to
talk of consequences, but I suppose, as far as we can
judge of them, that no one thing would tend more entirely
to throw us back and undo what little good may have
been done of late. As to the question itself, I am really
too ignorant of the parts of history to which you refer
to say a word; but can it be that the evidence seems
so overpowering as to amount to moral certainty? and
if not, ought not but a small probability on the other
side to weigh against it practically?

"You see my deep feeling about your withdrawing
from your ministerial place refers almost wholly to what

I fear might come after; if I were secure against such consequences, I cannot say that I should think it wrong, great as the alarm would perhaps be for a time, and the loss too in many respects.

"One thing occurs to me. Do you not think it possible that you may have over-estimated the claims of Rome in your later studies from a kind of feeling that your earlier expressions had done her wrong? and now that you have retracted them, would it not be well to examine the matter over again, free as you would be from that particular bias?

"And now, my dearest Newman, I have one most earnest request to make of you: that you will not in the smallest degree depend on my advice or opinion in this matter, for you do not, you cannot [*words struck out*] to advise with about it, in *every respect* but true love (I believe) towards you. It frightens me to think how rashly, and with how small preparation, I have been dealing with these great matters, and I have all manner of imaginations as to how my defects may have helped to unsettle people, and in particular to hinder you from finding peace. Yet do not suppose I would stop you from writing to me if it is the least relief to you to do so. On the contrary, not to hear from you would be a sad loss. All I want is that you should put no sort of implicit faith in me, but take up with what I say when you see anything in it that is reasonable and right, not otherwise.

"I still cling to the hope you taught me to entertain, that in the present distress, where the Succession and the Creeds are, there is the Covenant, even without visible inter-Communion.

"God forgive and bless us, and choose our burthen

for us, and help us to bear it; and if it be His will, may we two never be divided in communion.

"Ever your most grateful and affectionate

"J. KEBLE."

Again, on July 29th—

"You may well believe that I have been full of thoughts about you, the more in one sense that I feel so utterly helpless and unable to think of any-thing which I can suggest as good for a person tried as you are, except what I am sure you have thought of long ago. Thus sometimes I think it would be good for you to withdraw as much as possible for a while from theological study and correspondence, and be as entirely taken up with parochial concerns; but then I am met with the recollection that you expect so soon to be separated from poor Littlemore. Again, I think unre-served confidence in some *really worthy* confessor might be a great help to you at times—I mean the sort of submission which would make you put by a subject if he bid you, without his assigning any reason. And I suppose it may be well for one to watch and pray, especially against the temptation of always being on the move, which I suppose is the portion of some minds."

On Jan. 22, 1844, he writes—

"These are some of my impressions. First, I feel more strongly with every month's, week's, day's experience the danger of tempting God, and the deep responsibility I should have to bear were I to forsake this Communion; and yet with the same lapse of time one seems to feel more and more the truth and beauty and majesty of so much which they have and we seem at least to have not. Secondly, one is at times very very strongly impressed with the thought of the Evil One, how surely he would endeavour to ruin the good work, supposing it begun, in the English Church, by laying hold of any undiscerned weakness or ill-tendency in the agents to entice or drive them out of it; such tendencies one can imagine in your case—among the rest a certain restlessness, a longing after something more, something analogous to a very exquisite ear in music which would keep you, I should think in spite of yourself, intellectually and morally dissatisfied wherever you were. If you were in a convent, you would be forced to subdue it and as it were swallow it down; may it not perhaps be your calling now to do the same, though under no such definite rule, for others' sake as well as your own? May it not be your duty, according to your own line of argument just made public, to suppress your misgivings—nay, what seem your intellectual convictions, as you would any other bad thought, making up your mind that the conclusion is undutiful, and therefore there must be some delusion in the premises? Another thought one has is of the utter confusion and perplexity, the astounding prostration of heart and mind into which so many would be thrown, were their guide and comforter to forsake them all at once, in the very act, as it would seem to them, of giving them directions which they most needed. I really suppose that it would be to *thousands* quite an indescribable shock, a trial almost too hard to be borne, making them sceptical about everything and everybody. Surely, when it is a person's duty (as St. Paul's) to take such a step as that, the tokens from above will be such (one naturally expects) as no one could mistake; and may we not piously believe that when it is the will of Divine.

Providence that such persons as Pusey, for example, should leave their present Communion, something equivalent to that voice will occur, such as an unequivocal act of heresy on the part of our Church, leaving no doubt on the mind, and that till such tokens are given, it is His will men should stay where they are? I am running on, I fear, not very wisely; and I wish I may not be distressing you, but if I could express myself better, I believe I really mean what I have learned from yourself.

*   *   *   *   *   *

"I am writing in great ignorance, and very likely quite beside the mark; if I pain or disturb you, forgive me. Somehow or other I was almost forced to write. You know I see you looking at me day after day, and I *must* speak to you now and then, and when I speak, I must say what is in my mind. May it do no harm, if it does no good. I am sure my account is heavy enough without that."

This extract from a letter of March 3rd is interesting—

"My grand swallow of pain on the subject was perhaps three-quarters of a year ago, when I received a long letter of yours, and retired into a dirty old chalk-pit to read it. I cannot tell you with what sort of fancy I look at the place now."

In June, he was pained by the publication of Arnold's *Life and Letters*, and he writes—

"You will readily understand what is the bitterest part of one's feelings in the whole matter, both in respect of Arnold and of your change, not that I mean to compare the two subjects in the least degree in point of distressfulness, but in both one has a sad depressing thought, that if one were or had been other than one is, the anguish might have been averted or mitigated. To think that you remember me continually is indeed a most consoling thought. May it always be so, and may I be more worthy of it."

In November, 1844, he sends him an extract from a letter of Judge Coleridge about the gratitude, veneration, and love which many in the English Church feel towards him, and adds—

"Therefore, my dear Newman, do not in any case imagine that you have not hundreds, not to say thousands, sympathizing with you, and feeling indeed that they owe their very selves to you. I can only speak for *one* of certain knowledge. Your sermons put me in the way, and your healing ministration helped me beyond measure. This is certain knowledge of mine, ... and wherever I go there is some one to whom you have been a channel of untold blessing. You must not be angry, for I feel as if I could not help saying it, and I am sure the very air of England all around you would say the same, if it could be made vocal. They have had unspeakable help from you, and it is now their turn to help you with their prayers and good wishes, now that you seem to be called for a while to be patient in comparative silence and inactivity."

On February 20, 1845, he writes an affectionate birthday letter, recalling the bright associations of the day in which the first stone of Littlemore Church was laid. This is printed in Newman's Letters, and need not be repeated here; but the following letter, which closes the correspondence, though already published, is too touching to be omitted.

"*October 3rd*, 1845.—I feel as if I had something to say to you, although I don't very well know what it will be; but Charlotte's illness having for the present at least abated, I find that I am better able than I have been for near a fortnight past to think and speak coherently of other things, and what can I think of so much as you, dear friend, and the ἀγωνία which awaits us with regard to you: except, indeed, when my thoughts travel on to Bisley to Tom's bedside; for there, as well as here, everything almost seems to have been, perhaps to be, hanging by a thread. At such times one seems in a way to see deeper into *realities*, and I must own to you that the impression on my own mind of the reality of the things I have been brought up among, and of its being my own fault, not theirs, whereinsoever I am found wanting, this impression seems to deepen in me as Death draws nearer; and I find it harder and harder to imagine that persons such as I have seen and heard of lately should be permitted to live and die deceiving themselves in such a point, as whether they are aliens to the grace of God's Sacraments or no.

"*October* 11*th, midnight.*—I had written thus far about a week ago, and then left off for very weariness, and now that I am thinking of going on with my writing, I find that the thunderbolt has actually fallen upon us, and you have actually taken the step which we greatly feared. I will not plague·you, then, with what I might otherwise have set down—something which passed directly relating to yourself in what fell from my dear wife on this day fortnight, when in perfect tranquillity and self-possession, having received the Holy Communion, she took leave of us all, expecting hourly to sink away. By God's great mercy she revived, and still continues among us, with

I trust increasing hopes of recovery; but the words which she spoke were such that I must always think of them as of the last words of a saint. Some of them I had thought of reporting to you, but this at any rate is not the time.

"Wilson has told me how kindly you have been remembering us in our troubles; it was very kind, when you must have so much upon your own mind. Who knows how much good your prayers and those of other absent friends may have done us both here and at Bisley? for there too, as I dare say you know, has been a favourable change, and a more decided one, I imagine, than here—at least their doctor has told them they may make themselves comfortable, which is far beyond anything that has yet been said to us. But his recovery is very very slow. There too, as well as here, everything has fallen out so as to foster the delusion, if delusion it be, that we are not quite aliens, not living among unrealities. Yet you have no doubt the other way. It is very mysterious, very bewildering indeed; but being so, one's duty seems clearly pointed out: to abide where one is, till some new call come upon one. If this were merely my own reason or feeling, I should mistrust it altogether, knowing, alas! that I am far indeed from the person to whom guidance is promised, but when I see the faith of others, such as I know them to be, and so very near to me as God has set them, I am sure that it would be a kind of impiety but to dream of separating from them.

"Besides the deep grief of losing you for a guide and helper, and scarce knowing which way to look (though I trust, thanks (in good part) to your kindness in many ways, I am not in so wretched a condition as I was),

you may guess what uncomfortable feelings haunt me,
as if I, more than any one else, was answerable for
whatever of distress and scandal may occur. I keep on
thinking, 'if I had been different, perhaps N. would
have been guided to see things differently, and we
might have been spared so many broken hearts and
bewildered spirits.' To be sure, that cold hard way of
going on, which I have mentioned to you before, stands
my friend at such times and hinders me, I suppose,
from being really distressed, but this is how I feel
that I ought to feel, and [*words struck out*] I tell you
[*words struck out*] and how I wish you to help me. That
way of help, at any rate, is not forbidden you in respect
of any one of us.

"My dearest Newman, you have been a kind and
helpful friend to me in a way in which scarce any
one else could have been, and you are so mixed up
in my mind with old and dear and sacred thoughts,
that I cannot well bear to part with you—most
unworthy as I know myself to be, and yet I cannot go
along with you. I must cling to the belief that we are
not really parted—you have taught me so, and I scarce
think you can unteach me—and having relieved my
mind with this little word, I will only say, God bless
you and reward you a thousandfold all your help in
every way to me unworthy, and to so many others. May
you have peace when you are gone, and help us in
some way to get peace ; but somehow I scarce think
it will be in the way of controversy. And so with
somewhat of a feeling as if the Spring had been taken
out of my year,

"I am always your affectionate and grateful
                                            "J. KEBLE."

CHAPTER VI.

LYRA INNOCENTIUM.

" Or if perchance a sadden'd heart
  That once was gay and felt the spring,
Cons slowly o'er its alter'd part,
  In sorrow and remorse to sing,

Thy gracious care will send that way
  Some spirit full of glee, yet taught
To bear the sight of dull decay,
  And nurse it with all-pitying thought ;

Cheerful as soaring lark, and mild
  As evening blackbird's full-toned lay,
When the relenting sun has smiled
  Bright through a whole December day.

These are the tones to brace and cheer
  The lonely watcher of the fold,
When nights are dark, and foemen near,
  When visions fade and hearts grow cold."
  The Christian Year. SS. Simon and Jude.

THE years between 1841 and 1846 were years of intense strain and weary waiting. Where were things tending ? Would the Church of England refuse to answer to the high call made upon her ? What would J. H. N. do ? If he went to Rome, ought others to follow ? What would be his own duty ? Such questions were pressing upon Keble's heart, and the tension

K

once more found relief in verse. Once more, as in the early days in Gloucestershire, there is strong feeling and there is tranquillity. Once more Keble goes back to his ideal. The vision of innocence and of holiness refreshes him again, and it is seen mirrored in the faces of young children. "Those who christen children," he said, "have a right to love them."

In the lines of the *Christian Year*, quoted above, he had described the comfort which the young could bring to the sad; and he found tones to brace and cheer him in the simple village children of Hursley, and in the growing families of Sir W. Heathcote at the Park and of Dr. Moberley, whose children spent the holidays in a farm-house in Hursley parish.

As early as 1841 he edited *The Child's Christian Year.* This is essentially a book for children; it had been compiled by Mrs. Yonge for the parish school at Otterbourne, under Keble's supervision. Four only of the hymns have since been reprinted as his own.[1] The object of the book, as described in the Preface, was " to bring ordinary parochial teaching into unison with the tone of the Prayer-book, and by consequence with that of the Ancient Universal Church; and for this purpose to raise and purify the standard by which the poor judge of religious teaching. Incidentally it is hoped that attention to this part of education may do much towards preparing another generation for something like a revival of Discipline—the only Church Reform which can really deserve the name. As things are at present, to speak of such a thing sounds almost like talk in a dream; yet if the well-disposed of our young people were trained up in the tone of the Ancient

[1] *Miscellaneous Poems*, pp. 103—109.

Church, were taught to sympathize with her and look to her for sympathy, the spirit of discipline, it would seem, could not fail to revive, and what are now mere forms would again take to themselves power." [1]

This was written on November 6, 1841. During the following years his own poems on childish life grew apace; and in 1845 an external circumstance decided him to publish them. He had made up his mind to restore the church at Hursley. Coleridge, Dyson, and Patteson advanced him money for this on the security of the copyright of the *Christian Year;* but this was not sufficient, and the need of further funds led to the publication of the *Lyra Innocentium,* which appeared— but without the author's name—in the beginning of 1846. This is not, like the compilation of 1841, a book *for* children; it does not profess to be; according to its title it is a book "*on* children; their ways and privileges"; and so it is a "mother's book"—"a sort of *Christian Year* for teachers and nurses." It is not so well known as the *Christian Year,* for it does not appeal to so wide a circle, and yet in two respects it may rank above it. First, there is more of lyrical freedom, more of metrical variety and of musical melody. *The Song of the Manna Gatherers* is more dramatic, and has perhaps more vigorous movement in it than any of his poems. *The Offertory* and *Continual Services* have

---

[1] On a stray piece of paper still preserved in Keble's writing are found the following "principles in choosing and correcting hymns "—

"(1) Always use 'we' instead of 'I,' or nearly always.

(2) Insert as many touches of doctrine as may be.

(3) Under every head have at least an ancient or archaic hymn."

The paper is undated, and probably refers to a later date (1856), when he was helping Lord Nelson edit the *Salisbury Hymnal.*

a charm, the one of bright joyousness, the other of quiet harmony, that are wonderfully in keeping with their subject.

Again, there is more brightness, more inspiriting hopefulness about its tone. The tone of the *Christian Year* had been sadder; it always assumed that the Church is in decay; the poems of the *Lyra Apostolica* had been more defiant against its foes; whereas these are gladsome with the signs of life and tokens of revival that are already to be seen in the Church. Jeremiah has given place to the stripling David, advancing hopefully and trustfully against Goliath.

In 1826 he had written, " I hold it to be a selfish and dangerous sort of thing for people to be always turning their eyes inwards ": and perhaps it is not untrue to trace in the brighter and less subjective tone of the *Lyra* some result of the discipline which he had exercised over himself in this matter.

In the poetic imagery there is the same loving—sometimes over-strained—use of Holy Scripture. There is less of the mystical interpretation of Nature; more, as is perhaps natural in dealing with children, of illustrations from animal life,

> " The Lord lends His *creatures* all,
> A tongue to preach His will,"

and the young in the nest, the hen gathering her brood under her wing, the redbreast carolling during Service, form some of the softest touches in the picture. The *Christian Year* stands to the *Lyra Innocentium* as Ps. xix. does to Ps. viii. In Ps. xix. the glory of the heavens, and the undefiled purity of the Law of the Lord giving wisdom unto the simple, leads up to the cry to be saved

from presumptuous sins. Such is the *Christian Year.*
In Ps. viii. the glory of the heavens pales before the
witness of little children, by whose means God stills
the enemy, in whom man is seen crowned with glory
and worship, and all dumb creatures are in subjection
under his feet. Such is the *Lyra Innocentium.*

Innocence is the keynote of the whole; the love of
holiness is the emotion which has inspired it. The
thankful harmony of Nature is lovingly described, and
even the *Christian Year* has no more beautiful expression of it than is to be found in *Continual Services*—

> " His spheres, recede they or advance,
>   Before him in mysterious dance
>   Keep tune and time ; nor e'er
>   Fails from this lower world a wreath
>   Of incense such as sweet flowers breathe
>   And vernal breezes bear.
>   Only man's frail, sin-wearied heart
>   Bears, half in sadness,
>   A wavering intermitted part
>   In that high gladness."

But the innocence of childhood and its winning ways
are most prominent. No beauty in flower or gem can
show half so fair as the charms of the new-baptized; as
in each dew-drop is mirrored some glory of heaven's
great sun, so in each baptized child some ray of the
Father's likeness. The tender, spotless child rehearsing
his Creed has visions of spiritual truth which his elders
lack; his presence has more than angelic power to scare
away thoughts of evil and of sadness—

> " A little child's soft, sleeping face
>   The murderer's knife ere now hath stayed ;
>   The adulterous eye, so foul and base,
>   Is of a little child afraid."

Babes have a sympathy with dumb animals, and

animals with them, which Eastern sages might explain
as due to transmigration of souls, but which is part of
the heritage of Eden ; their ready praise and willingness
to give their toys away is a type of Christ's largess on
the day of Pentecost ; their shyness is a germ of the
true silent awe which all ought to feel in the Presence
of God, and especially the pastor who has to work for
Him. Their life is like that of the angels, in their
white robes, in their ready prayer and praise, in their
willingness to serve—

> " As angels wait in joy
> On saints, so on the old the *duteous-hearted* boy "

(p. 250). And the angels catch up their prayers for
home and parents, and expand them and interpret them
before God as prayers for the Church and her Priests.

Duteous — duteous-hearted — that is the special
quality chosen for praise ; but even child-life suggests
notes of warning too. The mother as she looks on the
child cannot but be anxious ; fear's chastening angel
must, for Love's sweet sake, dwell with the child. David
too was a generous boy with open brow ; the mother of
Judas must have looked on him with joy and hope ;
as the mother's prophet eye reads even in their sports
her child's future life and character, it must be in
" hope and agony " that she prays ; for that life may be
soiled by violent passion or by sullen moroseness, by
neglect of childhood's simple courtesies, by irreverence,
by " the blight of thankless eye," by " the quick untrem-
bling gaze," by the love of praise making the child rest
in earthly things ; too great display may be as fatal to
the child's future as Hezekiah's display of his treasures
to the ambassadors of Babylon—

> " For busy hands and an admiring ken
> Have blighted ere its time full many a rose."

The child has had the sign of the Cross put upon it ; therefore it must be ready for suffering, ready to find its life thenceforward by daily dying.

This child-life is often used to point the contrast with the grown-up man ; his own sense of sinfulness breaks in upon the scene, and seems so black against its whiteness—

> " Jesus in His babes abiding,
> Shames our cold ungentle ways : "

and yet more often He comes in His children not to judge but to give life; with a hope and a suggestion of what even the sinner may be. The white apparel of the baptized child and the joyous white of the bride find their counterpart in the white robe of the penitent. There is still the same deep sense of sin and of unworthiness, but there is perhaps a yet stronger hold on the reality of absolution, a more lively hope that " the withered bough may blush with fruitage still "—

> " O fear, O joy to think ! and what if yet
> In some far moment of eternity,
> The love of evil I may quite forget,
> And with the pure in heart my portion be ! "

Others have come to him by this time for guidance in the hour of remorse and of perplexity; he has trusted that God will use even his unworthiness, and has found his trust true, and the witness of the reality of forgiveness in them has deepened it for himself. The sorrows of the time have drawn him out of himself and made him cling close to the Church, like a child clinging closer to its mother's robe among strangers, when it

can only see " far-reaching ways unknown and wide." [1]
But that touch has given him boldness, and made his
step free and light. He has learnt her power to train
her children, to minister to all the varied needs of life.
The tenderness of bright joyous children for a sister just
recovering from death, and the heartfelt prayer of the
parents for the child, have brought closer home to him
the sense of the love of God and of His Church for the
penitent.[2] Moreover he has learnt more of her doctrine;
" When I wrote the former book," he says to Judge
Coleridge, " I did not understand (to mention no more
points) either the doctrine of Repentance or that of the
Holy Eucharist as held e. g. by Bishop Ken; nor that of
Justification, and such points as those must surely make
a great difference." [3] There is certainly greater definiteness in this volume on several points. There is a
stronger sense of " the living dead"; " the pure and
childlike dead," watching our lives and joining in our
prayers. The saints have grown dearer to him, and he
loves to trace in the baptized not only the signs of filial
likeness to the Father which is in heaven, but of likeness to its brothers the saints, whether they recall the
penitence of St. Peter, the loving smile of the loved
disciple, or the purity of Blessed Mary. Especially is
the reverence towards the Blessed Virgin marked—her

> " Whom the awful blessing
> Lifted above all Adam's race."

The orphaned child is taught to feel that not only her
own mother is praying for her, but also "A holier
mother rapt in more prevailing prayer." He had

---

[1] See the touching poem entitled *Separation*.
[2] Cf. *Languor*, "the tenderest of all the poems" (Miss Yonge).
[3] *Memoir*, p. 282. Cf. I. Williams, *Autobiography*, p. 117.

intended to prefix to the volume a poem written on December 8, 1844, and entitled *Mother out of Sight*,[1] in which the Blessed Virgin is " called blessed " as the one only instrument of the Incarnation, as the type of the Church, as the pattern of all purity, and in which, though we may not adore her, we are urged to seek the love and fear "which bring thee with all saints, near and more near," and suppliants are invited to greet her with an " Ave," as

> " Children with ' good morrow ' come,
>   To elders in some home,"

and in this spirit to invite the saints to join in our prayers. Such language goes indeed very little, if at all, beyond that of the *Christian Year*, but Coleridge, Dyson, and other friends dissuaded him from publishing it. The poem tells of doubt and perplexity, of the wonder of many whether Mother Church could really be found in the Church of England, yet it bears witness that he himself is convinced that God's signs are still around us; there is no hint of disloyalty; there is a sense that the Church places too low the honour she pays to the highest of God's creatures ; but he is content to wait, even as, while grieving over the disuse of Infant Communion in another poem, he was willing to wait and take such part as the Church—"she whose laws are sealed on high "—ordains. His feeling towards other Churches was at the time one of *neutrality;* he would recognize each as separate parts of one great stream, destined to be united hereafter, but for a while flowing apart. This is illustrated in the poem called *The Waterfall;* there the value of each separate Christian

---

[1] Printed after his death in *Miscellaneous Poems*, p. 254.

life is illustrated by the various streams that rush
together from all sides to make up the glory of Lodore;
but he is clearly thinking more of Churches than of
individuals as he draws the application—

> " E'en so the mighty sky-born stream :—
> 　Its living waters from above
> All marr'd and broken seem,
> 　No union and no love.
>
> Yet in dim caves they haply blend,
> 　In dreams of mortals unespied ;
> One is their awful end,
> 　One their unfailing guide.
>
> 　.　.　.　.　.　.
>
> 　.　.　.　.　.　.
>
> And Christ hath lowly hearts, that rest
> 　Amid fallen Salem's rush and strife ;
> The pure peace-loving breast
> 　Even here can find her life.
>
> What though in harsh and angry note
> 　The broken flood chafe high ?　They muse
> On mists that lightly float,
> 　On heaven-descending dews,
>
> On virgin snows, the feeders pure
> 　Of the bright river's mountain springs,
> And still their prayers endure,
> 　And Hope sweet answer brings.
>
> If of the Living cloud they be
> 　Baptismal drops, and onward press
> Toward the Living Sea
> 　By deeds of holiness,
>
> Then to the Living Waters still
> 　(O joy, with trembling !) they pertain,
> Join'd by some hidden rill,
> 　Low in earth's darkest vein."

Baptism and the struggle for holiness are to each

sufficient assurance that he belongs to the Church ; the signs of spiritual life around them are full of hope. So it has been throughout the book. The possibilities of true spiritual life in the English Church are hinted at by dwelling upon all that it does for children, by trying to picture something of what their pure vision sees in it ; the hope of the penitent is rekindled by recalling to him his childish innocence, and by pointing to the hope of re-winning that. So it is that in the Preface which he substituted (on February 8, 1846), he prays that God may pardon his sin, and strengthen him that he may guide the perplexed along their path,

" And with no faint or erring voice
    May to the wanderer whisper, 'Stay ' :
God chooses for thee : seal His choice,
    Nor from thy Mother's shadow stray :
For sure thy Holy Mother's shade
    Rests yet upon thine ancient home ;
No voice from Heaven hath clearly said,
    ' Let us depart' : then fear to roam.

Pray that the prayer of Innocents
    On earth, of saints in heaven above,
Guard, as of old, our lonely tents ;
    Till, as one faith is ours, in Love
We own all Churches, and are own'd.
    Pray Him to save by chastenings keen
The harps that hail His Bride enthron'd
    From wayward touch of hands unclean."

A copy of the book was sent to Newman with the accompanying message—

" I hope you will receive a little book along with this, which I have asked Copeland to forward to you. You will kindly take it as a pledge of (I hope) unabated love and gratitude and constant remembrance; though confidence (sad to say) cannot be what it was. *That* is a very bitter feeling, but it will do one good, if one can at all adequately perceive and feel that it is one's own fault.

"May I say God bless you, very dearest friend?— being always

"Your affte. and grateful

"J. KEBLE."

CHAPTER VII.

RECOVERY.   1846—1860.

"And now what time ye all may read through dimming tears his
    story,
How discord on the music fell and darkness on the glory ;
And how, when one by one sweet sounds and wandering lights
    departed,
He wore no less a loving face because so broken-hearted,

He shall be strong to sanctify the poet's high vocation,
And bow the meekest Christian down in meeker adoration ;
Nor ever shall he be in praise by wise or good forsaken,
Named softly, as the household name of one whom God hath
    taken."—MRS. BROWNING : *Cowper's Grave.*

"The place where the priests' feet stood firm."—*Joshua* iv. 3.

IT will have been noticed that in the letters to
Newman there are erasures from time to time.   These
were made by Cardinal Newman, when he deposited
the originals in the library of Keble College, and he
prefixed to the correspondence of 1843—1846 the
following note—

"In the letters which follow I have made erasures,
which may seem strange and arbitrary, unless I say
something to account for them.

"Let me observe, then, that dear John Keble's heart
was too tender and his religious sense too keen, for him
not to receive serious injury to his spirits and his

mental equilibrium by the long succession of trials in which his place in the Oxford movement involved him.

"The affair of No. 90, Williams's failure in his contest for the Poetry Professorship, the Jerusalem Bishoprick, Young's rejection when offering himself for Orders, Pusey's censure by the six Doctors, the promotion of Thirlwall and others, my own religious unsettlement and that of so many others, the charges and hostile attitude of the Bishops, the publication of Arnold's life and letters, and the prospect of the future opened upon him (not to dwell upon the serious illness of his wife and his brother), were too much for him, and threw him into a state of extreme depression, which showed itself to his intimate friends in the language of self-accusation and even of self-abhorrence.

"This heartrending trial, of which perhaps I saw more than any one, is remarked upon by Sir John Coleridge in his *Life of Keble* (p. 283, &c., ed. 1), though he has not attempted any sufficient explanation of it. He seems to attribute what was a surprise to him to the intense self-disparagement which, however strange to the run of men, is natural to a mind so religious as Keble's. Others have supposed it was a point of duty with Keble thus to speak and write, as being a proper form of introducing a religious sentiment, or what was called in a Bishop's charge some forty years ago, a sort of 'mystic humility'—an imputation most untrue to Keble's nature. It is more exact to say that the idea had grown upon him and vividly possessed him, that he had allowed himself for the last ten or twelve years to be engaged in deep religious questions, and in controversy rising out of them, without adequate preparation. He had set off in the company or at the head of many others, on a road which he had not explored, and as he might think, he had been 'the blind leading the blind.' And, in particular, he considered himself at least indirectly, if not positively, the cause of my own abandonment of the Church of England.

" This impression, however, unless he had been at the time so worried and broken in heart, as I have supposed, would not have been enough in itself to account for the *obiter dicta*, the ejaculations, the single words and half sentences, the language, so shocking to one who knew and loved him so well as I did, in which he expressed his sense of the difficulties of the moment and his own responsibility in relation to them.

" To me nothing is more painful than the contrast between the cheerfulness and playfulness which runs through his early letters and the sadness of his later. This must remain anyhow ; it is founded on the successive circumstances of his history ; it is part of his life ; nor could one expect it to be otherwise ; but I could not be so cruel to that meek, patient, and affectionate soul, to that dearly, deeply beloved friend, as to leave to a future generation the exhibition of those imaginary thoughts about himself which tormented him, which grew out of grave troubles, which were very real, and which are sufficiently recorded for posterity, when they serve, as in a notice like this, to suggest to a reader the weight of those troubles."

It is only fair to the reader to print also a short memorandum added by Dean Church on the sight of the above note.

" Nov. 10, 1879.—I was not sure, and I am not sure, about the accuracy of the impression which such

a notice might leave, as to Keble's own state of mind
—whether it would not suggest the reflection, 'Poor
Keble, he felt the earth reeling and opening round
him—the foundations are cast down.'

"Great as Keble's troubles were, I do not suppose
that this was his permanent state of mind; nor does the
notice say so; it only speaks of the distress of the friend
and the brother workman. But I wish, what is too
much to expect, that the distinction had been acknowledged or remembered between Keble the broken-
hearted friend, and Keble the priest of the English
Church. Because about this, in all his griefs, he never
lost his head or his faith; though if anything could
have made him do so, it would have been the event of
1845 and the parting with Newman.

"But it is a very natural account for N. to give; and
it is full of his matchless tenderness and considerateness
and surprising affectionateness."

It needs the combination of these two judgments
to do justice to Keble's feelings at this crisis. On no
one person did the blow fall with heavier weight.
All his affection for Hurrell Froude had passed over to
Newman when Froude was taken away; to Newman he
had given his heart and his generous sympathy to the
last; he had trusted him when his Bisley friends were
distrustful; he had accepted his intellectual position
and entered into his imaginative enthusiasm for all
that was good in the Church of Rome, and could
understand its attractiveness probably more than Dr.
Pusey, and yet he stood firm under the shock. The
strongest link at the moment was formed by the
evidence of true spiritual grace which he saw on what
seemed to be the deathbed of his wife at Hursley, and

of his brother at Bisley; but this was but one instance of the reality of that spiritual life to which he had been accustomed from childhood. "*Every day*," he wrote, "*things are happening*, especially in our two sick-rooms, which make it more and more impossible for me to do as he has done." [1]

The first result of the blow was to deepen the sense of humility and of repentance, both in him and in Dr. Pusey; each accused himself of failures and sins which had caused the loss of their fellow-worker. Their first common act was to unite with the other Tractarians, who remained loyal,—and Newman was the only Tract writer who at any time joined the Church of Rome,— in preaching at the consecration of St. Saviour's, Leeds, a church which had just been built as an act of gratitude by "a penitent," who wished to give expression to the revived Catholic doctrines in the midst of a busy town. Keble was himself unable to go, but he sent three sermons on God's judgments and upon Hell, which were read by Dr. Pusey, save that in the last the tone of sternness about God's judgments was so awful that even Dr. Pusey could not read parts of it. From this time forward the two were drawn more closely together, and kept up an active correspondence with each other, in which each heartened the other in his moments of difficulty, and pleaded for the other's prayers that he himself might be truly contrite.

But the second result was a strong, vigorous effort on the part of each on behalf of Church principles. The sense of the reality of spiritual life within the Church was the strongest link that held them loyal;

[1] Letter to Dyson, Oct. 12th (Coleridge, p. 308).

L

if they had not followed Newman, at any rate the
world should see that it was not that self-sacrifice could
exhibit itself less really in the English Church. Active
life went forward without any break and developed
itself in new ways; the Church lengthened its cords
and strengthened its stakes; in 1836 the first bishop
had been appointed for Australia; in 1840 Bishop
Blomfield had made his great appeal for an extension
of the Colonial Episcopate, which resulted in the
bishopric of New Zealand in 1841, of South Africa in
1847, and of many others. At home the deepening
sense of sin caused the more frequent use of confession,
and the desire for entire self-devotion in the religious
life led to the formation of sisterhoods at Devonport,
at Wantage, and at Clewer, all within a few years of
Newman's secession. In Oxford Charles Marriott was
collecting funds for a new Church College for men of
humbler means, a scheme which failed only through his
illness; at Hursley the sign of reviving life was seen in
the restoration of the parish church, which was opened
in 1848. Thus, "*things were happening,*" not only at
Hursley, but throughout the whole Church, which made
it more and more impossible to leave her. But all this
was not effected without struggle and loss. The
controversy around Tract 90 and Ward's *Ideal* had at
any rate laid bare the weak spots in the life of the
Church, and each had to be made good. There were
still losses by secession in the course of this; there
were exasperating appointments to bishoprics; there
were decisions of the Privy Council which seemed to
threaten the very central doctrines of the faith. But
gradually the ground became clearer, and Churchmen
came to see how little the real being of the Church

could be touched by such a secular court as the Privy
Council or even by the individual utterances of
bishops, and step by step was gained in securing the
free legislative action of the Church. It will be
impossible to deal with all these cases, and we must
select but a few to illustrate Keble's action.

First it became necessary for the leaders who
remained to reassure their followers, to re-examine and
re-assert the grounds on which the claims of the Church
of England were based. At first, in their affection
for Newman and their belief that God had some special
work for him to do in reuniting the Church, they were
content to acquiesce in a position of pure neutrality
towards Rome; but this became impossible to maintain
as the converts took the offensive. In order to meet
the mere logical appeal to the abstract principle of
authority, "it was necessary further to realize the limits
of pure logic, to distinguish theoretical and practical
issues, and to feel in its fullness the close connection
of all questions of authority with those of practical
life." [1] A short paper suggesting subjects for mutual
intercession, viz. the unity and peace of the Church,
the conversion of sinners, the advancement and
perseverance of the faithful, was circulated among
friends by " J. K., E. B. P., and C. M." (Charles Marriott).
Dr. Pusey threw all the weight of his learning into
the controversy, and gradually built up the great
defence of the Anglican position, of which the *Eirenicon*
was the chief outcome. Keble's line was naturally
different. He was quite clear about his position; and
when Dr. Pusey wrote in 1847 that there was a
widespread rumour that "you are going to leave us,"

[1] *The Guardian*, July 20, 1892.

he answered, "I scarcely think it can do much harm; it is so utterly without ground or foundation; however, I have authorized two persons to contradict it as publicly as they please." And there is no trace of any hesitation on his part. He did, no doubt, from time to time, face the possibility of resigning his Orders, or even of giving up communion with the Church; but the position he contemplated was one similar to that of the Non-jurors. He never showed a desire to join the Church of Rome. But he was not a controversialist. Although he had expressed as early as 1836 an intention to write a course of Bampton Lectures on Romanism, yet he had never found time for it, and always felt that he did not know the controversy as a controversy. He, too, was at first inclined to neutrality; but as time went on, his exasperation at the underhand methods used by some of the later converts, and the unfairness of their attacks on Dr. Pusey, and the growing sense that separate conversions did not promote peace and unity, made him more strong in his insistence upon the errors of the Church of Rome.

For the present his contribution to the cause was the publication of a volume of *Sermons, Occasional and Academical*. One of these—the sermon which he had prepared for St. Andrew's Day, 1841—dealt directly with the question of loyalty to the English Church, but the argument of it was now expanded into a long and careful Preface, which is the fullest passage in his writings on the subject. In it he makes no attempt to deal with the controversy controversially: as always he protests against treating any question on mere intellectual grounds; moral considerations must also be weighed. Hence he does not primarily ask, What is

true ? but, What is right to do ? He attempts calmly, and
" without consternation and amazement," " to direct a
simple man's practice." The method is that of Butler's
Analogy. He will not allow the question to be settled
by *à priori* considerations of what the Church ought to
be, without regard to historic facts; but assuming that
historic facts point to a divided Church and prove that
the Church of Rome does not preserve all the notes of
an ideal Church, assuming further that the controversy
is a doubtful one, on which there is much to be said on
both sides, he asks, What is the *safe* course to pursue ?
The safest course is that which satisfies our moral sense
of what we owe to God as a Father ; in other words,
it will be that course which is most likely to promote a
spirit of acquiescence in His will, of intellectual modesty,
of contrition, of generous recognition of holiness in
others, and which is least likely to give offence to
others. Such a course is supplied by remaining loyal
to the English Church, for as she is less attractive to
the imagination, loyalty to her will show a generous
contentment, like the conduct of one who is not
ashamed of lowly parentage. On the other hand
secession implies a great act of private judgment, and
the power of deciding a number of controverted
questions; it would also minimize the sense of
contrition for the past, because it minimizes the sense
of privilege enjoyed, and would make us disparage the
saints of the English Church, whereas *we* are free to
reverence all saints of the Roman Communion ; finally
it would cause pain to some and throw others into
scepticism.

He tries to show that such an argument would not
apply equally to Dissenters and unbelievers, because

they disavow nothing on becoming Catholic Christians; they only add to the substance of their faith and practice; and they have stronger and clearer evidence on which to act; nor does it put the English Church in the position of the Donatists, for we do not anathematize other Christians, and the difference between us and Rome is of detail rather than of principle, and it will probably decrease. We do not deny any important doctrine, but, at the worst, only tolerate error through want of strong discipline.

If it is urged that the Roman Church can give a clearer guidance, the answer is that guidance in all essentials was provided before the division of the Church, that the promise of guidance to individuals is always conditional, and that a reasonable hope is a more wise trainer of character than a perfect assurance.

Our unity is that of a divided family, and therefore implies the duty of all the charity and tenderness which brothers would feel to each other; but the English Churchman must remain loyally where he is, as the position is not one of his own choosing, whereas to change would be to take the management of his soul into his own hands. The Church of Christ in England is a true branch of the Catholic Church; it retains the essential notes of a Church; but it is hampered by want of discipline, by toleration of error, by low ideals of life; hence it must be a Church in penitence, and a Church under appeal to an Œcumenical Council, whenever such can be summoned.

Such an argument is in a very minor key, and would not convince, though indeed it might solemnize and give pause to one who was keenly interested in the controversy; but at any rate it makes the appeal to the whole nature of man; and Keble might well answer that the question never arises whether a man should choose in the abstract between England and Rome, without reference to previous claims and obligations upon him.

Two storms followed in 1847 which both seemed at first to threaten shipwreck to the Church, but which she weathered safely. In November Dr. Hampden, who was still under University censure for heterodoxy, was nominated by Lord John Russell to the Bishopric of Hereford. Keble at once consulted Coleridge as to the legal course to be proposed by the opponents of the nomination. With the help of Dr. Pusey he drew up the articles of the charge against Dr. Hampden; he used every influence he could command with the Dean and Chapter, and the Dean was induced to oppose the confirmation of the election in Bow Church; but his opposition was overruled, and the new Bishop was consecrated. Nothing was directly gained, but it had been clearly shown how the Church was fettered by the State in the choice of her own officers, and the primary result was the formation of Church Unions both in Bristol and in London to watch over the interests of the Church; their special aims being the increase of the Episcopate, the provision of some valid security against unfit appointments, the revival of the Church legislature, and the restoration of discipline. The ultimate result was the revival of Convocation in 1852.

One extract from a letter written by Keble to Dr. Moberley on March 6, 1848, will illustrate his ultimate feeling about the importance of the question. Dr. Moberley had consulted him on behalf of some one

who was perplexed by the consecration and inclined to
take this as a sign that the Church was no true
Church. He, in his answer, is inclined to regard
such a seeking for a sign as, at the bottom, a profane
and heathenish state of mind, and he adds: "But is
this *such* a sign? I mean, if persons have thought
it their duty to bear with the Puritans and Latitu-
dinarians of times past, so far as not to give up the
Church of England to them, nor to acquiesce in
their interpretation of its formularies, what is there
in this case to make them take a different view?
We are not bound in any manner to express
approbation of Hampden's notions; we are not at all
committed by them: we have protested against them
as far as we are able, on the ground that they are
contrary to the Prayer-book, and yet were we to retire
from the Church of England because of them, must it
not be on the very ground that his was the right
interpretation of the Prayer-book? It would be another thing were we called on as a condition of Churchmanship to subscribe to his views or to refrain from
holding and teaching our own. As I understand it,
so far from retiring on account of the mistaken toleration of such views, it is an additional reason for every
one of us to keep his post and do his best, as I understand St. Basil and others to have done with the Semi-
Arian bishops of their time. As long as the formularies
continue unchanged, I cannot see how the toleration
even of heresy in this or that bishop, or even in the
whole Bench, can be other than a question of discipline,
not of doctrine, and I thought it had been ruled ever
since the days of Donatus that questions of discipline
affect the well-being, not the being of the Church. . . .

As to the Erastianism, the more I think it over, the more I seem to see that we are on a better ground than we have been, at least since the Revolution, and if people will now be patient and persevering, we have every chance of making that ground good. The one thing to ruin us would be impatience."

Meanwhile, the Gorham case, which seemed more serious still, as appearing formally to authorize false doctrine as the teaching of the Church, and which proved more serious in the secessions which it caused, had already commenced. In June, 1847, the Lord Chancellor presented the Rev. G. C. Gorham to a living in the diocese of Exeter, but Bishop Phillpotts, having already had knowledge of his denial of the doctrine of regeneration in Baptism, formally examined him on the subject, and as he would only admit a conditional regeneration, the Bishop refused to institute him, in March, 1848. Mr. Gorham appealed to the Dean of Arches, who pronounced judgment in August, 1849, in favour of the Bishop. Against this Mr. Gorham appealed to the Queen in Council; and the Committee of the Privy Council, consisting of six laymen, with the two Archbishops and the Bishop of London as assessors, gave judgment on March 8, 1850—the Bishop of London alone refusing to concur—against the Bishop of Exeter. The Judgment did not assert that conditional regeneration was the doctrine of the Church, but it did decide that it was not so clearly condemned by the Church that a bishop could refuse to institute one who held it. The Bishop of Exeter still refused to institute, but the Archbishop, in spite of the Bishop's threat to refuse to hold communion with him, instituted Mr. Gorham. The Bishop was defeated in an attempt to provide a more satisfactory Court of Appeal, but he summoned a Diocesan Synod in 1851 which formally declared its firm and immovable adherence to the article of the Creed, "one baptism for the remission of sin." Again the evil was overruled for good; the unsatisfactory character of the Court of Appeal was brought home to the consciences of Churchmen: a precedent was set for the revival of the synodical action of the Church, which greatly helped forward the movement for the revival of Convocation.

During all this anxious time Keble was incessantly active. His correspondence and his publications were occupied with two problems: How could the Church be freed from any complicity with the judgment? and how could the younger Churchmen who felt the attraction of Rome, and they were many—Allies, Dodsworth, Maskell, Manning, and, dearest to his heart, his old Southrop pupil, Robert Wilberforce—be kept loyal in the face of such a judgment?

In January, 1850, he consulted Sir John Awdry on the legal position. His own opinion was that as the prerogative of deciding doctrine lay with the Bishops, and as this was a lay Court never formally accepted by the Church, he was not bound in conscience by its decisions, but might ignore them and still hold his position in the Church, because his oath to admit the Royal Supremacy was taken with the understanding that the supremacy would be constitutionally exercised. But others had taken counsel's opinion on the matter, which was that they were bound to accept the decision of the Court, and therefore he asks for guidance. Sir John Awdry's answer was quite clear: (1) that not every usurpation in a Church, such as *ex hypothesi* that of this Court was, would justify secession, and (2) that no judicial decision, though it turn on a matter of doctrine, binds the conscience; it is only the expression of the opinion of the judges, which may be treated as a precedent, but is not law; as one who thinks some of the decisions of the House of Lords in secular matters erroneous is not less a loyal subject, so would one be no less a loyal member of the Church if he treated a decision of this Court of Appeal as erroneous, and if he continued to teach and preach Baptismal Regeneration as the doctrine of the Church, even though the Court should hold that unsoundness about it was not a ground on which a bishop could exclude a presentee from preferment.

This letter cleared away any doubts in Keble's mind, and he threw himself actively into the controversy. He published two short papers on *Church Matters in 1850*, which are among the most clear, pointed, and vigorous of his writings. The first, *The Trial of Doctrine*, was published before the judgment, and is a protest against the whole constitution of the Court; on the grounds that it consisted of laymen, without any security that they should be members of the Church, so that the vote of a Nonconformist might decide a case in a matter of doctrine; that it had never been accepted by the Church, for it was not the same as the old Court of Delegates, being neither accompanied by the same safeguards nor appointed by the same authority: hence the clergy are not bound by their acknowledgment of the Royal Supremacy to obey it, for that assumes a constitutional exercise of the Supremacy in religion as well as in secular matters. A judgment by it cannot affect the being of the Church, but it can its well-being,

as it will cause confusion and distress, especially if the
Court has to deal with deeper questions still, such as
Inspiration or Eternal Punishment.   Hence the duty of
Churchmen is to petition for some Court with Synodical
authority, and meanwhile to let Christendom ring with
our appeal, and to continue our struggle.

"All this we must do; and there is something else
which must nowise be left undone.   For, τοῦτο τὸ γένος
οὐκ ἐκπορεύεται εἰ μὴ ἐν προσευχῇ καὶ νηστείᾳ (St. Matt.
xvii. 21).

As soon as the judgment was declared, he circulated
a petition in his parish praying the Bishop of the
diocese to help them, owing to the doubt which has
arisen, " Whether or no the Church holds it needful to
be believed that by the Blood and merits of our Saviour
Christ, Original Sin is remitted to all infants in Holy
Baptism ?" and this received over 200 signatures, and
was forwarded with a letter assuring the Bishop that
the names had been put down "with intelligence and
hearty goodwill," and imploring him to repudiate the
decision in order to avoid a distressing separation from
the Establishment.   On July 20th he published another
vigorous tract, entitled *A Call to Speak Out*, in which he
urges that though those who hold communion with the
Archbishop after his sanctioning of the heresy would
not formally be guilty of heresy, yet they must protest
against his action and the Court.   The State must
allow the decision to be reviewed by the proper
authority, or else the Church's rulers must disregard the
decision.   If not, we must agitate for a change in the
relations of Church and State.   We have a right to
declare our own doctrines, to confirm, vary, and repeal
our canons, to have a voice in the nomination of our

chief pastors, and to grant or withhold our sacraments according to our proper rules. "We had rather be a Church in earnest, separate from the State, than a counterfeit Church in professed union with the State." Clearly his mind was already facing the possibility of disestablishment.

In the autumn of the same year the Church Unions stirred themselves to unite Churchmen in common action against the judgment. In the Bristol Union an unwise attempt to combine the question with an expression of antagonism to Rome nearly caused a split among its members, and there seemed for a moment the fear of Keble and Pusey taking opposite sides. The more conservative group of Churchmen, led by William Palmer, Archdeacon Prevost, and others, wished to make an expression of such antagonism a test of membership of the Union. Dr. Pusey offered his strongest opposition to this: it seemed to him that a statement of antagonism was never a true basis of union, and that at this time antagonism to Rome might easily be perverted into repudiation of much that was true and Catholic. Keble, though opposed to a test, was inclined to a declaration of similar effect. To this too Dr. Pusey was opposed. It was a moment of severe strain for him, for nothing would induce him to appear publicly in opposition to Keble; yet at the same time he knew that such a declaration would alienate waverers. He was on the point of leaving the Union, but ultimately the test was withdrawn, and a declaration of willingness to live and die in the Church of England was substituted for it. Meanwhile in London a great meeting was summoned on July 23rd at St. Martin's Hall. The Eucharist was celebrated in several of the London churches for God's blessing upon the meeting. When the hour came, the number who attended made it necessary to have an overflow meeting in the Free-masons' Tavern, and at both resolutions were passed appealing to the Queen that the power of Convocation might be revived, that ecclesiastical cases might be submitted to spiritual judges; appealing to the arch-bishops and bishops to support these movements and to pronounce independently in favour of the Church doctrine; appealing to all Churchmen in all lands to uphold the doctrine, and thanking the Scotch bishops for a Synodical statement which they had recently issued about it. Both Pusey and Keble spoke. Keble pleaded for hopefulness and perseverance: hopefulness because he found that even his simple village poor cared so much for the doctrine, and were preparing to defend it; perseverance because the Church of the fourth century had even a longer struggle to endure before the doctrine of the Incarnation was established, and we in our present state had more difficulty in reasserting true doctrine. If any were inclined to mistrust the Church of England and to leave her, "the whole air of England seemed to ring with voices from the dead and from the living, especially from the holy dead, all to this effect, 'Stay here, think not of departing, but do your work.' If it seemed to any unsatisfactory, let him consider that we were under appeal, and had been so for three hundred years, and that must be unsatisfactory, like a piece of music not come to its natural close: but what then? It was the condition of the Church in the time of the blessed saints he had referred to for two whole genera-tions, and if we had to leave it so to those who came after us, he knew not himself that he could say a better

word, were it the last word that he had to say, than to
bid men persevere in hope."

During the whole year Keble used in the public
services at Hursley a special form of prayer for the
distress of the Church, and when the Bishop of Exeter
prepared to summon his Synod, he issued a pastoral
letter to his parishioners, explaining that he had done
so because the judges had decided against baptismal regeneration, and so encouraged people to think less of
their sins; because these judges had no right to decide
at all; because the Church was no longer free to elect
her bishops; and because, on account of this, many
were inclined to leave the Church, while others were
slandering her work.

When the Synod was over, he wrote an article in the
Christian Remembrancer of December, 1851, reviewing
the gains of it. This is one of the brightest and most
sprightly of his prose writings, characterized by much
humour and delicate satire. He has recovered his
buoyancy of spirits; he admits that the Church of
England can only be a Church under appeal, and doing
penance, but at any rate she is sound at the core; she has
justified herself. The eye of faith can see in her action
God's hand helping us in our troubles; the Church still
witnesses to the belief in Sacramental Grace; she speaks
with a living voice, and therefore there is no ground for
despair.

Others, however, had less of hope and patience than
himself; the influence of Keble kept Robert Wilberforce loyal till 1854, but among others, Allies, Maskell,
and Dodsworth in 1850, and Manning in 1851, joined
the Roman Church, as the immediate result of the
Gorham decision.

The position of Keble and Pusey was made more difficult because, during these years, 1851-52, Bishop Wilberforce informally and privately inhibited the latter from officiating in his diocese, fearing lest his adaptation of Roman devotional books and his practice about confession was tending to lead people to Rome. Throughout the whole difficulty Keble, both by letter and by personal interview, acted as a mediating influence. "I say to myself," he wrote, "here are two persons who really ought to understand one another, and it seems quite a judgment upon us that they cannot act together"; and by a combination of outspoken expression of his agreement with Dr. Pusey, of bold protest against unfairness in suspending him without a hearing, and by insistence upon all that was to be said on his behalf, as actively keeping back waverers from Rome, he contributed to the happy result that the Bishop removed the suspension in 1852.

Two events in the next ten years turned Keble's attention mainly to the defence of the other great Sacrament. These were the trial of Archdeacon Denison in England, and the censure of Bishop Forbes in Scotland, for teaching the doctrine of the Real Presence and of the Eucharistic Sacrifice. In 1853 Archdeacon Denison preached two sermons in Wells Cathedral on the Real Presence, the orthodoxy of which was challenged by his neighbour, the Rev. Joseph Ditcher, and on his refusal to retract them, he was tried in 1856, in the Pro-Diocesan Court at Bath, before the Archbishop of Canterbury, who called upon him to retract the statements that the Body and Blood of Christ is received by those who eat and drink unworthily, and that worship is due to the real though invisible presence of the Body and Blood of Christ in the Holy Eucharist under the form of bread and wine.

On refusing to retract he was deprived of his vicarage and archdeaconry, but the sentence was overthrown by the Final Court of Appeal in 1858. During the process of the case both Dr. Pusey and Keble had done what was possible to guide and advise Archdeacon Denison. Keble had indeed been very doubtful on the point of the reception by the wicked, but ultimately was convinced by Dr. Pusey, and on the question of Adoration he felt very keenly. As soon as the first judgment was delivered these two circulated a protest, for the matter was more serious in one respect than the Gorham case; the decision being that of the Archbishop without any interference of the State Courts. This protest was signed by eighteen clergy, and consisted of a re-statement of their belief that the doctrine of the Real Presence had been held as a point of faith from the earliest times; that the most common view held in the Church had been that the wicked do eat and drink unworthily to their own condemnation the Body and Blood of Christ, which they do not discern, and that the practice of worshipping Christ then and there, especially present after consecration, had been common throughout the Church. They therefore protested against anything in the judgment which contradicts these statements, and appealed from it to a lawful Synod of the Bishops of the Province of Canterbury, and, if need be, to a free and lawful Synod of all the Churches of our communion. As a report was circulated that they intended to form a Non-juring Church, they published a letter stating that they should regard such an act as a betrayal of a sacred trust; that no sentence of one

M

archbishop could bind the conscience, as only the voice of the whole Church could do that; but that they had felt bound in honesty to declare their intention of continuing to teach what they had always taught, and of taking the consequences.

Keble followed up the protest by a careful treatise on Eucharistical Adoration. This consisted partly of a careful examination of the grounds of the practice, partly of a consideration of the duty of Churchmen in face of the judgment. The object was, not to reason out at large what he calls "that great and comfortable, and I will add necessary, truth of the Real Presence," but rather, "calmly, and not without deep reverence of heart," to allay troublesome thoughts which interrupt devotion. Following the method of Hooker in the fifth book of the *Ecclesiastical Polity*, he brings the practice to the test of natural piety, of the teaching of Holy Scripture, of the Primitive Church, and of the Church of England. The argument starts from the premise that natural piety suggests adoration wherever Christ is present, and especially in this Sacrament, because of the greatness of the gift given, of the individual character of the blessing, and of the condescension of Christ in giving it. "It is as impossible for devout faith, contemplating Christ in this Sacrament, not to adore Him, as it is for a loving mother, looking earnestly at her child, not to love it." The sense of such a gift calls for the most unreserved surrender that a man can make of himself, his whole spirit, soul, and body, *i. e.* for the most unreserved worship.

Such an instinct would naturally be followed, unless it was definitely forbidden. But the reverse is the case: the New Testament shows us that special reverence was paid to Christ in every detail of His humiliation, especially in His death; that virtue was regarded as proceeding from His Body, which was treated with reverence in death, and which even then retained its cleansing power; that it treats Him as really present in the Eucharist, both as Priest and Victim. It was natural then that this reverence should be transferred to the sacramental elements, so expressive of His humiliation, "as being in themselves so cheap and ordinary, and as representing especially His Death and Passion"; and, as a matter of fact, the early Liturgies and the language of the Fathers bear witness to such transference of reverence to the sacred Body and Blood in the Eucharist. Further, the Church of England has always insisted on reverence at the Liturgy, and there has been a continuous teaching of the Real Presence, though sometimes it has been attacked, "like Jehoshaphat in Ahab's robes," because it has been mistaken for Transubstantiation. The doctrine has never been formulated about it by any Council, and therefore error about it is not formal heresy, so that we are not bound to refuse to communicate with an archbishop who decides against it: but it has been continuously taught, and no judicial interpretation has the right to narrow the liberty allowed by the Church in the expression of her doctrine. The only course then for those who believe in the doctrine, is prayer, willingness to suffer for the truth, formally expressed protest, and appeal to an Œcumenical Council.

The subject is, as Keble admits, not exhaustively treated, but nothing could be more of a model of the right tone of sacred controversy, making each reader feel that he is dealing with a subject, real, solemn, and vital. One extract may be given, in which the act of sharing in the Eucharist is shown to typify faith in the whole Creed.

"By receiving His creatures of bread and wine we acknowledge Him (as St. Irenæus argues) Creator of heaven and earth, against all sorts of Manicheans; receiving Christ's Body is confessing His Incarnation, and adoring it, His Divinity; it is the memorial of His death, and the participation of that Sacrifice which supposes Him raised and ascended into heaven; it is obeying His command so to show forth His death till He come; it is drinking into one Spirit: it is partaking of that one Bread which makes us one body, the Holy Catholic Church; it is the Communion of Saints; it is the Blood shed for the remission of sins; it is the last Adam coming to be in us a quickening spirit, to seal us for the Resurrection of the Body and the Life Everlasting."

In the preface to the second edition he expressed a hope that that might be the last time that he would have to deal with the subject in a controversial way; but this prayer was not to be granted.

In August, 1857, Bishop Forbes of Brechin delivered his Primary Charge to his clergy, the substance of it being a full statement of the doctrine of the Holy Eucharist, emphasizing its sacrificial aspect and the mystical identity of it with Christ's own offering of Himself, and drawing out the inference of the duty of adoration of Christ present in the elements. About the same time Keble, who was an honorary canon of the college of Cumbræ, sent his own Tract to the Scottish bishops. The Bishops met in Synod in December, but after discussion postponed any action about the charge.

Three of them, however, the Bishops of Edinburgh, Argyll, and Glasgow, put out on their own account a joint declaration on the subject of the Eucharist, protesting against any adoration of the elements, and against the doctrine that the offering in the Eucharist was anything more than a commemoration of the Offering upon the Cross. Keble received a copy of this declaration, and imagining under a mistaken impression that it was intended as a criticism upon his own Tract, and that it had been sent to him by the Bishop of Edinburgh, wrote to him a long letter of queries, criticizing the language and arguments of the declarations.[1] In May, 1858, an extraordinary episcopal meeting was held, and the Bishops, although they refused to allow the Bishop of Brechin to be represented by a legal adviser, and in spite of his protest that they were acting *ultra vires*, issued a pastoral letter to their clergy, regretting the publication of the charge, as containing views unsound, erroneous, and calculated to lead to grave error on the two points of adoration to Christ in the gifts, and of the transcendental identification of the Sacrifice of the Cross and the Sacrifice of the Altar. They then lay down the lines of teaching which they wish the presbyters to follow, and issue the letter as words of fatherly guidance and admonition, "by a right essentially inherent in a provincial episcopate."

Owing to Dr. Pusey's illness at this time, Keble had been the Bishop's chief adviser through the whole discussion ; he was, moreover, an honorary member of the Church of Scotland, and he felt that by former publications he had incurred a deep responsibility in the matter. Accordingly, as an effort towards truth and

---

[1] This is quoted in full in Mackey's *Life of Bishop Forbes*.

peace, he addressed to the presbyters of the Scotch Church a pamphlet of "Considerations" on the pastoral letter. He urges that the letter is not a Synodical act, because presbyters have a right to be present at a Synod, and because the discussion was carried on with closed doors, and the judgment given without any statement of the reasons; hence the presbyters are not bound to accept it as authoritative. They can either acknowledge the receipt of it and take no further action, or discuss its statements in full. In view of the possibility of this latter course being taken, he argues the points at length. He acknowledges with great gratitude the facts that the Bishops appeal to the consent of the Undivided Church as the ultimate ground for decision, that they have not thought the Bishop of Brechin liable to a judicial presentment, and that there is so much positive teaching in their statements on the reality of sacramental grace, on the objective Presence even for condemnation to unworthy recipients, and on the sacrificial character of the Eucharist. But he criticizes the negative statements, showing that the denial of the statement that the Substance of Christ's Body and Blood, still less His entire Person as God and Man, now glorified in heaven, is made to exist *with*, *in*, or *under* the material substances of bread and wine, tends to Nestorianism, "which in one shape or another bids fair to become the prevalent tendency among the religionists of our day." On the point of the Sacrifice he proves that the Fathers have always held that Christ is the real Priest, and that the offering in the Eucharist is really identical with, not the Sacrifice on the Cross, but rather with the present offering of Himself by Christ in heaven; the same Person offers the same Body and Blood, but for different purposes—"on the Cross for expiation of sin, with vicarious suffering, pain, bloodshedding, and death; in heaven for pleading and application of those atoning pains." Further, he urges that adoration is implied in the fact of the Real Presence, that it never has been condemned, that all which the Bishop is pleading for is a toleration which has always been permitted.

Here he pleads against limitation of toleration; and indeed the whole argument is a plea against limitation. He will not have truth limited by the objection that a particular doctrine is "Roman"; though we cannot accept their terms of communion, yet "we ought always to be glad to agree with them, when we can do it with a safe conscience:" surely the right way must be in this or any other question, "calmly to apply the proper standards, Scripture as interpreted by our own formularies, and where they are ambiguous or silent by the consent of the Undivided Church; and if the conclusions come out agreeable to what the rest of Christendom has received, thankfully to welcome such agreement: if not, humbly and reverently to commit the cause to Almighty God, and to such authorities as it may hereafter please Him to raise up for the healing of the wounds in His Church." So, too, he will not limit the *Presence* of the Lord by our possibility of understanding it, "shedding, as it does, such a glory over the celebration of the Holy Eucharist." "It were better philosophy and not worse devotion here, if anywhere, to apply the maxim of the wise man, ' When you glorify the Lord, exalt Him as much as you can: for even yet will He far exceed: and when you exalt Him put forth all your strength, and be not weary: for ye never

can go far enough.'" [1]   For there is One walking about
who wishes to make us forget that "as Christians we
are altogether in a supernatural· condition, that the air
around us is full of miracles, full of great, intense
realities, of which the things that we see are for the
most part faint shadows."

The "Considerations" had little effect.   In October
1859, Bishop Forbes was formally presented for trial;
the case was postponed till February 1860, and judgment
delivered in March, a formal declaration of censure
being passed, but no penalty imposed.   On both of
these last occasions Keble was present at Edinburgh,
in order to help the Bishop by his wide knowledge of
the controversy; and although he blamed himself for
the line that he had taken at times during the controversy, yet it was mainly through his agency that
at once truth and peace were secured, and that the
Bishop was kept loyal to the Church even under these
difficulties.

Three other subjects, partly academical and partly
political, on which Keble published pamphlets during
those years, deserve a passing notice. In 1852 the
opposition to Mr. Gladstone's re-election as Burgess for
the University drew from him a smart and spirited
protest against the unfairness of charging that statesman with inconsistency in dealing with the Church, on
the ground of his support of the admission of Jews into
Parliament: and in 1854 he tried to rally Churchmen
to a determination to disavow, deprecate, and resist to
the uttermost the attempt to admit Nonconformists to
the University, and threw out the suggestion that the
difficulty might be met by affiliating to the University

----

[1] Ecclus. xliii. 30.

denominational colleges, even though situated at a distance.

But the point which always stung him to the quick was any attempt by Parliament to interfere with the sanctity of the Marriage Law. In 1849 he issued a short appeal *ad populum* against the Deceased Wife's Sister Bill, or, as he called it, against profane dealing with Holy Matrimony in regard of a man and his wife's sister; and he obtained 10,000 ladies' signatures to a petition against it, which he forwarded through Sir G. Grey to the Queen. In 1857, in opposition to the Divorce Bill, he wrote a careful, scholarlike treatise on the indissolubility of marriage. The treatise was an attempt to explain the difficulty which dutiful children of the Church might feel in the fact that while the Church forbade divorce altogether, our Lord seems to permit it under the condition given in St. Matt. v. 32, xix. 9. Keble's line of defence was that this limitation was not meant for Christians at all; that it was only preserved in St. Matthew, the specially Jewish Gospel; that it occurred in contexts in which Christ was not speaking to His disciples alone, but to the Jewish multitudes, and was interpreting rather than adding to the Mosaic law, and that the limitation was only meant to apply as long as the Mosaic law was in force. This was followed by a laborious examination of all the Canons and Patristic references to the subject, with the result of showing that, in spite of some conflicting evidence, there was a continuous stream of opinion against divorce for any reason among Christians, and against the re-marriage of either party after a separation.

In these, as in all his treatises, the moral considerations are the primary with him. He discusses the

Levitical prohibition, but he does not lay much stress
upon it, because whatever it may require, the "spirit of
the Christian dispensation is to require more of man in
proportion as it gives him more grace." He is especially
indignant at the unfairness with which the two sexes
were treated by the proposers of each measure, and
contrasts it with the language of the Fathers ; [1] he lays
stress on the indissolubility of marriage, because that
gives it a sacramental character, and makes it affect the
whole life ; on the prohibition of re-marriage, because
it leaves room for penitence on the part of the guilty
party, and reconciliation. He pleads that sad experience
has taught him how terribly strong is the feeling among
the poor that marriage erases the blot of previous un-
chastity, and though they have now a horror of adultery,
he dreads the power of One who may avail himself of
the change to suggest to them that offences of that kind
also may be salved by after-marriage.

The pamphlet did not avail to save England from a
Divorce Bill; probably of greater avail to deepen the
religious sense of marriage, and so to avoid divorce, has

---

[1] *E. g.* St. Augustine (*Serm.* 392, vol. v., p. 2) : " Who would
endure an adulterous wife ? Yet the woman is bidden to endure
an adulterous husband. What justice ! Why, I ask thee ?
'Why ? because I am the man.' Thou the man ? Let us prove
thy manhood by thy fortitude. Thou the man ? Overcome lust.
How art thou the man, whose wife is braver than thou art ?
Thou art the head of the woman, the man : it is true. If he is
the head, let him lead, let the wife follow. Only take heed which
way thou goest. Have thou no mind to go where thou wouldest
not have her to follow."
And the Emperor Antoninus, as quoted by St. Augustine :
" Care must be taken to enquire whether thou by living chastely
hast been a pattern of good conduct to her. For it seems to me
most unjust that the husband should exact from the wife the
chastity which he does not practise himself."—*De Conjug. Adult.*
§ 5.

been the hymn which he wrote while the pressure of
the controversy was upon him—

> "The Voice that breathed o'er Eden
> That earliest wedding-day,
> The primal marriage blessing,
> It hath not passed away.
>
> Still in the pure espousal
> Of Christian man and maid,
> The Holy Three are with us,
> The threefold grace is said."

CHAPTER VIII.

THE END. 1860—1866.

" Wait humbly till thy matin Psalm
Due cadence find in evening calm."
Lyra Innocentium.

THE reader will probably have gained the impression
that Keble's interest was only in controversial questions;
but the case was really much the same as with the
history of the Church. The controversies come to the
front, and must be noticed by the historian. To a reader
of the history of the first four centuries it might seem
that the Church was mainly occupied in a series of
uninteresting speculations and antagonisms; but behind
the controversy lay a spiritual body, moving through
the world ministering comfort, absolution, inspiration to
its own members, moulding by silent influence the
customs and laws of the world outside it, and so gradually
winning its way to establishment and supremacy. So
behind the controversial writings by which Keble came
before the world, there was the quiet constructive work
both of the student and of the parish priest. As a
student he was engaged through all these years on his
careful translation of Irenæus for the *Library of the
Fathers,* and also on the life and edition of the

works of Bishop Wilson. The former was not published until after his death, but the latter issued from the press in 1863. The motto prefixed to it, " The care of Discipline is Love," shows the aspect of the good Bishop's work, whether in self-discipline or in the discipline of his diocese, which had specially interested his biographer. Alike the century and the man attracted him. Around the Bishop's youth were memories of the Cavalier struggles ; during his life there were glimpses of the struggles of the Non-jurors, and, carefully treasured up, just here and there, sayings and deeds of Bishop Butler. The struggle between Bishop Wilson and the representatives of the Earl of Derby, who at one time boldly claimed that the Earl and not the Archbishop was the Metropolitan of the Church of Man, reminded him of the struggles in England under Henry II. and Henry VIII., and made the annals of the small island of Man seem to be a miniature reflection of far more important histories. It seemed to his heart, saddened by the decay of faith around him, that Man had preserved later than any other part of England that simple faith in the reality and grievous effect of excommunication, and in the solemn seriousness of an oath, on which alone ecclesiastical discipline could be based.

No less was he in hearty sympathy with the teaching and personal character of the Bishop. The sobriety of his teaching, his readiness to recognize the Roman Catholics as a real part of the Holy Catholic Church, the absence of any insistence on the necessity of sensible conversion and assurance of personal salvation, his principle that it is safer to obey authority with a doubting conscience than with a doubting conscience to

disobey, the public spirit which made him feel national
troubles as keenly as private calamities, his interest in
missionary work and in education, his pastoral spirit,
his care with his candidates for Ordination, some of
whom lived in his house for a year before being ordained, his own methodical intercessions, his insistence
on family prayer, his loyal use of the daily offices of
Matins and Evensong,[1] his simple Prayer-book-like
outspokenness in preaching or writing on subjects of
delicacy, his sternness with all breaches of the marriage
laws, his prompt and fearless exercise of discipline, his
equitable desire to make allowances for difficulties, his
liberality to the poor, extending ultimately to the be-
stowal in charity of one-half of his income ; above all,
his reality, his sense of his own personal sinfulness, his
realization of the Communion of Saints, and his gratitude to God for even the least mercy of his life—every
point found an answering note in Keble's own heart.

He approaches his subject therefore with the greatest
reverence and desire to do it justice.   He tries to find
explanation or at least excuse for the few points in the
Bishop's life which he cannot approve.   Unstinted
pains are taken in verifying each place and explaining
each allusion ; the relations of the Earl of Derby to the
Island and the conditions of Manx land tenure are
traced out with painstaking accuracy.   Some scenes, such
as those of the Bishop's imprisonment and of his struggle
with the civil powers, are painted very graphically ; but

---

[1] This was impressed upon the Bishop by his friend the Rev.
M. Hewetson, on his ordination as deacon in 1686, in the church
of Kildare.   The whole of Hewetson's *Memorandum* is a very
striking proof of the strength of Church feeling and practices in
the Church of Ireland at the end of the seventeenth century (vol. i.
pp. 22-23).

it must in fairness be admitted that the details rather overwhelm the general effect, and that the whole is wanting in a due sense of proportion.

But the main staple of his life was the work, the incessant, anxious, unsparing, loving work, of a parish priest. From the first he had held daily service in his church. For at least four years, during the Gorham controversy, he said the Litany on Wednesdays and Fridays at 5.30 a.m., "to give those who fear God and believe His sacraments and love His Church, a chance of calling upon Him in the early morning, while they are on their way to their day's work." [1] He would stay behind in private prayer for an hour or half an hour. One hour every morning and two hours every Sunday were spent in teaching in the school. When a boy had been turned away from school for disorderliness, he would take him and train him privately. The preparation for Confirmation was especially careful, sometimes lasting for a whole year, as he went through with the candidates the whole of the Baptismal and Eucharistic services, as well as the Catechism. If any boy or girl lived too far off to come to the classes, he would walk out himself at night with a lantern and teach them in their cottages after their work was over. He went on with the training until he could win them to come to the Holy Communion, once getting them to sign the following paper: "In the presence of Almighty God, I seriously declare that I am turning my mind towards Holy Communion: that I hope before very long, by God's mercy, to be fit for it; that I will pray to God to make me fit, and that I will come to Mr. Keble or

---

[1] Cf. *Sermons:* Septuagesima to Ash Wednesday, p. 358, and Preface, p. vi.

Mr. Young from time to time if they wish me to do so, to have their advice about coming or staying away." When he was away from home he used to receive accounts of each individual from his curates, and when absent once from the Confirmation itself, sent a short, earnest-pastoral letter to the candidates. His favourite text was, " Ourselves your servants for Jesus' sake"; his favourite expression, that of *waiting* on the sick, ever suiting himself to their hours, delighting if they asked to receive the Sacrament, but always waiting for the suggestion to come from them, that it might be a real act of their own spiritual will. His interest in missions had always been great, and it developed in later years when his personal interest in Bishop Selwyn and Bishop Patteson, and his ecclesiastical sympathy with the struggle of Bishop Gray for the faith in South Africa, made the life of the Colonial Church so much more real to him. After 1861 he sanctioned cricket on Sundays at the suggestion of Sir W. Heathcote, partly because he found that otherwise the men played, though under the conviction that it was wrong, and partly influenced by the fact that the chief Evangelical families who might have been offended had left the parish. So wrapped up was he in his parish that the villagers had no conception of the part which he played in the Church, and a new school-mistress, who came to the place with an enthusiasm for the author of the *Christian Year*, found it hard to convince the children that the Vicar was as clever as the School Inspector, and cleverer than herself.

The succeeding chapters on his preaching and spiritual guidance will complete the picture of his more constructive work; but as in the days of Nehemiah "the builders every one had his sword girded by his side, and so builded," so it was in these years. Even in old age his interest was as keen as ever in all that concerned both Oxford or the Church. Dr. Pusey shared with him all his plans about the prosecution of Professor Jowett and the endowment of the Greek chair. Before the election of 1865 he wrote a strong incisive letter to the *Guardian*, pleading for the re-election of Mr. Gladstone on the ground of that statesman's real services to the Church, especially with regard to the Divorce Bill, the Burials Bill, the Royal Supremacy and its relation to the Final Court of Appeal. "Were I asked," he ends, "to add my name to the list of his opponents, I should answer, No! a thousand times No! for prudence' sake, for justice' sake, for Oxford's sake, and most of all for the Church's sake."[1] In the same year he was interested in the proposals for the extension of the University, and warmly approved of the report of Dr. Shirley's Committee, which afterwards was taken as the outline on which the charter of Keble College was framed.

But the chief interest of these years lay in the struggles caused by the publication of *Essays and Reviews*. In 1850 he had contemplated the serious issues which must arise if such a Court as the Judicial Committee of the Privy Council were to deal with subjects of such delicacy and seriousness as the Inspiration of the Bible and Eternal Punishment; and these were the very two points on which they were called to decide. The book was published in 1860; in 1861 Dr. Williams was prosecuted by the Bishop of Salisbury for virtually denying the Inspiration of the Holy

[1] *Guardian*, Dec. 7, 1864.

N

Scriptures; Mr. Wilson by the Rev. J. Fendall on the
same charge, and also for denying the doctrine of the
Eternal Punishment of the wicked. Both clergy
were condemned in 1862 by the judgment of Dr.
Lushington in the Arches Court. But in both cases
the judgment was overthrown on appeal to the Privy
Council in 1864. The Court consisted of four lay judges
and three spiritual, the two Archbishops and the Bishop
of London. Its policy was to limit the issues before
it, and treat them with the most exact legal technicality;
holding that it could take no cognizance of anything
outside the extracts from the *Essays* laid before it,
and of the Articles referred to in them. It passed no
opinion upon the general teaching or tendency of the
whole *Essays*, but decided that on the subject of
Inspiration the extracts did not contain any statement
inconsistent with the exact words of our formularies;
and further that "we do not find in the formularies to
which this article refers any such distinct declaration of
our Church upon the subject as to require us to condemn as penal the expression of a hope by a clergyman
that even the ultimate pardon of the wicked who are
condemned in the day of judgment may be consistent
with the will of Almighty God."

It may be that if the distinction between a judicial
decision in a penal case and the formal legislative
expression of the real mind of the Church had been
clearly grasped, the judgment might have been
acquiesced in. But such a distinction was by no means
clear then : even with the limitation imposed by the
Court's ruling, the two Archbishops refused to concur
in the judgment. The cry of determined, uncompromising protest was more loud even than after the

Gorham judgment; leaders who had been opposed to each other through all the Sacramental struggles joined hand in hand now. More than 11,000 clergy and 137,000 laity signed declarations affirming their belief that the Church of England and Ireland, in common with the whole Catholic Church, maintains without reserve or qualification the inspiration and divine authority of the whole Canonical Scriptures, as not only containing but being the Word of God, and further teaches, in the words of our blessed Lord, that the punishment of the cursed, equally with the life of the righteous, is everlasting.

Keble was indignant alike at the substance of the decisions and at the composition of the Court which had given them. A strong movement was made to get it altered, and when this was ridiculed by the *Times* he wrote a letter to that paper justifying the agitation, as being the constitutional method of remedying a grievance;[1] criticizing acutely the assumptions of his opponents, and showing that his action rested upon the belief that "it is better to have a *real* Church; that a real Church cannot exist without dogma, and that the action of this Committee, tending as it does to do away with all dogma, tends of course to the annihilation of the Church." In the following month he read a paper at the Bristol Church Congress, in a discussion on Church Synods, admitting that there was much to be said *à priori* for such a court, but that it had proved a failure, and that the failure was due to its being based upon a wrong principle. It was an infringement of the rights of the Bishops; it was a human invention; its principles for deciding doctrine, and its procedure,

---

[1] *Times*, Sept. 22nd; *Guardian*, Sept. 28, 1864.

by which dissentients could not justify their opinions, were alike anomalies. He also alluded to the seriousness of the points at issue, quoting the saying of a woman in his parish, who had a son who had been a great trouble to her because of his wicked habits, and who, on hearing that the doctrine of eternal punishment was being called in question, said, "Oh, what an effect it will have, when my son hears of it, on him! What will become of him?" The lines on which he would have liked to see reforms are indicated in the following suggestions embodied in a letter to Judge Coleridge.

"1. Whether it is impossible to obtain a law taking away all temporal penalties annexed to excommunication, and leaving the Church really free to enforce its own rubric and canons in case of notorious sin and unbelief?

"2. Might there not be a declaratory Act to the effect that the formularies must always be interpreted agreeably to Holy Scripture and general consent? . . . To which Act the assent of Convocation should be obtained and recited, as in the Act of Uniformity.

"3. After providing in the completest way for perfect investigation and exact legality, still might not the Bishops in Provincial Council, with full publicity to all their proceedings, be made judges in the last resort?"[1]

But it was not only with the Court that Keble was indignant. Both the decisions touched him to the quick. His knowledge of the Bible was remarkable; he knew large parts of it by heart, and his sermons, no less than the Tract on Mysticism, are steeped in the mystical use of its language, and marked by a striking insight into its principles. And his reverence for it

[1] Coleridge : *Memoir*, p. 488.

was no less striking. " His manner of reading Holy
Scripture was very remarkable. In its extreme simplicity it was like that of a reverent child; and yet
probably all who were in the habit of hearing him
have felt the wonderful charm of it, and that he made
them understand the Lessons better than any one else,
conveying to them also in some measure his own intense
feeling of the *sacredness of every inspired word*. He
always paused before reading the Bible, often putting
his hand to his forehead (as was often his way), and
after the Lesson was ended he made the same pause. . .
In some sermon of his he takes it for granted that the
custom of pious people would ﹐be to pray inwardly
before and after reading any portion of Holy Scripture." [1]

That he might contribute his part to a true belief in
Scripture, he set himself to work at a Commentary on
St. John's Gospel, and composed the fragment on Chap.
i. 1-18, afterwards printed in the *Studia Sacra*, the
rich spiritual suggestiveness of which causes regret that
it never was finished. He circulated a protest against
the judgment for signature in his parish. In a letter
to the *Times* on the whole subject, he urged that the inspiration of the Bible was a part of the " common law "
of the Church, and therefore as really binding as a
formulated decision; and spoke of the inspiration
of the various parts of the Bible in a way that shows
alike reverence and wisdom.

" The New Testament declares the Old Testament to
be inspired of God; accordingly, the Book of Esther to
be as really inspired as the Evangelical Prophet, *as
really though not as largely*. But since it is so inspired
men know that they are bound to believe every word

[1] M. T. in Coleridge : *Memoir*, p. 604.

of it, and if contradictions appear, to feel sure that they
will one day disappear, either by amended readings or
by satisfactory explanations. All will prove true, all
exactly what was needed for its own peculiar purpose.
But there may be any degrees of difference in love and
fear, the awe and the gratitude with which Almighty
God means us to receive one portion and another,
according to the measure in which He vouchsafes to
disclose Himself, or to draw nearer to us; and again,
according to the measure in which His several gifts of
grace are allowed to manifest themselves through the
several human writers. *In this respect* we may imagine
a scale ranging from the mere adjustment of a genealogy
in the Chronicles up to the first chapter of St. John.
All are equally true, although all do not contain an
equal amount of Divine Truth."

The denial of the doctrine of Eternal Punishment
seemed even more pressing as a matter of practical
importance. He had an almost Calvinistic sense of
the corruption of the human heart; he knew how
simple villagers are wont to regard the utterance of
the law as the sole standard of truth; he believed in
the power of the Evil Spirit who was always anxious to
lower the standard of truth and of morality. "We cannot spare one of the severe but most fatherly sayings
by which our loving Lord has revealed to us the issue
of the broad way; least of all can we spare the thought,
the conviction, of eternity."

Early in 1864 he published a *Litany of our Lord's
Warnings*, for use by those "whose hearts are aching at
the recent decision." The Litany recalls all the great
acts of God's justice, and His words of warning in the
Bible; and in the light of them prays for mercy, for

protection from all that can blind men's eyes to the truth, and for guidance to the Church, the Queen, the Parliament, and for all who are in danger of neglecting this special truth.

In the same year he was invited by Bishop Wilberforce to preach the sermon at the commemoration of Cuddesdon College. With this subject in his mind he preached one of the most solemn and touching of his sermons, on "Fear as a Gift of the Holy Spirit," and drew out the true fear of God that should be in a Christian's heart. There is the fear of judgment, of hell—the lowest form, yet still quite necessary for ourselves and for others; for " little do they know of their brethren, how high soever their own rate of goodness may be, who depend on winning souls without it." Then there is the nobler fear of losing Christ, the object of our love; this remains in the converted soul, and grows with the growth of our love for Him. Both these fears will cease with this life, but still beyond the grave there will be the highest fear, the deep awe and trembling reverence before God as God, an intense, unspeakable adoration, a bowing down before the Light unapproachable; and this awe begins here, for even here it is our privilege to be living in a supernatural state. Thus, as the *Christian Year* ended with the " Spirit of God's most holy fear," so his last published sermon ended with the fear of God's Holy Spirit.

One other public utterance must be noticed. In 1865 the Bishop of London was pressing for a Royal Commission to deal with the Ornaments Rubric, and some High Churchmen were inclined to support him. To one of these Keble wrote a letter,[1] very strongly

---

[1] *Literary Churchman*, January 13, 1866.

deprecating such a course. It seemed to him suicidal
to invite Parliamentary interference in spiritual matters,
when it was sure to be exercised in an anti-dogmatic
direction. As it was, the Church of England, through
the struggles of the Reformation and Restoration, had,
under Providence, retained the rubric, and so expressed its doctrine as to assert the reality both of
the Presence and of the Sacrifice in the Eucharist;
but further legislation in a moment of excitement might
easily upset the exact proportion of the truth, destroy
the equilibrium of parties in the Church, and quench
all the fond hopes of reunion among Christians, "which
just now appear to be dawning on us from various
quarters." While treating the disregard of the rubric
as a real blemish in our ecclesiastical practice, and
rejoicing whenever the revival is tranquilly accomplished, he pleads for equity and candid allowance and
charity in the revival, and protests against the scornful,
disparaging tone in which some were speaking of midday Communions, "with small consideration for the
aged and infirm, and for such as cannot come early,"
and against the practice of urging all men indiscrimin-
ately to be present at the Holy Mysteries.

In his private life there was sadness and happiness,
partings and reconciliations, towards the close. In 1860
his sister Elizabeth died, "for twenty years of health
and fifty of sickness always at hand or within reach,
and never a look nor a word that I know of but was
wise and kind with the true kindness and wisdom."
His great friend Dyson died the same year. From
that time onward Keble's own health was very pre-
carious, and constant visits to the seaside kept him a

good deal from his parish work; and on St. Andrew's Day, 1864, he was seized with a slight stroke of paralysis, after which he never preached again.

In the course of 1863 he had received an account of the proceeds of the *Lyra Apostolica*, and this led to a letter to Newman thanking him for it, and sending him his own Life of Bishop Wilson.

"August 4, 1863.

"MY DEAR NEWMAN,

"It is a great thing, I know, for me to ask, after so many years, that you should look kindly upon what comes from me. For I cannot conceal it from myself, nor yet acknowledge it without a special sort of pang, that what I have heard occasionally from Crawley and Copeland, of your feeling as to your old friend's silence, touches me perhaps as much or more than any, and it is one of the many things which now in my old age I wish otherwise. I ought to have felt more than I did what a sore burthen you were bearing for conscience' sake, and that it was the duty of us all to diminish rather than aggravate it, so far as other claims allowed. In point of fact I rather imagine the last communication was on my part, with the *Lyra Innocentium*. Since then I have been more than once about to write; but something always happened which seemed to check me, and I suppose I said to myself, 'It will be but cold and constrained after all,' and so I gave way to my dilatory habits; and it frightens me now to think how nearly the time has passed away. I can but ask that if I have been towards you too much as if you had been dead, you will now be towards me as if I were dying; which of course must be nearly my condition, for though (D. G.) wonderfully well, I am in my seventy-second year. Do then, my dear old friend, pardon me what has been wrong in this (I can see it in some measure, but I dare say there is more which I do not see), and let me have the comfort of hoping that your recollection of me will not henceforth be embittered by anything more than is inseparable from our sad position, as I am sure your kindness to me has always been the same. . . . And now, dear N., let me say 'God be with you; and may He forgive and bring us all together, as He will and when He will.' I know that you will let me have a line or two, to say that you will believe me still and always

"Yours affectionately,

"J. KEBLE."

This renewal of correspondence led to the visit of Cardinal Newman in October, 1864, when, almost by accident, Dr. Pusey also was present. Newman has himself described the strange meeting of the three friends, each scarcely recognizing the other through the great changes which time had made. It was necessarily a meeting at once joyful and painful. Keble seems to have formed some idea that Newman was uneasy in his position; but it is very doubtful if there was any ground for this. Newman was probably more ready than he had been to do justice to the reality of spiritual life in the English Church; but there was to be no closer, no more visible, union on this earth. For that he could only wait till beyond the grave; for the present he might have taken on his lips almost word for word, the speech which Browning attributes to Pym at his parting from Strafford:

" . . . . I love him now,
And look for my chief portion in that world
Where great hearts led astray are turned again.
(Soon it may be, and, certes, will be soon :
My mission over, I shall not live long.)
Ay, here I know I talk—I dare and must—
Of England and her great reward, as all
I look for here ; but in my inmost heart
Believe, I think of stealing quite away
To walk once more with Wentworth—my youth's friend—
Purged from all error, gloriously renewed."

"Certes, it will be soon." In the winter of 1865 he moved to Bournemouth on account of his wife's illness. He himself was well, able to attend service regularly in St. Peter's Church; but she grew weaker, and as the spring came he was daily expecting her death. But he was taken first from her; he suffered what seemed to be another stroke of paralysis on March 22, 1866. He lay ill for a week. "Whether wandering or clear-minded, he was constantly intent on holy things or in actual prayer; he uttered fragments or ejaculations in the former case, which showed the habitual prayerful-ness of his heart; he repeated, or composed as it seemed, prayers; the Lord's Prayer he uttered most commonly."[1]

He passed away on March 29th, and was buried at Hursley on April 6th. When she heard that he was gone, she thanked God that he had been spared the trial of surviving her, and she said that she knew that in his dying thoughts were the words of the *Christian Year* for Good Friday—

" Lord of my heart, by Thy last cry,
    Let not Thy blood on earth be spent—
Lo, at Thy feet I fainting lie,
    Mine eyes upon Thy wounds are bent,
Upon Thy streaming wounds my weary eyes
Wait like the parched earth on April skies.

---

[1] Coleridge : *Memoir*, p. 559.

Wash me, and dry these bitter tears,
  O let my heart no further roam :
'Tis Thine by vows, and hopes, and fears,
  Long since—O call Thy wanderer home ;
To that dear home, safe in Thy wounded side,
Where only broken hearts their sin and shame may
    hide."

Who can doubt that they were in her thoughts too, when she followed him on the eleventh of the following month, and they who for thirty years had shared every hope and prayer and plan for the Church, were not divided in their death ?

CHAPTER IX.

THE PREACHER.

"To gentlest touches sweetest notes reply.
  Still humbleness with her low-breathed voice
  Can steal o'er man's proud heart, and win his choice
  From earth to heaven, with mightier witchery
  Than eloquence or wisdom e'er could own."

J. K. : Misc. Poems, p. 217.

"IF I were to say what I really feel," wrote Newman in 1837, "I should say plainly that no greater benefit could in my opinion be granted to the Church than the publication of sermons from you, and that on account of their matter, not only of the authority of your name." [1]

Yet the only volume of sermons which Keble published in his lifetime was the *Sermons, Academical and Occasional* (1847), with the preface on the Roman question, about which I have already spoken. This volume consists mainly of University sermons, preached as Select Preacher, containing among others the famous Assize Sermon of 1833, and the Winchester Sermon on Tradition.

The history of two of them has special interest.

On St. Andrew's Day, 1841, Keble was appointed to

[1] *Letters*, ii., p. 229.

preach before the University. He prepared a sermon upon the duty of acquiescing in imperfections in the Church rather than hurriedly leaving the Church for some other body, and sent it to Newman for his approval; but he dissuaded him from preaching it. The sermon is the clearest and most vigorous statement anywhere to be found in Keble's writings, of the duty of loyalty to the English Church, and puts, perhaps even more effectively, the line of argument afterwards worked out in the preface. Newman, however, thought it would add to the excitement without effecting any object. "It will increase," he wrote, "upon a separate authority, the impression which is not well founded, that there are men in Oxford who are on the point of turning to Rome, with a sort of confession to the world at large, and as a triumph to the foe over you and us. I know of none such. There is doubtless great danger in prospect, but the persons in danger are far too serious men to act suddenly or without waiting for what they consider God's direction, and I should think very few indeed realize to themselves yet the prospect of a change—nay would change, provided our rulers showed us any sympathy, or their brethren kept from saying or believing of them that they would change." [1]

Whatever may be thought of this opinion in the light of subsequent events, Keble at least acquiesced in it. "I shall never be able to thank you enough," he wrote on December 12th, "for sending back that sermon of mine." In its stead he preached a most excellent spiritual sermon on "Counsels of Perfection," showing deep insight into the secret forces

[1] J. H. N. : *Letters*, ii., p. 370.

of character, and drawing out most subtly the dangers
to which religious people are exposed. Both these
sermons were now published.

It is not necessary to dwell at any length upon this
volume. The first three sermons deal with the grounds
of faith, and anticipate much of the preface. They are
slightly laborious in style, but full of quiet, thoughtful
reasoning, steeped in Aristotle and Butler, " one of
the safest teachers of religion, natural and revealed,
that ever blessed the Church."

While emphasizing the essential value of the
" implicit faith " of the simple Christian, which may
seem to be bigotry and yet is true practical wisdom,
" abiding by the dictates of experience, not in defiance
but in default of theoretical and argumentative knowledge," he yet insists on the duty of each man enquiring
for himself into the grounds of his faith; in a true
pastoral spirit he pleads that even the poor can understand more than we give them credit for: " the
recollection that ' proving all things ' is as much the
duty of the unlearned as it is of the educated, should
make us less afraid to trust them with reasoning than
in matters of this sort we commonly are." One passage
—preached in 1822—is pathetically prophetic in the
light of the subsequent history of the movement. " Not
being quite satisfied concerning some part of religious
truth, and ill-enduring the condition of doubt and
discomfort (which after all would do them no great
harm, if they would be careful always to take the safe
side in practice), subtle and ingenious men set themselves to devise argument after argument in its behalf,
and thus they have often succeeded, to a wonder, in
strengthening and extending the fabric of theology,

perhaps to the benefit of others, without having been
able to find under it any shelter, final and complete, for
their own harassed and perplexed spirits. Thus the
Church has witnessed more than once the sorrowful
spectacle of orthodox teachers falling off in their latter
days from the very truth which they had themselves
before most triumphantly defended ; the law of compen-
sation, which has so wide a range in the natural world,
extending, apparently, in this among other instances, to
the moral world also; in that the versatility and ingenuity which enable men to devise new modes of
evidence, are too often accompanied with a disposition
to be restless and unsatisfied with the old."

One other extract from a sermon preached at a
school at Harrow Weald in 1846 shows the spirit in
which he wished to see boys trained in order to fit
them for the difficulties of life : " We hope and pray
that from this day forward this place may begin to be
a nursery, not only of sincere Christians, but of Christians
willing and able to serve the Church of God at home or
abroad in her roughest and barest paths of duty; and
it is obvious that to this end they must be trained to
endure hardness, to love the poor and low places of the
earth, to give up their own wills more unreservedly than
is expected in a common way, even of those who are
brought up in our Church."

But it is as a parish preacher that Keble will be
best known. Since his death, Dr. Pusey and other
friends have seen through the press twelve volumes of
sermons on the *Christian Year*, one volume of *Sermons,
Occasional and Parochial*, a volume on the *Baptismal
Office*, and a volume of *Outlines of Instructions or Meditations for the Church's Seasons*, consisting of notes for

sermons. This last volume does not lend itself to quotation or analysis but it deserves a special mention. From 1855 onwards, Keble nearly always preached extempore, and scarcely any written sermons are preserved after that date; but these notes date mainly after that year, and so contain his ripest thought. For suggestions for preaching or for individual meditation on the Bible, they are admirable, being stimulating and original and marked, like all his work, by a simple, humble, deep reverence for Holy Scripture.

Of the more finished sermons, Dr. Pusey has said that the chief characteristics are affectionate simplicity and intense reality.

" Mr. Keble was not a great preacher, was he?" said one soon after his death to the landlord of the village inn at Hursley. "Well, I don't know what a great preacher is," was the answer, "but he always made us understand him." That is exactly it: he is never thinking of himself, but of his hearers. He said himself, when weighing the relative merits of written or extempore sermons, "That course is probably best for each which most enables him to forget himself, and to think only of God, his hearers, and his subject." [1] There is no display, no elaborate ornament, there is only the desire that he shall be understanded of the people. The sermons are what his favourite Bishop Wilson said sermons should be, " pious instructions to lead men to heaven and save them from hell." [2] "In delivery he did not give his sermons the advantages of an ordinarily eloquent preacher, but he was eminently winning; he let himself down—I do not mean in language or argument, but in simplicity and childlike

[1] *Occasional Papers*, p. 370.   [2] *Life*, ii., p. 875.

humility—to the most uneducated of his audience; he
seemed always to count himself one of the sinners,
one of the penitents, one even of the impenitent and
careless whom he was addressing, and the very quietness, the almost tearful monotony of his delivery
became extremely moving when you recollected how
learned, how able, how moved in his own heart, and
how earnest was the preacher."[1] "He spoke of good
angels," says Miss Wilbraham, "their loving ministry
and their presence in church, briefly but in words so
simple and real that it seemed as if the rustling of their
wings were close around."[2]

This simplicity is very striking in contrast with the
academical sermons, and it is more marked in his later
style : it was indeed the result of a very deliberate
effort on his part. "They said to me," he told Dr.
Pusey, "that I was preaching over the people's heads,
and so I changed my style."[3]

For our purpose it will be enough to take one volume
of his sermons, the course on the Baptismal Office, delivered after this change in the years 1849-50, to
serve as a specimen of this village preaching. "Affectionate simplicity" is everywhere—yes, very affectionate,
but also very stern ; very winning in charm, but very
clear in warning. Let us analyze the charm of them
a little more exactly. First there is the clear determination to be understood. He reverences the
intellect of his simple country folk; he treats it as
worth while to spend trouble in making things clear to

---

[1] Sir J. Coleridge : *Life*, p. 439.
[2] *Musings on the Christian Year*, p. cx.
[3] E. B. P. : Preface to the *Village Sermons on the Baptismal
Office*.

them. The principle of each rubric is drawn out; every possible misconception of the Church's teaching is guarded against. Thus on the essentials of Baptism (p. 247): "The two together, the words and the act, make up (as the Catechism says) the outward visible sign or form in Baptism. It would not be Baptism were a child washed or dipped in water in silence with only good thoughts—no, nor if he were washed and dipped with the best and most beautiful prayer. It would not be Baptism unless the very words which our Saviour appointed were used, 'In the Name of the Father, and of the Son, and of the Holy Ghost.' So on the other hand, neither would it be Baptism were this most Holy Name ever so solemnly repeated over the child, with the Amen of the whole Church. This would not, I say, be Baptism, unless the child or person at the same time were actually washed or dipped in the water." Again on the doctrine of Baptismal Regeneration (pp. 273-4): " We are to say distinctly, ' This child is regenerate,'—if there were any doubt, the Church, I suppose, would bid us say, ' *We hope* that this child is regenerated.' There is no reason against our saying that, if it were more according to the truth, according to our Lord's sayings, and the mind of His Holy Church. We might say, we hoped this child was regenerate, just as we say in the Burial Service, 'our hope is' that our brother or sister is now resting in Christ; the word would have been just as easily spoken. But instead of saying ' we hope,' we say positively, 'it is regenerate.' We say it concerning every child: no distinction is made between this one and that one. Why should we say it if we are not to believe it ? Surely the Church meant us all to believe it, and if we will be true Churchmen we

must believe it.   I say it over and over again, and
I wish you to take notice of it, and always remember
it, that over every child without exception, immediately after it has been baptized, the Priest is
desired to say, 'This child is regenerate,' not, 'it
may be,' or, 'we hope it is,' but plainly and distinctly,
'it is.'"

The illustrations are drawn from the ordinary details
of village life.   The nurse's care to hold a child carefully and not let it drop, leads to the thought, "If
helpless mortals can do so much for those little ones,
how much more may we make ourselves certain that
the Everlasting Arms will not fall from under us; that
Jesus Christ will never of His own accord cease to bear
us in His loving embrace."   When the Church asks
God to receive the child according to His promise, this
is "much in the same way as a person might present
a ticket of admission to a hospital, or an order to receive
a little bread or money or clothing, and, if signed by
the proper person, it would ensure him the gift."   The
sign of the cross is like the mark with which shepherds
put their master's name upon each lamb separately,
when it has been washed and shorn.   The sponsors
can truly say, "That is my desire," on behalf of the
children, being "so very certain that, if the children
could know, they would desire it above all things.   Just
as if one had a humble petition to make to the Queen
for any child who was too young to know the meaning
of it, to have its property taken care of or the like, one
should present it in the name of the child and call it
that child's petition.   Or if an infant was crying at the
door for hunger, though it were too young to understand its own wants, or at all to speak them out in

'words, yet we should not scruple to say 'the child is longing and asking for bread.'" The whole service is "as if a father sending his child a journey should first give him instructions what to do, then make him solemnly promise to do it, and lastly cause him to kneel down and bless him very religiously before he set out." The good behaviour of children at school before a holiday or festival is a type of what our conduct should be .in expectation of the great day of Judgment and Glory. Nay, more boldly still—the anger of the tidy housewife, when things are wilfully or wantonly stained or sullied, is a type of the anger which the Lord must feel when, having washed us clean in His own most precious Blood, He finds us by our own fault all foul and filthy again.

Some of these extracts lead up naturally ¸to the second characteristic note of the preaching: its unshrinking clearness of doctrine. The statements are clear, definite, yet always in due proportion; one side of truth does not crowd out another. Quite clear is the sense of the power of original sin, owing to which the child is born a child of wrath; quite clear the power and the personality of the Evil Spirit; but equally clear and far stronger is the power and the personality of God, coming to save the child in Baptism. There the child is saved, is regenerate: it is newborn unto righteousness and made a new creature. "Henceforth One abides in this child, greater than he that is in the world. A spark of holy fire is lit up in him, which if it be duly attended to will consume all that is gross and earthly, and purify him altogether in the likeness of Jesus Christ." The child receives justification, which is, being made a member of Christ the Righteous;

and justification brings with it pardon and peace;
pardon for sins past, for original sin, and grace to do
well for the time to come.   But then, as natural birth,
so far from relieving man of the necessity of food and
growth, absolutely requires them, so spiritual regeneration must be followed by spiritual growth, and that
life must be sustained by spiritual food, "the spark
must be kindled into a flame by the unceasing wonder-
working Breath of God, *i. e.* His Holy Spirit."   "We
must be made and continue members of Him.   *That* is
being saved by Him."   "From beginning to end of
the Baptismal Office two doctrines go together, or
rather two parts of one doctrine.   The one that every
baptized babe is regenerate by the Holy Ghost, the
other that every one who lives to the age of actual sin
will stand in need of further grace—the grace of perseverance and improvement, most likely of conversion
also, that he may not after all be a castaway."   "Pardon
and grace come first in Holy Baptism, and for the time
they come completely, they save us until they are
forfeited by sinful relapsing; but as we grow older and
temptations come on, new supplies of grace and pardon,
new ways of partaking of Christ the God-man are
needed, and most especially the Sacrament of Holy
Communion."

Now, the secret of this dogmatic clearness is no mere
love of intellectual precision, it is the singleness of
spiritual vision.   Priest and friends and nurse seem to
pass away : he sees only the Presence of the Lord
Jesus Christ and the Church to which the Lord
commits the child.   As clearly as to the eyes of the
mothers by the Lake of Galilee, the Lord is there to
his eyes; the Lord with His individualizing love, He

who had died to redeem this little one, and who loves
it as though there were no other child in the world.
He now takes him into His loving arms, pours the
water upon him, and blesses him with the very
greatest of His gifts, the Holy Spirit. "The goodness and bounty which is offered to all the world is
here attracted as it were to the soul and body of that
one little boy or girl; as when the lightning which is
mysteriously and invisibly floating above us in the
whole heaven is attracted to a particular point and
strikes upon it." Saints and angels watch in wonder
at the greatness of the gift. "It is in fact no less than
the Day of Pentecost over again, so far as that infant
is concerned." The Lord, when He said to His Apostles,
"Suffer them to come to Me," implied that there was
something in them, some instinct, which would cause
them, if let alone, to come; and if we only look reverentially, we may discern the new man in the baptized,
in their loving and confiding ways, in their little acts
of self-denial, in their contrivances how to be kind and
dutiful and obedient.

Such a vivid sense of the reality of the scene tends
naturally to the last point which needs to be noted, the
solemnity, the sternness, the almost awful sternness of
the tone. "The thought is *very* blessed, and therefore
very fearful." "Baptism lifts us to a far higher Heaven
or sinks us into a lower and more miserable Hell."
"We never can be as if our promise in Baptism had
not been made. We are baptized, and do what we will,
be as wicked as ever we may, we cannot unbaptize
ourselves. We may turn our Baptism into a curse, but
we cannot get rid of it altogether. We cannot be as if
we had never made any promise to God. His mark is

set upon our foreheads, and although by wilful sin
unrepented of we wear out all its beauty and glory, all
its saving grace and virtue, we cannot altogether wear
out the mark itself. It will be there to our worst condemnation, if it is not there to save us."

This solemnity is pressed home to all present. It is
pressed on the parents; they pretend to love their
children, but "how is it possible you can truly love
them, if you are not very full of love towards Him who
so chooses them out and blesses them, who is even now
taking them in His arms to save them from Hell? And
if you love Him, you will try to please Him; you will
not pass slightly over any of His commands, especially
His last dying command, 'Do this in remembrance of
Me.' Your love to your child, if you really believe in
Christ's blessing given to that child in Baptism, will be
enough by God's grace to make you a good Christian."
It is pressed also on the sponsors; they are not merely
friends of the parents, but deputies appointed by the
Church to offer and present the young child to its
Saviour. It is an honour done to them, that they are
allowed to take charge of the Church's children. "They
ought to feel as if God had put into their hands something of a father's or a mother's trust." The least they
can do is to wish and pray in their hearts that the little
one for whom they answer may keep his vow. But
this they cannot do, they cannot really wish and pray
for the child's soul, except they be really in care for their
own souls also. It is pressed alike upon all present:
they being made witnesses of the baptism are bound
thenceforward to treat the child as a Christian, to pray
for him, and to show all brotherly love to him. They
are reminded of their own past promises, and called to

repentance as far as they have been untrue to them.
" As we feel uneasy if any little child belonging to us
is left unbaptized, so should we long to confess our own
sins, which may have brought us perhaps into a worse
than unbaptized condition." For the standard to which
baptism commits us is a standard of willing obedience
and of steadfast faith, a faith not of the tongue only, or
of the mind only, but of the heart. " Consider what it
is to be steadfast in faith. It is to look to the great
things out of sight, not only now and then, but continually and regularly. It is to remember every morning
you have an account to give and every evening that you
are so much nearer, that your doings are being put down
there. It is to turn your heart to Jesus Christ, God
and Man, crucified for you, and to refrain from sin for
His sake ; not merely to speak affectionately and to be
at times touched with the thought of Him. To be
steadfast in faith is, moreover, to believe our Lord when
He says that we must take up our cross, we must lead
strict lives, and be zealous and repent." The volume
closes with words of mingled hope and warning—the
last note a note of warning. " O that it would please
Him to pour out upon us, even now, His good and
loving Spirit, upon *us*, I say, who are here present, that
we might from this very hour begin, one and all of us,
to show forth our baptism in our lives far more truly,
far more courageously, far more lovingly than we have
yet done ! And one fruit of that Good Spirit will
assuredly be, that parents and teachers, godfathers and
godmothers, will go on making more and more of their
precious and tender charge, the little ones of Christ.
If we make much of our own souls and of theirs, they
will learn themselves to make much of them also. If

we make light of them, fearful indeed is the end we must expect, both to them and to us."[1]

The extracts given above are sufficient to show the extreme simplicity and directness of style; from time to time this is lit up by a touch of poetic imagery. Baptism is a coronation, in which we are made kings, "to reign over our own hearts and imaginations, and to command and order all outward things so that they shall work together for our good"; it is a marriage in which we are wedded to the mystical body of Christ: it is like a fresh morning breeze: "The recollections of this deep Baptismal Love breathe over our hearts like fragrant airs of a summer morning." Again there is a frequent mystical use of the Old Testament, verging at times on what would seem to be fanciful; but even this use is rare. Everything is chastened and subdued. Everywhere the tone is of one living in the Presence of a Truth which he fears to sully by ornaments of his own; of one sitting hushed and silent in a beautiful grove lest words of his should stay the sweet warbling of the birds or drown the music of the clear rill which is trickling through the flower-clad banks. It is the tone of one who brings with him and tries to win others to bring with them, to such a scene,

> "a heart
> That watches and receives."[2]

---

[1] It will be no surprise to the reader after this to hear that the Evangelical party in Oxford recognized in Keble, in spite of his maintenance of Baptismal Regeneration, a spiritual man : or even that a sturdy Baptist, who used to attend Burthorpe Church when Keble was curate there, gave it as his reason that he there "heard the gospel." Newman, *Letters*, vol. i. p. 115 ; Sir J. Coleridge, *Memoir*, p. 64.

[2] Sermons vi. xiv. xviii. and xxx. are specially recommended as specimens of Keble's style.

The three chief gifts which make a great preacher in all times and countries have been recently described to be "the sympathy which can move and lift the hearers, the insight into spiritual facts which can present them as luminous realities, and the enthusiasm for a sacred cause which can fire the soul with a congenial devotion." [1] Certainly if these make a great preacher, Keble was such.

[1] Dr. Bright's *Lessons from the Lives of Three Great Fathers*, p. 62.

CHAPTER X.

THE SPIRITUAL ADVISER.

"ὁ ἐπικληθεὶς Βαρνάβας ἀπὸ τῶν ἀποστόλων, ὅ ἐστίν μεθερμηνευόμενον Υἱὸς Παρακλήσεως."—Acts iv. 36.

FROM earliest days Keble's advice had been asked by college friends on religious matters or on such deep questions of practical life as the choice or change of a profession, for his friends knew that all such questions would be pondered over and decided in the light of the highest motives. From 1840 onwards he was frequently consulted by strangers needing direction for their own spiritual life or guidance in ecclesiastical questions. Often, too, he would himself take the initiative, when a call was made upon his prompt sympathy; his had been "a soul in suffering tried," and so was quick to bear aid to his "suffering brethren's side." There had always been at home anxieties arising from ill-health. "Oh what a day of joy a day of perfect health would be in our family" (he had written in 1814); "we are all so united, so fond of home, and just separated enough to know the value of each other's society." The deaths of his two sisters, Sarah and Mary Anne, of his mother and his father, of Hurrell Froude, the frequent illness of his wife and care for his invalid sister, Elizabeth, the loss of Newman's friendship and companionship, fell with heavy weight but also with fruitful power upon his heart; and so there was no grief from which his alembic could not distill some drop of consolation. Or, again, he would take the initiative even to rebuke; his sense of justice, his jealousy for the good name of those for whom he cared, made him bold to speak in very clear language, whether it were to a stranger—as in the plain speech of the letter " to the Father of an Illegitimate Child," printed in the *Letters of Spiritual Counsel*— or privately to friends. But whether he was writing spontaneously or in answer to appeals, whether to console or to rebuke, the language is always gentle, humble, courteous, full of delicate suggestion rather than command, of apology, of self-distrust, even at times of self-abhorrence. " You have a way of saying things which does not annoy," [1] wrote J. H. Newman in 1838. " You write so humbly, it would perplex me at times; only I construe it in my own way," [2] wrote Dr. Pusey in 1848.

The reason of this tone is due to two things. It was caused partly by his high standard of Christian and especially of clerical duty, emphasizing his own sense of personal unworthiness. The language that he uses of himself both in the *Confessions* of his poetry, and in the simple prose of his correspondence, is language of such deep self-accusation that Sir J. Coleridge, in writing the *Memoir*, and Mr. Wilson in editing the spiritual letters, have both felt that it is liable to misinterpretation, and have both borne their witness to the purity of every word and act of his life. Each reader will be tempted to interpret such hints by the worst with which his

[1] *Letters*, ii., p. 238.   [2] July 9, 1848.

own conscience has to reproach him, but each will probably be wrong, unless he brings to the consideration a sense of sin which shall include "rude bad thoughts" and "cold, ungentle ways" as absolutely defiling, and a conception of the holiness of God and the possibilities of human holiness such as does not enter into the heart of most men. Keble's standard was that of life as one bright joyous service, with every thought brought into subjection to Christ, with constant praise of God, with frequent intercession for man. This was his ideal. Sin was to him, in St. Anselm's phrase, "nothing else than the failure to render God His due"; and therefore, if ever thoughts of worldly promotion and ambition had filled his mind, if "rude bad thoughts" had soiled it, if praise had been cold or intercession had been neglected, if some hasty word of his had offended a brother or done harm to the cause of the Church, these fell on his "sensitive, dutiful mind" (it is Dr. Pusey's phrase) with a greater weight than gross acts of sin fall upon a less tender conscience. "My own notion is," he said, "that clergymen generally have more to blame themselves for as to neglect in the way of example and the way of special intercession than in the way of direct warning" [1]; and again, when saying that the anxieties of a clerical life overbalance any sense of comfort, he adds, "If not, it is, I am afraid, because we are not considerate enough about the unspeakable awfulness of our trust, and are therefore too soon satisfied with ourselves; or else because we do not rate what God requires of Christian people high enough, and therefore are too soon satisfied with our flocks." [2]

But there is a second, very different reason, which

---

[1] *Letters*, ix., p. 23.   [2] *Ibid.*, vii., p. 13.

worked to the same end, viz., the deep sense of the responsibility of each individual in religious matters—in a word, his reverence for Christ's Presence in each soul. One who knew him well has said, " What I think remarkable was not how many people loved him, or how much they loved him, but that everybody seemed to love him with the very best kind of love of which they were capable. It was like loving goodness itself: you felt that what was good in him was applying itself directly and bringing into life all that was best in you. His ready, lively, transparent affection seemed as if it was the very spirit of love opening out upon you and calling for a return such as you could give." [1]

This reverence was kept alive by frequent special intercession; the morning hour at 9 a.m. was set aside for remembrance of those who had been brought into spiritual relation to himself. " I have never, I believe, gone a day without thinking of you," is his language to one whom he did not know personally, but who had written to him under temptation; and the language finds frequent echoes throughout his correspondence. He encourages one correspondent to send him written reports of spiritual progress, and assures him that no other work shall interfere with his attention to such a case. " I scarce know what could be of more consequence, *to me*, than helping such work . . . . be it only by affording you a means of relieving your mind." This patient intercession kept alive in his own heart a hopeful faith in his penitents, which was ever urging them to have " root in themselves," to try " to swim without corks," which was guiding their eyes away from himself to the Saviour. It is true that he often

---

[1] Quoted in the Preface to Coleridge's *Memoir* (ed. 2), p. 92.

counsels direct auricular confession ; at one time, when
oppressed by the feeling of his own inefficiency in his
parish, he writes, "Whoever can discreetly and effec-
tually bring in Confession will do, I should think,
one of the best things for this poor Church, as she
is at present." [1]   Again, he expresses his opinion that
when outward Communion becomes more common and
more frequent, "we shall find it impossible to get on
without the discipline of confession more or less strict.
It seems as if it would be the next thing that would
agitate the Church of England. God send us well
through it, and then, by His blessing, we shall stand
better than ever since the Reformation." [2]

When mediating between **Dr. Hook** and the clergy at
St. Saviour's, Leeds, he was very clear that Confession
should be treated as a means of grace, and not merely
as a means of comfort. For dealing with certain sins
he is persuaded that "in most cases regular confession
and not occasional only will be found the best help by
way both of precaution and remedy." [3]   Yet he will
not shift responsibility from the penitent's shoulders
to his own. "The wish for an infallible guide to
relieve one of responsibility is plainly very natural, but
as plainly not intended to be granted in this world."
"I consider that English priests are not only permitted
but commanded to leave to their penitents a certain
discretion with regard to those rules" (*i. e.* of communicating without a fresh confession). "The stricter rules of
the foreign Churches would make one's task easier, but
the line which our Church has taken compels us to
modify them in very charity to the many souls that
would, I fear, otherwise be repelled from the best hope

[1] *Letters,* xxi.   [2] *Ibid.,* cxvii.   [3] *Ibid.,* cxiv.

of recovery." To an undergraduate, who had asked his advice about Confession, he writes—

"Whatever people do or decline to do as to confession should (1) not go upon feeling one way or the other, but upon calm consideration with prayer ; (2) should not be allowed to lessen their own sense of responsibility. (3) To whomsoever the confession is to be made outwardly, it should be made distinctly to our Lord beforehand, in the conviction that He knows it all beforehand, and has declared His will that it should somehow be made known" (St. Luke xii. 2).[1] He suggests again and again to his penitents that they should make their own rules and even choose their own penances for themselves. This respect for their own sense of responsibility appears even in a tart sharpness, which he sometimes uses when he thinks that his correspondents are playing with him, that they have really made up their minds, but want their own opinion sanctioned by him, and "seek direction with an instinctive purpose of directing the director." "Excuse my saying, I deeply wish you had not said this," is his criticism on one piece of shallowness. "Will you excuse my saying that you do not now seem to me to have really put your mind to these considerations." "If you cannot help feeling displeased with me, do not therefore cast aside what I have said until you have well and long considered it *your own self*, not borrowing the eyes of others" (pp. 241, 259, 266, 267).

The best statement of his feeling with regard to Confession in relation to parish work is to be found in his review of Monro's *Parochial Work*.[2] He is quite

---

[1] *Letters*, xcvi.
[2] Reprinted from the *Christian Remembrancer* of 1850, in *Occasional Papers and Reviews*.

clear that real pastoral efficiency must rest upon
the pastor's personal intercourse with his people ; that,
like a doctor, he ought to know the real evils with
which he is dealing. The fear of the priest enslaving
the spirit of an English yeoman or peasant seems to
him foolish and unreal. Those who have once fairly
accepted the doctrine of judgment to come can never
wish to free themselves of their sense of responsibility.
" Their very object in seeking the benefit of absolution
together with ghostly counsel and advice, was to enlarge
their responsibility by obtaining deliverance from the
chain of past sin and better principles to guide them
for the future." At the same time he would avoid the
technical terms of "direction" and "auricular confession,"
" because they are associated in almost all minds with
something more absolute, peremptory, and indispensable
than we should practically mean by them." He is
especially anxious to avoid interfering with that happy
unconsciousness which is the natural ground of true
Christian simplicity ; anxious again to check any risk
of hero-worship, and determined to avoid minute and
incessant direction, as the desire of it seemed to him to
be a form of self-will. But all these abuses can be
guarded against. " They have no force against the legitimate mode of personal intercourse which the Prayer-
book enjoins," and it seemed to him that the rubric
requiring notice to be given beforehand of the intention
to communicate, and that which required each com-
municant to communicate three times a year, gave
sufficient vantage-ground for such personal intercourse.
" These two rules, duly made known and followed up,
would constitute a regular and effectual system of
Church discipline with adults, even as the rules about

sponsors, catechizing, and Confirmation would secure a complete Church education for children. Let there be a religious and living sense of Church authority, and the work of discipline, as well as of doctrine, is done for us."

But to return to the spiritual letters. Their tone is always this, " I am a very bad person for you to have come to; I have had little experience and little knowledge. I need your prayers and forgiveness much more than you need mine, and whatever I say, you must see if it is right and then act upon it." But this is not the whole; he always goes on to stay himself upon the Presence of Christ and His promise to be with His ministers. The thought of the Atonement braces him to fresh effort. " It is a fearful thing to think that one owes a heavier debt than one's fellows to the great Owner of all. Aye, so fearful that nothing could enable one to support the thought except it were the same recollection with which I ended the last paragraph, and with which, if we brought it in as often as we have occasion, we should end every paragraph and every sentence which we write or speak—i. e. that we have One who has redeemed our debt as well as promised us unfailing supplies for the future." He reminds a priest who felt that he had too lightly undertaken his office of the duty of showing his penitence by all diligence and activity, and quotes the words of Bishop Bull: "Having laid ourselves at God's feet, let us not lie idly there, but arise and for the future do the work of God with all faithfulness and industry." So there is always something inspiring and hopeful about his advice. Under all the gentleness and hesitation there is very seldom anything but definiteness of advice; there is always in it a strain

of sober practical common sense, even in the earliest
letters a strange maturity of wisdom which inspired
confidence.

This mellow wisdom is equally noticeable whether
he is dealing with the problems of individual life or
of Church organization. In each he starts with a
high ideal; but he is so impressed with the great
degeneracy of the Church, and with the power of
the Evil Spirit, that he does not hastily expect great
progress or startling changes. In the individual life
the one thing necessary is that the motive should be
true; if that is set on the active service of Christ,
he is ready to make any allowance for differences of
character and of circumstance. Each man has to ask
himself what is reasonable for such an one as he to
do for Christ; and then set calmly and gently about
his own work without breaking through established
customs where they are innocent. There must be a
resolute guard over thoughts and senses, and a control
of the feelings. He is especially distrustful of the
feelings, whether of melancholy or of remorse, or of
excited assurance, or of sorrow. They must have *relief*,
but they must never be our masters. To one suffering
from a sense of loneliness and want of sympathy he
writes, " One thing occurs to me as a possible help in
soothing and relieving your pent-up feelings, viz., that
you should, if circumstances allow, get into a regular
course of some kind of charitable visiting among poor
and distressed people. Music heard and practised,
poetry read and written, drawing, scenery, gardening
and all kinds of out-door recreations, if not too exciting,
may be made useful in this way, but the specific is
works of charity and devotion." Overmuch sorrow for

the dead, and even remorse for our sins towards them, have to be put aside. "No person who believes in the Atonement ought to indulge in bitter remorse." To Dr. Pusey, when his wife lay dying and he was feeling it as a punishment for his own sins, Keble wrote—

" I want you to be on your guard against *bitter* self-reproach—against that kind of remorse which I know is apt to come over one when a blessing of which one feels one's unworthiness seems taken away ; a feeling, I mean, which would benumb and prostrate, instead of softening and quickening our faith. Surely in such matters, as in all others, we do well not to think or *feel* as if we knew positively the cause of God's dealing with us. The tone of the Prayer-book seems to me so beautiful, ' For whatsoever cause this sickness is sent unto you,' without pretending to search it out or to encourage the sufferer to do so with anything like certainty. The thought that it *may* be this or that, seems to me the intended way of humbling us. If we go on to treat ourselves as if we *knew* it to be this or that, perhaps we go beyond God's will."

So even with regard to our feelings towards God ; we have no right to demand of God or to be uncomfortable if we do not feel sensible comfort or the certain assurance of salvation. " To say that such assurance is a sure and necessary sign of God's favour must be a mistake, if it were only that it contradicts our Lord's agony and the feeling that He had upon the Cross, not to speak of many saintly examples in Scripture." Even more strongly, " The whole of this doctrine of the necessity of assurance is to me not left doubtful but contradicted by such places as Philippians ii. 12, 13 ; indeed by the whole gospel, our Lord's own teaching in particular; and I pray God to keep us all from it." [1] For such assurance tends so readily to a low standard of life, and to that which seemed to him the most fatal thing to spiritual life, the feeling of self-complacency. "You must pray especially against this," he writes to one lady, "you must do penance for it by trying inwardly to turn away from and be pained at the affectionate praise, even of those whom you would most wish to approve you" (p. 151). Even assurance of the purity of our motive may be denied to us, and we must not be over-anxious even then. One short letter [2] may be quoted in its entirety to illustrate this:

"MY DEAR CHILD,—My entire conviction is that your anxiety about your motive for what you do in the way of penitence is carried too far. He on purpose for the most part hides that point from us; so that few, if any, shall be able to say in what measure they are influenced by love, in what by fear and shame and indignation, and such inferior yet legitimate motives. You must learn to bear this painful doubt, and to be thankful that He releases and keeps you from wilful sin *anyhow.* You must pray and strive for love, but not be violently grieved nor angry with yourself should you still feel as if the lower motives alone, or nearly alone, were yours. Do not allow yourself to sit for many minutes moody and dreaming. Your judgment, your conduct, your feelings towards others—that is where your minute watchfulness should be, *there* will be the proof of your grief being accepted as real contrition,

---

[1] See the whole of this letter, "On the Religious Revivals in Ireland," cliii.
[2] Letter lxx.

much more than in any consciousness you may seem to have of it at the time.

"Your loving father in Christ,

"J. K."

Such absence of feeling may be a punishment for past sins, and "the truly filial feeling is to accept the punishment of one's iniquity, praying that it may be in time, not in eternity." (p. 189). It may, too, throw us out of self on to the Lord. An old clergyman who had known him in younger days was dying, with a deep sense of his own sinfulness and a fear that he was not forgiven, and the absence of comfort in prayer. He longed to see Keble. "Oh, that John Keble was here!" That could not be, but Keble wrote to him a letter which brought him quiet happiness, and of which the following is an extract—

"I could say, for one thing, make your account beforehand with this trouble coming upon you, as you would with a fit of bodily pain, to which you might know yourself liable; and offer it to God as you would the bodily pain, in deep resignation, giving yourself up to Him, to deal with you in this respect also as He knows best. And, as we know that in some mysterious way our bodily sufferings are united (if we take them rightly) to those of our Lord on the Cross, so we may venture to associate these sadder misgivings of the soul with the deep agony and sense of desertion which He vouchsafed to endure for us. And we may believe that in ways known to Him they are made instrumental to our final purification and salvation. One way in which this may happen, we may well believe, is this: the more entirely we are made to feel the worthlessness

of all that we have ourselves been or done, the more
are we thrown, wholly and solely, upon Him who is our
only Hope ; and this deep and bitter feeling may be
our Lord's providential way of causing you to cast all
your care upon Him as you no doubt endeavour to do,
but feel that you do it but inadequately ; this distress
may render you more earnest in doing so ; and 'if there
be first a willing mind '—you know the rest, and how
fully it applies to the inward offering of Faith and
Repentance, as well as to the outward one of Alms.
Once more : I should wish to say, I am continually
saying, in effect, to persons in such trouble as you
sometimes feel, 'Which do you really want of the
Almighty ?   Comfort now, or pardon and acceptance
hereafter ?'   The latter, of course ; and it may be that
the imperfection you complain of in the former, may
greatly help towards that better thing, for the peace
of God passeth all understanding.'   Many, having it,
feel as if they had it not ; but many, alas! wanting it,
feel (like the Pharisees) as if they certainly had it.
Which is better : to kindle a fire of one's own, and
compass oneself about with sparks, and have to walk in
that light ; or to walk in darkness, and have no light,
only trusting (*i. e.* unweariedly trying to trust) in the
Name of the Lord, and 'staying yourself as you may
'on our God' ?

"Let me beseech you, dear sir, to go on trying this ;
and in a short time you will see and know what a Rock
you have been indeed standing on."

All sorrow is handled with delicate tact, for he
believed so much in its purging power. "The Almighty
has stores of chastening secret to us as well as of
mercy in its more placid form ; and I believe that

those whom we have every reason to believe His most
beloved have always most earnestly welcomed those
pains which they hoped in some unsearchable way
might help to purify them." " These sufferings are, in
one way, the Father's mode of applying the Cross to
us, as His Sacraments are in another way."[1] Or,
again, he asks the special prayers of a friend "now,
when affliction has brought you, in a manner, unusually
near the Throne." Sorrow may be penal, but it may also
be a mark of chastening love, and we are inquiring too
far if, in every case, we are anxious how far and for
what exact sin it is penal.

In the same way it is with a soothing tenderness
that he speaks of death and of "the living dead." In
one letter (cliv.) the whole of the Burial Office is analyzed
to show that it is not merely a form for the burial of
the body, but one of commending the whole person,
body and soul, to Almighty God. It assumes the continued existence of the departed ; it implies our hopes
that the promises may be true of them ; we may believe
that they still sympathize with us in our prayers ;
everything is aimed at " lessening the weary interval
between the bereaved and the departed," and so it
becomes a form of communion with the dead. So he
loves George Herbert's phrase that the departed have
only gone into another room in the Father's house ; they
are "entering into their rest, *or rather His rest*" ; the
bereaved are earnestly pressed to lose no time in using
themselves " to speak freely and calmly to one another
of those who are out of sight, as though they were, as
they are, only out of sight." God is sure to accept the
efforts which affection prompts us to make in the way

[1] Letter lxiii.

of doing that of which the departed would most approve.
The recovery of the practice of prayer for the departed,
which had come with the study of the ancient Church,
seemed to him to compensate for the trouble and
annoyance of the times; in 1837 he regrets the cessation
of prayers for the Founders in the College chapels, " nor
do I think we shall ever be quite right till it is restored ;"
and he sends to a friend the following prayer from
Bishop Andrewes, " which one very unworthy person at
least has used for years with far greater comfort than
he deserves."

"Remember Thy servants and handmaidens which
have departed hence in the Lord, especially .... and all
others to whom our remembrance is due; give them
eternal rest and peace in Thy Heavenly Kingdom, and
to us such a measure of communion with them, as Thou
knowest to be best for us. And bring us all to serve
Thee in Thine eternal Kingdom when Thou wilt and as
Thou wilt, only without shame or sin. Forgive my
presumption and accept my prayers, as Thou didst the
prayers of Thine ancient Church, through Jesus Christ
our Lord."

A few points of more ecclesiastical interest may be
added here, as they arise out of his letters and will in
the main illustrate the mellow wisdom of his advice.
In relation to Dissent, while clear of its sinfulness and
of the harm which it causes, he would deal lovingly and
forbearingly with Dissenters, " as being, alas! the wronged
party in bygone times." He would have each parish
priest regard himself as still responsible for them,
though all appeals to them will require much discretion
and charity. To a young lady who had been brought
up unbaptized and wished for baptism, as she supposed

against her parents' wish, he advises that clearly she must make her profession of faith, that it would be unreal to receive Dissenters' Baptism, that it would be very undesirable to go away and be baptized without her parents' knowledge. "It has an air of undutifulness, mistrust, and concealment which ought by all means to be avoided, if possible." Therefore she must tell her parents of her wish, and be content to wait for many months, in the hope of getting their consent or even winning them to Baptism. Meanwhile, she will hear what she believes in ill-spoken of, and be tempted to speak and think the worst of Dissenters; and so he adds his parting advice, "Force yourself, I beseech you, rather to keep silence, unless there be some grave duty in speaking, and to be glad, really glad, when you can speak and think well of them."[1]

Liberalism and speculative unbelief was much more trying to him than inherited Dissent; it seemed so often to go hand in hand with a spirit of irreverence; yet he would apply the same measure to liberalists, and of one such case he writes : "With regard to the very painful subject with which your letter concludes, I have been used to think that we are in no sort judges how far 'invincible ignorance' may excuse a person in the sight of God for any degree of speculative unbelief, provided he really tries to act up to the light vouchsafed. This way of thinking the fathers of old applied to the cases of the good and virtuous heathens, and, by parity of reasoning, it may, one should think, apply to many cases among ourselves whom the letter of our formularies would seem to condemn. Why, then, may you not hope humbly, that at some time, in some state

[1] Letter lx.

or other, the true faith and the mercy which it reveals
may, in some degree at least, reach to such an amiable
person as you describe, though we may not see or know
how? In the meantime, your speaking or not on
such matters is surely a question of expediency depend-
ing on the chance of doing good. You can but watch
and pray for opportunity and guidance, and help to
make the most of any opening that may be granted.
Sayings, doings, and looks, which seem very slight in
themselves, have often a good deal of virtue, I believe,
in such cases; and waiting on sickness or decline, gives
occasion sometimes to unexpected ways of helping those
whom we love."

In dealing with the three branches of the Catholic
Church, his main wish was that each member should
be faithful to his own branch, without any feeling of
jealousy or hostility to the others; he would gladly
have maintained neutrality towards Rome, but the
attitude of some of the converts made this more and
more difficult. In 1846 he wrote to Dr. Pusey, "I am
afraid from little symptoms that feelings are growing
bitterer between the converts to R. C. and those whom
they have left behind. Everything indicates that such
separate conversions, whatever else they may be, are not
the way of peace and unity." The truer way seemed
to him to be to labour and pray, not controversially but
practically, for that holiness which alone can truly unite
men, and which, if generally revived, would no doubt
bring back with it visible unity. .

The letter [1] which he wrote on the subject of Non-
Communicating Attendance at the Holy Eucharist, may
serve as a final specimen of the cautious way in which

[1] Letter cxxviii.

he handled a subject on which his own feelings were admittedly strong.

"I cannot deny that I have a strong feeling against the foreign custom of encouraging all sorts of persons to 'assist' at the Holy Eucharist, without communicating. It seems to me open to two grave objections. It cannot be without danger of profaneness and irreverence to very many, and of consequent dishonour to the Holy Sacrament; and it has brought in and encouraged, or both (at least so I greatly suspect), a notion of quasi-sacramental virtue in such attendance, which I take to be great part of the error stigmatized in our Thirty-first Article. Even in such a good book as the *Imitatio Christi*, and still more in the *Paradisus Animæ*, one finds participating 'in Missa vel Communione' spoken of as if one brought a spiritual benefit of the same order as the other. This I believe to be utterly unauthorized by Scripture and antiquity; and I can imagine it of very dangerous consequence. But whatever one thought of this, the former objection would still stand, and it would not do to answer that the early Church allowed, or even encouraged, the practice, because, even if that were granted (I very much doubt it, to say the least), the existence of discipline at that time entirely alters the case. I used to argue in this way with poor R. W., but I could never get him to mind me.

"Yet of course I cannot deny that there may be any number of cases in which attendance without communicating may be morally and spiritually (I could not say, sacramentally) beneficial; and in default of discipline, I should advise any person who thought that such was his own case, to consult with his Spiritual Adviser, and act accordingly ; the clergyman of the particular church not objecting." [1]

[1] The books which he most usually recommends are—*De Imitatione Christi;* Hooker's *Sermons on the Certainty and Perpetuity of Faith in the Elect,* and a *Remedy for Sorrow and Fear;* J. Taylor, *Holy Living,* and *The Golden Grove;* Bishop Andrewes, *Prayers;* Bishop Wilson, *Sacra Privata;* Law's *Serious Call,* and *Christian Perfection;* Kettlewell, *Companion for the Penitent;* Bund, *Aids to a Holy Life; Meditations of J. Bonnell, Esq.* (S.P.C.K.) ; I. Williams, *Commentary on the Gospels.*

CHAPTER XI.

CHARACTERISTIC AND INFLUENCE.

"Love is a present for a mighty King."—G. HERBERT.

> "The Gods approve
> The depth and not the tumult of our soul,
> A fervent, not ungovernable, love."
>> WORDSWORTH, *Laodamia.*

"Let it be your great care to go down humbly to your grave."
J. K. : *Sermons for the Christian Year,* Lent, p. 70.

"How shall I profess to paint a man who will not sit for his picture?"[1] These were Newman's words when asked to describe Keble, and they seem to point to the central feature which explains his character, a keen sensitiveness of nature, an instantaneous quickness of response to every influence from outside, opening out to the slightest breath of that which was akin to his true nature, shrinking into itself, and clinging closer to its native rock, at the approach of an alien hand. His was a nature of strong and permanent emotions : in childhood and youth the love of parents and brothers and sisters, in later years that of friends and of children, laid hold upon them and drew out all his happy, droll playfulness of wit and manner. "In power of exceeding

---

[1] J. K. : *Occasional Papers and Reviews,* Preface, p. xiii.

enjoyment, in positive admiration he was an unusually
happy man; children, high characters, good people,
noble actions, fine prints or pictures, music, scenery, all
gave him such great delight."[1]   But the nature needed
sympathy to draw it out.   He was shy and awkward
with strangers.   He would never, his sister said, have
written verses were it not for the encouragement he
met with in his own family.[2]   Hence any interruption
of a friendship was a terrible strain upon him.   After
his mother's death he could not restrain his emotion
while examining in the Schools, as one of the candidates
translated the farewell of Alcestis to her children; and
more than thirty years afterwards he wrote to a friend,
"Assuredly the world can never be the same again to
any one when one's mother is no longer in it."   On the
Sunday after receiving the news of Hurrell Froude's
death, he broke down with emotion while celebrating
the Eucharist; he was seen at times to come away
in tears from the sick-bed of a parishioner; and the
parting with Newman seemed to "take the very spring
out of his year."[3]   Such quickness of feeling led to
quickness of expression.   Mr. Wilson, on becoming his
curate, was startled by his ready outspokenness, by the
comprehensive and startling enunciation of principles;
an unsympathetic critic could speak of him as one who
quickly lost his temper [4]—nay, he could speak of himself

---

[1] *Musings on the Christian Year*, p. xlv; cf. J. B. Mozley,
Letters, p. 77 : " Keble is certainly great fun."

[2] I. Williams, *Autobiography*, p. 69.

[3] How striking to notice his other use of this same phrase :
"It would indeed be *taking the spring out of the year* were we
to doubt or deny a special Presence of our High Priest, God and
man, to solemnize with us the feast." *Euch. Ador.*, ed. v., p.
253.

[4] Mozley, *Reminiscences*, p. 220.

in later days, in intimate correspondence, as "a certain testy old clerk whom you know of." It led again at times to moods of morbid melancholy, against which he set himself to struggle by active kindness to others and by falling back upon the deepest religious motives. It was ever craving for itself some vent, some method of relief. To one friend he recommended Bishop Wilson's practice of keeping a journal of one's religious feelings in cypher, because the very act of devising the cypher withdraws the mind a little from itself; and "something in the nature of a journal is a kind of medicine to many persons." [1]   Poetry was another method of relief; and his whole theory of poetry sprang from this thought. Prayer was another, as he thought of the souls distressed by Church perplexities—"Oh, indeed it is a real trouble to think of them; it is a real relief to pray for them." [2]   Penance was thought of, partly, as a relief to souls oppressed with the sense of sin, and this was part of the attraction of a daily service for him, that "amid the wear and tear, the forebodings and misgivings incident to the cure of souls, it was well that one anxious and determined to spend and be spent should have a place where he might go and rest awhile in the Life-giving Presence, and keep up his heart and strength for the work." [3]

But all this quickness was kept in check with a hand which grew more strong and dominant as time went on. There was an almost provoking refusal to display his power or abilities when people looked for them; "he was jealous of anything brilliant and on his

[1] J. H. Newman, *Letters*, ii., p. 80.
[2] *Pastoral Letter*, p. 7.
[3] *Occasional Papers and Reviews*, p. 362.

Q

guard against anything hollow." Whatever he might
be in speech, he was always very careful and guarded
and fair in what he wrote, and his speech too was
controlled. "That is a subject that won't bear talking
about," is a frequent refrain in his letters whenever he
has been drawn on to speak of himself and his own
feelings.[1] Thus, as self became eliminated, the quickness of feeling was transmuted into a tender sensitiveness for others. There was the sensitiveness for the
honour, the purity, the freedom of the Church, firing
up with indignation at each act of State aggression, at
each unjust taunt of her foes, but most of all at each
unworthy act of her own children. His earlier writings
are full of protests against the spirit of Fatalism, which
would fold its hands and acquiesce in evil. In every
ecclesiastical event that happened between the years
1833 and 1886, he was a force that had to be reckoned
with, for " all his serious interests were public ones."[2]

There was an equal sensitiveness for individuals,
"always chivalrous enough to take the cause of the
weak,"[3] stirred at once by any symptom of injustice,
in act or judgment. We see this sensitiveness in his
reverence for each individual soul, in his respect for the
poor, always believing in their power to understand
spiritual truth and to enter into the real moral bearings
of Church doctrine, so that he associated them in his
protests against the Gorham case or against the Privy

---

[1] His comment upon the title " The Word " as applied to Christ
is, " He in whom we are to be restored to God's Image in vouch-
safing to call Himself the Word and Wisdom of the Father, plainly
teaches us that to be negligent in ordering and guarding our own
thought and speech is in a special manner pouring contempt upon
that Divine Image." *Studia Sacra*, p. 8.

[2] Dean Church, *The Oxford Movement*, p. 22.

[3] J. H. Newman, *Letters*, ii., p. 285.

Council.   Thus in his lectures he argued against the theory that the poor could not appreciate the beauties of Nature or of Poetry.   Their fondness for the place of their birth and youth, their tender speech about the dead and anxiety to obey their wishes, their external and half-superstitious forms of reverence, all seemed to him to betray unconsciously a mind instinctively poetic.[1] " I won't have my poor fellows laughed at," was his quick protest when some one had called them clod-hoppers.[2] We see it in his generous trust of Newman till the last moment before his secession; in the respectful, delicate suggestiveness of the correspondence of those sad years that preceded it.   We see it in the treatment of those who put themselves in his hands for guidance, strong and tender, and gradually leading them to self-confidence.   We see it in his desire to put the best interpretation on people's language;—" I am most anxious that we should make the best instead of the worst of the feelings and opinions of earnest men of all sections, that we should neither scorn nor ignore the very large amount of real faith and devotion to a Real Presence of Our Lord's Humanity, even among those who in words would perhaps think themselves bound to disavow it."[3]   We see it in the quick outgush of sympathy towards any friend in trouble or anxiety; or in the thoughtfulness which made him induce Miss Yonge not to use insanity as a topic for fiction, through fear of the harm it might do to excitable natures.

Yet this reverent sensitiveness had no weakness in

[1] *Prælectiones*, i., pp. 17—20.
[2] T. Mozley, *Reminiscences*, ii., p. 250 : cf. I. Williams, *Autobiography*, p. 20.
[3] Letter to Archdeacon Wilberforce : Bishop Wilberforce's *Life*, ii., p. 256.

it, for it was a reverence not for what men were, but
for what they might be. He was quite fearless, ready
to speak very frankly and boldly even to friends, if
their conduct seemed in any way unworthy of their
cause; very stern and severe if ever he had to deal
with cases of disgraceful marriage in his parish. One,
who was then a child, recalls the flashing eye and the
stern satisfaction of his voice, as he read out that a
certain murderer who had escaped had been caught and
would be hanged; adding, " his fierce indignation with
wrong-doing was very terrible, for he always seemed
to be repressing so much that he did not say." [1]

The secret of this " blended strength and sweetness "
was that it " glowed from touch of love Divine." He
looked not to others for his standard or his approval,
but only to the Perfect Example and the judgment of
God. His soul, with all its sensitiveness, seemed to

" Lie bare to the universal prick of light."

Each aspect of truth, each claim of holiness, seemed
to make its way through and to find its response.

It was so with truth. Wherever he saw it, he felt a
reverence for it. To him there was somewhat of a
sacramental character in poetry, even in the poetry of
Paganism; Nature was reverenced as the veil of the
supernatural; and this feeling came to its climax in
dealing with the Bible, the least approach to irreverence or flippancy in dealing with which was checked
by him at once. Hence one side of his teaching was a
constant protest against narrowness, against anything

[1] Newman (*Letters*, ii., p. 474) thus describes St. Philip Neri—
" He was formed on the same type of extreme hatred of humbug,
playfulness, nay, oddity, tender love of others and severity, which
are lineaments of Keble."

which would limit truth.   This caused his feeling against the old evangelical party; he was attracted by their personal devotion to the Lord, and always said that they had far more in common with him than they knew, but he felt that their system appealed too exclusively to the emotions and did not satisfy the intellect or the imagination.   As against their narrowness, he would neither exclude the truth that was in Paganism because it was Pagan, nor the truth that was in Roman Catholicism because it was Roman Catholic.   The same feeling made him revolt against the intellectualism of Whateley and his followers; with them the intellect seemed to have usurped the whole function of judgment and to have driven out the emotions.   He revolted against their utilitarian tests of truth, and as against them was always pleading for the instincts of the heart, for consideration for the poor and the simple, for the moral bearings and spiritual tendencies of a theory. "Ingenuity in an argument," he wrote, "should always put us on our guard, because it is in some sort an appeal to our vanity."   No less in the controversy with Rome was his position a pleading for *width;* those who sided with Rome seemed to him to press one logical position, the note of unity in the Church, as though it were the whole; but clearness and symmetry of doctrine seemed dearly purchased when Christian truth and duty were impaired for their sake, and he would never ignore, or allow others to ignore, the facts of the existence of the Eastern Church, or the past history of our own branch of the Church, or the duteousness which its members owe to it for blessings received through it in their own lives.   Truth was to him always a sacred thing; but it was sacred as a gift, a tradition, an heirloom. It has been well said that there are two kinds of lovers of truth; there is one whose instincts are conservative, who loves truth as a possession, who desires to have his results right however gained, who cares more for his conclusions being true than for the arguments being sound, who is satisfied to accept his conclusions already demonstrated, and has a loyal and sincere devotion to them. On the other hand the typical liberal thinker loves truth as an object of quest, it is a holy grail to him, nor does he much grieve if he does not find it; he cares more for the soundness of his methods and the diligence of his studies, than for the certainty of the result.[1] Keble decidedly belonged to the first rather than to the second of these classes. He was indeed ready to receive a new truth if it came from a quarter that he trusted, but he hated the spirit of eclecticism which would pick and choose at one's own pleasure amid the doctrines of the Church. Truth was a master to be served, not to be criticized and patronized; it was like the ark which he dreaded to touch with unconsecrated hand; it was there, embodied in the Bible and the Church; he shrank from harming it, and above all, he shrank from exposing it to those who would harm it and would harm themselves by rash and ignorant treatment of it, and that because it was a truth which affected spiritual life. He was pained by any heresy or disloyalty to an extent which made others think him intolerant, but it was because he saw so clearly what was at stake. All his struggles about the doctrine of Baptismal Regeneration—all these, he said, "come not of jealousy concerning clerical prerogatives, nor of a longing to complete and round off an ecclesi-

[1] *Church Quarterly Review*, January, 1876, p. 346.

astical theory, nor even of tenderness concerning any
single point of truth separately considered, but really
and truly of a wish to save our own souls and the souls
of our people—a fear lest the great things which God
Incarnate has done for us and in us should fail for want
of due appreciation on our part." [1] Such loving care for
truth begat in him caution and wisdom; he had spoken
at times hastily, and had been penitent for it; he had
come to see that "hurry is a cruel thing."   "It never
can be necessary for the Church that men should do
grave things in a hurry," he wrote to Newman; and so
his advice ever grew in wisdom. Dr. Liddon called
him the wisest man he had ever known; and Miss
Yonge said that she had never been to him to ask his
advice without getting an answer different from what
she expected, and one which showed that he had looked
the matter round on all sides.

But the sensitiveness to truth was surpassed by the
sensitiveness to holiness.   The Presence of God was
ever about him, with its loving and awful demand, " Be
ye holy, as I am holy."   The sense of the eternal issues
that hung upon life gave him a severity and dignity with
which it was impossible to trifle or take liberties. There
was a note of unearthliness about him; he was looked
up to by the younger Tractarians with a certain reverential awe —"The slightest word he dropped was all
the more remembered from there being so little of it,
and from its seeming to come from a different and holier
sphere.   His manner of talking favoured this, for there
was not much continuity in it, only every word was a
brilliant or a pearl." [2]   Meekness was the last word to

---

[1] *Occasional Papers and Reviews*, p. 302.
[2] *. Mozley, *Reminiscences*, i., p. 38.

apply to him, but humility was there in the sense that an eager, impetuous nature was ever controlled by a sense of God's Presence. This made him most severe with himself, in obedience to the rules of spiritual life— for instance, he always celebrated at midday fasting, and seldom broke his fast at all on Fridays till the evening. He was very generous in almsgiving, and "as time went on there was more and more a dispensing with matters of mere luxury and worldly requirements."[1] His ideal of the Christian life was that of the service of a loving son guided by a Father's eye, content with a reasonable presumption as to what his Father's wishes were and not asking for certainty or assurance. This affected his whole conception of the position of the Church; as he contrasted her ideal with her actual practice he felt that she too must be a Church in penitence, she must be content to work patiently for the revival of much that had been lost. For a time the success of the Tractarian movement and the contagion of Newman's sanguine temperament made him sanguine, but with the great change of 1845 this fell away, and he was content to walk humbly and to teach others to walk humbly, even in their hopes about the Church, though in perfect confidence that she was a true branch of the Catholic Church. And for himself, his humility was fostered by that which might threaten to kill it. "It must, I suppose" (he wrote), "be part of all persons' penitence in all ages and portions of the Church to bear with undeserved approbation, with being thought better than they are." The secession of Newman, of Manning, of Wilberforce, his friends and pupils, humbled him more, as he seemed to have had so little power to guide

[1] Miss Yonge, *Musings*, p. vii.

them right; his penitence poured itself out in language which to many would seem extravagant, and he could speak of "self-abhorrence as a duty, a necessity, and a joy." [1]

Yet such language was no exaggeration. Those who knew him best would combine to say that the words which he wrote of Bishop Wilson might be transferred to himself: "He never penned a sentence that savoured of unreality." It was no exaggeration, because the things of God were so intensely real to him; his penitence made his vision keener, and as he saw the perfection of the Perfect, he knew the blackness of a sin-stained life. He was so conscious of his own sinfulness that he really esteemed others better than himself, and treated them with a "humbling humility," as they found themselves looked up to and their judgment appealed to by him, and their prayers asked for him; so conscious of Christ's sympathy that his own seemed so poor to him; "one tries to feel it all" (he wrote to a friend in sorrow), "but is the more convinced that there is but One who really can do so."

Sensitiveness had passed into humility, humility into reality. He was real because the supernatural was real to him; the dead became the living dead to him; Baptismal Regeneration and the doctrine of the Real Presence were so vital because they told of the reality of a Living Christ touching and giving life to His members. The power of the Evil One was ever present to his thoughts as a real living personal power.

The writer to whom reference has been made above as having grown up as a child in friendly relations with him, has written thus of him and of Mrs. Keble (for

[1] Sermons for Sundays after Trinity.

indeed they were one in heart and method): "The impression left is of something intensely *alive*. There was such a combination of strong feeling and intelligence, a brimming over of poetical grace and tact, holiness which was so deep and true, that it seemed to enhance their common sense and made them free from any exaggeration of manner or judgment, a heavenliness and quietness which never failed to stir up and encourage one's own efforts, without producing the least desire merely to admire and honour them. They were eminently wholesome friends, for they first believed that we had feet and then made us stand upon them." One extract from one of his late writings will show how the sense grew upon him that the one question at issue in the conflict of Churchmen was the reality of the supernatural.

"Unless I am greatly mistaken, the real point at issue in most of the controversies which have troubled us in the Reformed English Church might be expressed as follows: 'Is the Church, mingled as we see it of good and bad, a supernatural body separated off from the world to live a supernatural life, begun, continued, and ended in miracles—miracles as real as any of those which befell the Israelites in the wilderness—as real but infinitely more gracious and awful; or is it only a body providentially raised up to hold the best and purest philosophy—helped as all good things are from above, but in itself no more than the heroical and divine phase of this present life?' It is plain at first glance which side of this alternative brings with it the more intense obligation to holiness, and represents sin as more exceedingly sinful." . . . "It is a sad habit of thought for a theologian to train himself up in—that of instinctively adopting, out of various expositions, that which is most earthly and least supernatural." [1]

What was his influence ? Is his life rightly included in a series of Leaders of Religion ? He certainly would have answered No, and indeed he was without many of the qualities which make a great leader; he was not great as a statesman; he was not an original genius as a thinker; his style has no attractive brilliance about it; his learning, though great, was not to be compared with that of Dr. Pusey. But, with all these deductions, he had qualities which made him a real leader. He was not a general to plan a campaign and marshal his forces, but he was a leader ready to throw himself into a breach and inspire enthusiasm by the fearlessness with which he led a forlorn hope. He was always, and more and more as time went on, one whose character could solemnize and awe those who were fighting on his side and make them feel the seriousness of the issues ; over all the conflict " he cast the cooling shadow of his lowliness," [2] and if he could not lead his followers to victory, he could and did lead them to that which is a truer part of religion—to penitence and deeper holiness. " Make a few saints," was once quoted by him as the test of success at which a good educator should aim; and his work will stand that test. Dean Church was inclined to attribute to Keble's influence the depth of the ethical tone which separated Dr. Arnold from the Oriel school.[3] With less hesitation we may point to those who have confessed the greatness of their debt to him—

[1] *Eucharistical Adoration*, Preface, ed. ii.
[2] Dr. Pusey, Sermon at the opening of Keble College Chapel, p. 25.
[3] *W. G. Ward and the Oxford Movement*, p. 41.

to Froude, to Robert Wilberforce, to Isaac Williams, to Newman himself,[1] to Dr. Pusey, to Dr. Liddon, to Miss Yonge; and these names are sufficient to show what he did for the Church of England. But we may claim more than the influence over individuals. There were moments when his action was the turning-point of a crisis. It was his influence upon Froude, passing through him to Newman, which formed a band of friends at Oxford ready to sacrifice themselves for a higher ideal of the Church; it was his sermon on National Apostasy which gave the signal for action; his mediating influence which drew together the two different elements in the Church party of those days; and when the break came in 1845, it was his influence, combined with that of Dr. Pusey, C. Marriott, James Mozley and others, which prevented the defeat from being a rout and rallied the forces for further fighting. And behind all these lay the influence of the *Christian Year*, winning a hearing for the deeper truths, and soothing and solemnizing and stirring the religious world, as no one other book has done in this century.

The points which he defined in 1837 as needing modification were that the Church should be less narrowly Anglican, and more ready to sympathize with all that was Catholic, that she should be free to exercise moral discipline over her members, that she should have a living voice which should be consulted in legislation about her own organization and her own officers. As we look at these we see indeed that much still remains to be effected, but still how much has been gained!

---

[1] Cf. *Letters*, ii., p. 87, ὁ πάνυ Keble. *Ibid.*, p. 155, "I am conscious I have got all my best things from Keble; you (Froude) and Keble are the philosophers and I the rhetorician."

How entirely different is the tone in which such subjects are discussed, how different the aspect of Church Life and Worship ! and this is due to those brave men, who amidst hostility and scorn, amidst suspicion and injustice, with loss of friends and much perplexity as to their own path, yet never permitted themselves to despair, and by dutifulness and laborious study and honest controversy spent their lives in adorning the Sparta in which their lot was cast. Of that band there was none whose words had more soothing power, whose life was more of a type of duteous-hearted loyalty than John Keble.

A few words should be added on his personal appearance. He was about middle height, with rather square and sloping shoulders, which made him look short until he pulled himself up, as he often did with sprightly dignity. The head was "one of the most beautifully-formed heads in the world,"[1] the face rather plain-featured, with a large unshapely mouth, but the whole redeemed by a bright smile which played naturally over the lips, and under a broad and smooth forehead, sheltered by thick eyebrows, "clear, brilliant, penetrating eyes"[2] of dark brown, with what Southey called a pendulous motion, lighting up quickly with bright merriment or kindling into fire in a moment of indignation. Mr. George Richmond, who twice painted it, described it as one of the most remarkable faces he had ever seen *for one who had eyes to see.* His first portrait, taken in 1843, when Keble was a little over fifty, is a three-quarter length water-colour, and gives very effectively the almost boyish sprightliness of

[1] T. Mozley, *Reminiscences,* ii., p. 58.
[2] Dr. Pusey, Sermon at the opening of Keble College, p. 32.

his figure, and the bright hopefulness of tone. It was
engraved by Cousins, who went to Hursley for the
purpose, and improved upon the original portrait. The
second portrait was a crayon drawing of the head, taken
not long before his death and engraved by the painter
himself. From it was enlarged the oil painting which
hangs in the hall of Keble College ; in this the hair is too
long and the whole is slightly idealized, but under the
mellowness of years is seen still the eager fire of the
eye and the sweet playful tender merriment of the
winning smile.

———————

"Comfort have thou of thy merit,
 Kindly unassuming Spirit,
 Careless of thy neighbourhood
 Thou dost show thy pleasant face
 On the moor and in the wood,
 In the land,—there's not a place,
 Howsoever mean it be,
 But 'tis good enough for thee."—WORDSWORTH.

APPENDIX I.

THE POEMS OF *THE CHRISTIAN YEAR*, ARRANGED IN THE ORDER OF COMPOSITION.

1819 or earlier	...	...	The Purification.
[„	„	...	First Sunday after Easter. Printed in *Miscellaneous Poems*.]
„	„	...	Whit-Sunday.
„	„	...	Nineteenth Sunday after Trinity.
1819	... ...	...	St. John's Day.
„	... ...	...	Septuagesima Sunday.
„	... ..	...	Tenth Sunday after Trinity.
1820	... ...	...	St. Mark's Day.
„	(Aug. 20)	...	Fourth Sunday after Trinity.
„	(Nov. 25)	...	The Evening Hymn.
„	... ...	...	St. Matthias' Day.
„	... ...	...	Palm Sunday.
1821	(Aug. 13)	...	Wednesday before Easter (The Lullaby).
„	... ...	...	Fourth Sunday after Easter.
„	... ...	...	Dedication.
„	... ...	...	Fifth Sunday after Trinity.
„	... ...	...	St. Bartholomew's Day.
„	... ...	...	St. Michael and all Angels.
„	(Sept. 16)	...	Thirteenth Sunday after Trinity.
„	... ...	...	Fourteenth Sunday after Trinity.
„	... ...	...	Second Sunday after Epiphany.
1822	(Jan. 27)	...	St. Andrew's Day.
„	(March 2)	...	The Conversion of St. Paul.
„	(April 6)	...	St. Luke's Day.
„	(April 18)	...	Easter Day.
„	(Aug. 7)	...	Second Sunday after Trinity.
„	(Aug. 13)	...	Ninth Sunday after Trinity.
„	(Aug. 23)	...	Twelfth Sunday after Trinity.
„	(Sept. 14)	...	St. Matthew's Day.
„	(Sept. 20)	...	The Morning Hymn.
„	(Sept. 27)	...	Sixteenth Sunday after Trinity.

1822 (Oct. 11) ... Seventeenth Sunday after Trinity.
[„ ... ... Third Sunday in Lent. An original draft,
                               much altered afterwards.]
  „ ... ... Fourth Sunday in Advent.
1823 [(June 1) ... The Annunciation. Printed in *Miscel-*
                               laneous Poems.]
  „ (June 5) ... Thursday before Easter.
  „ (July 15) ... Twenty-fifth Sunday after Trinity.
  „ (Sept. 25) ... Twenty-first Sunday after Trinity.
  „ (Sept. 28) ... Eleventh Sunday after Trinity.
  „ (Oct. 6) ... Eighteenth Sunday after Trinity.
  „ (Oct. 7) ... St. James' Day.
  „ (Oct. 7) ... Twentieth Sunday after Trinity.
  „ (Dec. 26) ... Advent Sunday.
1824 (Jan. 5) ... The Holy Innocents.
  „ (Jan. 20) ... The Circumcision of Christ.
  „ (Jan. 20) ... The Epiphany.
  „ (Jan. 20) ... Second Sunday in Advent.
  „ (Jan. 26) ... Third Sunday in Advent.
  „ (Feb. 9) ... St. Thomas' Day.
  „ (Feb. 18) ... Sexagesima Sunday.
  „ (March 6) ... Quinquagesima Sunday.
  „ (?) ... ... Second Sunday in Lent.
  „ (March 9) ... First Sunday in Lent.
  „ (April 24) ... Fifth Sunday in Lent.
  „ (May 17) ... First Sunday after Epiphany.
  „ (May 18) ... Fourth Sunday in Lent.
  „ (June 3) ... Fifth Sunday after Easter.
  „ (June 25) ... Sunday after Ascension Day.
  „ (?) ... ... Sixth Sunday after Epiphany.
  „ (?) ... ... Third Sunday after Epiphany.
  „ (?) ... ... St. Stephen's Day.
  „ (?) ... ... Christmas Day.
  „ (?) ... ... Easter Eve.
  „ (?) ... ... Tuesday before Easter. Printed as Six-
                               teenth Sunday after Trinity.
1825 (?) ... ... Tuesday in Whitsun Week.
  „ (May 15) ... St. Peter's Day.
  „ (June 7) ... Twenty-fourth Sunday after Trinity.
  „ (June 18) ... Ascension Day.
  „ (June 25) ... First Sunday after Easter.
  „ (July 4) ... St. Barnabas' Day.
  „ (July 14) ... Sunday before Advent.
  „ (Aug. 3) ... St. Philip and St. James' Day.
  „ (Aug. 15) ... First Sunday after Christmas.
  „ (Oct. 23) ... All Saints' Day.

1825	(Nov. 4)	...	Seventh Sunday after Trinity.
,,	(Nov. 12)	...	Twenty-third Sunday after Trinity.
,,	(Nov. 29)	...	Second Sunday after Christmas.
,,	(Dec. 19)	...	Fourth Sunday after Epiphany.
1826	(Jan. 15)	...	Monday before Easter.
,,	(Jan. 22)	...	Ash Wednesday.
,,	(Jan. 27)	...	First Sunday after Trinity.
,,	(Feb. 3)	...	Fifteenth Sunday after Trinity.
,,	(Feb. 7)	...	Twenty-second Sunday after Trinity.
,,	(Feb. 12)	...	Monday in Easter Week.
,,	(April 3)	...	St. Simon and St. Jude's Day.
,,	(April 7)	...	Third Sunday after Trinity.
,,	(April 11)	...	St. John Baptist's Day.
,,	(April 13)	...	[Eighth Sunday after Trinity. Printed as on Holy Baptism, composed on the baptism of his brother's eldest child.]
,,	(April 15)	...	Sixth Sunday after Trinity.
,,	(May 9)	...	Fifth Sunday after Epiphany.
,,	(?)		Good Friday.
,,	(?)		Tuesday in Easter Week.
,,	(?)		Third Sunday after Easter.
1827	(Jan. 31)	...	Holy Communion.
,,	(Feb. 9)	...	Third Sunday in Lent.
,,	(Feb. 16)	...	Catechism.
,,	(Feb. 21)	...	Confirmation.
,,	(?)		Communion after Matrimony.
,,	(?)		Visitation and Communion of the Sick.
[,,	(March 5)	...	Burial of the Dead. Published in *Miscellaneous Poems.*]
,,	(?)		Eighth Sunday after Trinity.
,,	(March 9)	...	Commination.
,,	(March 13)	...	Churching of Women.
,,	(March 17)	...	Tuesday before Easter.
,,	... ...		King Charles the Martyr.
,,	(Nov. 11)	...	Gunpowder Treason (address to converts from popery).
,,	(?)		Form of prayer to be used at sea.
,,	(?)		The Accession.
,,	(?)		Restoration of Royal Family.
1828	(March 28)	...	Ordination.

The following poems are not in the MS. books, from which these dates are taken.

(1) Second Sunday after Easter.
(2) Monday in Whitsun Week.
(3) Trinity Sunday.

APPENDIX II.

PUBLISHED WRITINGS.

1812. On Translation from Dead Languages. A Prize Essay, recited in the theatre at Oxford, June 10, 1812.

1827. The Christian Year (Anon.), 2 vols. [2nd Edition, 1827 ; 3rd Edition, 1828.]

1829. Six Queries by John Keble, tending to oppose Mr. Peel's candidature to represent the University of Oxford. Feb. 16, 1829, 4to.

1833. National Apostasy, considered in a sermon preached in St. Mary's, Oxford, before Her Majesty's Judges of Assize on July 14. [Oxford : J. H. Parker.]

1834. Ode for the Encænia at Oxford in honour of His Grace, Arthur, Duke of Wellington, Chancellor of the University of Oxford. [Printed in Oxford Prize Poems, 1839.]

Poems in Lyra Apostolica.

Tracts for the Times : Nos. 4, 13, 40, 52, 54, 57, 60.

Sunday Lessons, the Principle of Selection. No. XIII. of the Tracts for the Times. Reprinted in 1867. [Oxford and London : J. Parker and Co.]

1836. The Works of R. Hooker. A new edition, with additions, preface, fac-similes, indexes, arranged by Rev. J. Keble, 3 vols. [2nd Edition, 1841 ; 3rd Edition, 1845 ; 7th Edition, revised by Church and Paget, 1888.]

1836. Primitive Tradition recognized in Holy Scripture, a Visitation Sermon at Winchester. [2nd Edition, 1837 ; 3rd Edition, with postscript, to which is subjoined Catena Patrum, III. = Tract No. 78.]

1838. Remains of R. H. Froude, 2 vols. 8vo.

1839.   ,,   ,,   ,,   2nd Part, 2 vols., 8vo.

1839. The Psalter or Psalms of David in English Verse. (Anon.) [3rd Edition 1840.]

1839. The State in its Relation with the Church. British Critic, October. [Reprinted with a Preface by H. P. Liddon. Oxford and London : J. H. Parker, 1869.]

1841. On the Mysticism attributed to the Early Fathers of the Church. No. 89 of the Tracts for the Times. [Reprinted in 1868. Oxford and London : J. Parker and Co.]

1841. The Case of Catholic Subscription to the XXXIX. Articles considered in a letter to the Hon. Mr. Justice Coleridge. London. Privately printed. [Published in 1865.]

1841. The Child's Christian Year : Hymns for every Sunday and Holy-day. [Edited by J. K.]

1842. Protest against the Bishop of Winchester's Refusal to Ordain the Rev. P. Young. [Lithographed.]

1844. De Poeticæ vi Medica. Prælectiones Academicæ. 2 vols.

1845. Sermon on Psalm cxix. 164. In a volume of Sermons preached at Jedburgh.

1845. Jan. 16. Heads of Consideration on the Case of Mr. Ward. 12mo.

1845. Three Sermons [4-6] in Sermons preached at St. Saviour's, Leeds.

1845. Mutual Intercession : with Preface signed J. K., E. B. P., C. M. 16mo.

1846. The Duty of Hoping against Hope. A Sermon preached in the Chapel of Harrow Weald. [Privately printed.]

1846. Lyra Innocentium : Thoughts in Verse on Christian Children ; their ways and their privileges. [Anon.]

1847. Sermons Academical and Occasional. [2nd Edition, 1848.]

1849. The Strength of Christ's Little Ones. A Sermon preached at Coggeshall for the School. [Colchester, 1849.]

1849. Against Profane Dealing with Holy Matrimony in regard of a Man and his Wife's Sister. A Tract for English Churchmen and Churchwomen. [Oxford.]

1850. Church Matters in MDCCCL. I. Trial of Doctrine. II. A Call to Speak Out. [Reprinted with Preface by H. P. Liddon, 1877. Oxford and London : J. H. Parker.]

1850. The Danger of Passing by Christ. In Sermons preached at St. Barnabas', Pimlico. [London.]

1851. A Pastoral Letter to the Parishioners of Hursley ; occasioned by the Proposed Synodical Meeting in the Diocese of Exeter. Reprinted with Preface by H. P. Liddon, 1877. [1st and 2nd Editions. Oxford and London : J. H. Parker.]

1852. On the Representation of the University of Oxford. A Letter to Sir B. W. Bridges, Bart., M.P. [London: J. H. Parker.]

1853. Putting on Christ. In Sermons preached at St. Bartholomew's, Cripplegate, in 1852. [London: 1853.]

1854. A Few Very Plain Thoughts on the Proposed Admission of Dissenters to the University of Oxford. [Oxford: A. A. Masson.]

1857. (1) An Argument against immediately Repealing the Laws which treat the Nuptial Bond as Indissoluble. [Oxford: J. H. and J. Parker.]

1857. (2) Sequel to the Argument against immediately Repealing the Laws which treat the Nuptial Bond, etc.

1857. (?) Easter Joy and Easter Work. A Sermon preached on the Day of Thanksgiving for the Suppression of the Rebellion in India. [London: J. T. Hayes.]

1857. On Eucharistical Adoration. [Oxford and London: J. H. and J. Parker. 2nd Edition, 1859.]

1858. Considerations suggested by a Late Pastoral Letter on the Doctrine of the Most Holy Eucharist. [Edinburgh: R. Lendrum and Co. Oxford and London: J. H. and J. Parker.]

1858. A Sermon preached at St. Paul's Church, Brighton, on St. Luke's Day, 1858. [Brighton: A. Hawkins and Co.]

1858. The Rich and the Poor One in Christ. A Sermon preached in St. Peter's Church, Sudbury, August 3, 1858. [London: J. T. Hayes.]

1863. Women Labouring in the Lord. A Sermon preached at Wantage, July 22, 1863. [Oxford and London: J. H. and J. Parker.]

1863. Life and Works of T. Wilson, D.D. [Library of Anglo-Catholic Theology.] Oxford.

1864. Litany of Our Lord's Warnings, in larger or smaller forms: the larger with a Preface on the Privy Council decision about Everlasting Punishment. [Oxford and London.]

1864. Pentecostal Fear. A Sermon preached in the Parish Church of Cuddesdon, on May 24. [Oxford and London: J. H. and J. Parker.]

1866. A Letter to a Member of Convocation. Lit. Churchman, Jan. 13. [Reprinted June 1867. Oxford and London: J. Parker and Co.]

1866. Tracts and Extracts. No. 1. The Rev. J. Keble and the Ritual Question. An extract from his recent letter on that subject.

1868. Sermons Occasional and Parochial. [Oxford.]
1869. Village Sermons on the Baptismal Service. [Oxford.]
1869. Miscellaneous Poems. Edited by G. Moberley, D.D.
1870. Letters of Spiritual Counsel. With Preface by R. F. Wilson. [3rd, and fuller Edition, 1875.]
1875—1880. Sermons for the Christian Year. 11 vols.
1877. Occasional Papers and Reviews. With Preface by E. B. Pusey, D.D.
1877. Studia Sacra. [Commentary on St. John, i. 1-18 ; on Romans i.-vi. ; Note on the Procession of the Holy Spirit ; Analysis of St. Paul's Epistles ; Notes on Greek Testament.] Ed. J. P. N(orris).
1880. Outlines of Instructions or Meditations for the Church's Seasons. With Preface by R. F. Wilson.
1885. Sermons on the Litany, the Church, the Communion of Saints. Reprinted from Sermons for the Christian Year, with Preface by E. B. Pusey.

THE END.

A LIST OF NEW BOOKS AND ANNOUNCEMENTS OF METHUEN AND COMPANY PUBLISHERS : LONDON 18 BURY STREET W.C.

CONTENTS

OCTOBER 1892

MESSRS. METHUEN'S
AUTUMN ANNOUNCEMENTS

------◆------

GENERAL LITERATURE

Rudyard Kipling. BARRACK-ROOM BALLADS; And Other Verses. By RUDYARD KIPLING. *Extra Post 8vo, pp. 208. Laid paper, rough edges, buckram, gilt top.* 6s.

A special Presentation Edition, *bound in white buckram, with extra gilt ornament.* 7s. 6d.

The First Edition was sold on publication, and two further large Editions have been exhausted. The Fourth Edition is Now Ready.

Gladstone. THE SPEECHES AND PUBLIC ADDRESSES OF THE RT. HON. W. E. GLADSTONE, M.P. With Notes. Edited by A. W. HUTTON, M.A. (Librarian of the Gladstone Library), and H. J. COHEN, M.A. With Portraits. *8vo. Vol. IX.* 12s. 6d.

Messrs. METHUEN beg to announce that they are about to issue, in ten volumes 8vo, an authorised collection of Mr. Gladstone's Speeches, the work being undertaken with his sanction and under his superintendence. Notes and Introductions will be added.

In view of the interest in the Home Rule Question, it is proposed to issue Vols. IX. and X., which will include the speeches of the last seven or eight years, immediately, and then to proceed with the earlier volumes. Volume X. is already published.

Collingwood. JOHN RUSKIN: His Life and Work. By W. G. COLLINGWOOD, M.A., late Scholar of University College, Oxford, Author of the 'Art Teaching of John Ruskin,' Editor of Mr. Ruskin's Poems. *2 vols. 8vo.* 32s.

Also a limited edition on hand-made paper, with the Illustrations on India paper. £3, 3s. *net.*

Also a small edition on Japanese paper. £5, 5s. *net.*

This important work is written by Mr. Collingwood, who has been for some years Mr. Ruskin's private secretary, and who has had unique advantages in obtaining materials for this book from Mr. Ruskin himself and from his friends. It will contain a large amount of new matter, and of letters which have never been published, and will be, in fact, as near as is possible at present, a full and authoritative biography of Mr. Ruskin. The book will contain numerous portraits of Mr. Ruskin, including a coloured one from a water-colour portait by himself, and also 13 sketches, never before published, by Mr. Ruskin and Mr. Arthur Severn. A bibliography will be added.

Baring Gould. THE TRAGEDY OF THE CAESARS: The Emperors of the Julian and Claudian Lines. With numerous Illustrations from Busts, Gems, Cameos, etc. By S. BARING GOULD, Author of 'Mehalah,' etc. 2 *vols.* *Royal 8vo.* 30s.

This book is the only one in English which deals with the personal history of the Caesars, and Mr. Baring Gould has found a subject which, for picturesque detail and sombre interest, is not rivalled by any work of fiction. The volumes are copiously illustrated.

Baring Gould. SURVIVALS AND SUPERSTITIONS. With Illustrations. By S. BARING GOULD. *Crown 8vo.* 7s. 6d.

A book on such subjects as Foundations, Gables, Holes, Gallows, Raising the Hat, Old Ballads, etc. etc. It traces in a most interesting manner their origin and history.

Perrens. THE HISTORY OF FLORENCE FROM THE TIME OF THE MEDICIS TO THE FALL OF THE REPUBLIC. By F. T. PERRENS. Translated by HANNAH LYNCH. In three volumes. Vol. I. *8vo.* 12s. 6d.

This is a translation from the French of the best history of Florence in existence. This volume covers a period of profound interest—political and literary—and is written with great vivacity.

Henley & Whibley. A BOOK OF ENGLISH PROSE.. Collected by W. E. HENLEY and CHARLES WHIBLEY. *Crown 8vo.* 6s.

Also small limited editions on Dutch and Japanese paper. 21s. and 42s.

A companion book to Mr. Henley's well-known *Lyra Heroica*.

"Q." GREEN BAYS: A Book of Verses. By "Q.," Author of 'Dead Man's Rock' &c. *Fcap. 8vo.* 3s. 6d.

Also a limited edition on large Dutch paper.

A small volume of Oxford Verses by the well-known author of 'I Saw Three Ships, etc.

Wells. OXFORD AND OXFORD LIFE. By Members of the University. Edited by J. WELLS, M.A., Fellow and Tutor of Wadham College. *Crown 8vo.* 3s. 6d.

This work will be of great interest and value to all who are in any way connected with the University. It will contain an account of life at Oxford—intellectual, social, and religious—a careful estimate of necessary expenses, a review of recent changes, a statement of the present position of the University, and chapters on Women's Education, aids to study, and University Extension.

Driver. SERMONS ON SUBJECTS CONNECTED WITH THE OLD TESTAMENT. By S. R. DRIVER, D.D., Canon of Christ Church, Regius Professor of Hebrew in the University of Oxford. *Crown 8vo.* 6s.

An important volume of sermons on Old Testament Criticism preached before the University by the author of 'An Introduction to the Literature of the Old Testament.'

Prior. CAMBRIDGE SERMONS. Edited by C. H. PRIOR, M.A., Fellow and Tutor of Pembroke College. *Crown 8vo.* 6s.

A volume of sermons preached before the University of Cambridge by various preachers, including the Archbishop of Canterbury and Bishop Westcott.

Kaufmann. CHARLES KINGSLEY. By M. KAUFMANN, M.A. *Crown 8vo.* 5s.

A biography of Kingsley, especially dealing with his achievements in social reform.

Lock. THE LIFE OF JOHN KEBLE. By WALTER LOCK, M.A., Fellow of Magdalen College, Oxford. With Portrait. *Crown 8vo.* 5s.

Hutton. CARDINAL MANNING : A Biography. By A. W. HUTTON, M.A. With Portrait. *New and Cheaper Edition. Crown 8vo.* 2s. 6d.

Sells. THE MECHANICS OF DAILY LIFE. By V. P. SELLS, M.A. Illustrated. *Crown 8vo.* 2s. 6d.

Kimmins. THE CHEMISTRY OF LIFE AND HEALTH. By C. W. KIMMINS, Downing College, Cambridge. Illustrated. *Crown 8vo.* 2s. 6d.

Potter. AGRICULTURAL BOTANY. By M. C. POTTER, Lecturer at Newcastle College of Science. Illustrated. *Crown 8vo.* 2s. 6d.

The above are new volumes of the "University Extension Series."

Cox. LAND NATIONALISATION. By HAROLD COX, M.A. *Crown 8vo.* 2s. 6d.

Hadfield & Gibbins. A SHORTER WORKING DAY. By R. A. HADFIELD and H. de B. GIBBINS, M.A. *Crown 8vo.* 2s. 6d.

The above are new volumes of "Social Questions of To-day" Series.

FICTION.

Norris. HIS GRACE. By W. E. NORRIS, Author of 'Mdle. de Mersac,' 'Marcia,' etc. *Crown 8vo.* 2 vols. 21s.

Pryce. TIME AND THE WOMAN. By RICHARD PRYCE, Author of 'Miss Maxwell's Affections,' 'The Quiet Mrs. Fleming,' etc. *Crown 8vo.* 2 vols. 21s.

Parker. PIERRE AND HIS PEOPLE. By GILBERT PARKER. *Crown 8vo. Buckram.* 6s.

Marriott Watson. DIOGENES OF LONDON and other Sketches. By H. B. MARRIOTT WATSON, Author of 'The Web of the Spider.' *Crown 8vo. Buckram.* 6s.

Baring Gould. IN THE ROAR OF THE SEA. By S. BARING GOULD, Author of 'Mehalah,' 'Urith,' etc. Cheaper edition. *Crown 8vo.* 6s.

Clark Russell. MY DANISH SWEETHEART. By W. CLARK RUSSELL, Author of 'The Wreck of the Grosvenor,' 'A Marriage at Sea,' etc. With 6 Illustrations by W. H. OVEREND. *Crown 8vo.* 6s.

Mabel Robinson. HOVENDEN, V. C. By F. MABEL ROBINSON, Author of 'Disenchantment,' etc. Cheaper Edition. *Crown 8vo.* 3s. 6d.

Meade. OUT OF THE FASHION. By L. T. MEADE, Author of 'A Girl of the People,' etc. With 6 Illustrations by W. PAGET. *Crown 8vo.* 6s.

Cuthell. ONLY A GUARDROOM DOG. By Mrs. CUTHELL. With 16 Illustrations by W. PARKINSON. *Square Crown 8vo.* 6s.

Collingwood. THE DOCTOR OF THE JULIET. By HARRY COLLINGWOOD, Author of 'The Pirate Island,' etc. Illustrated by GORDON BROWNE. *Crown 8vo.* 6s.

Bliss. A MODERN ROMANCE. By LAURENCE BLISS. *Crown 8vo. Buckram.* 3s. 6d. *Paper.* 2s. 6d.

CHEAPER EDITIONS.

Baring Gould. OLD COUNTRY LIFE. By S. BARING GOULD, Author of 'Mehalah,' etc. With 67 Illustrations. *Crown 8vo.* 6s.

Clark. THE COLLEGES OF OXFORD. Edited by A. CLARK, M.A., Fellow and Tutor of Lincoln College. *8vo.* 12s. 6d.

Russell. THE LIFE OF ADMIRAL LORD COLLINGWOOD. By W. CLARK RUSSELL, Author of 'The Wreck of the Grosvenor.' With Illustrations by F. BRANGWYN. *8vo.* 10s. 6d.

Author of 'Mdle. Mori.' THE SECRET OF MADAME DE Monluc. By the Author of 'The Atelier du Lys,' 'Mdle. Mori.' *Crown 8vo.* 3s. 6d.

'An exquisite literary cameo.'—*World.*

New and Recent Books.

Poetry

Rudyard Kipling. BARRACK-ROOM BALLADS; And Other Verses. By RUDYARD KIPLING. *Fourth Edition. Crown 8vo. 6s.*

'Mr. Kipling's verse is strong, vivid, full of character. . . . Unmistakable genius rings in every line.'—*Times.*

'The disreputable lingo of Cockayne is henceforth justified before the world; for a man of genius has taken it in hand, and has shown, beyond all cavilling, that in its way it also is a medium for literature. You are grateful, and you say to yourself, half in envy and half in admiration: " Here is a *book*; here, or one is a Dutchman, is one of the books of the year."'—*National Observer.*

'"Barrack-Room Ballads" contains some of the best work that Mr. Kipling has ever done, which is saying a good deal. "Fuzzy-Wuzzy," "Gunga Din," and "Tommy," are, in our opinion, altogether superior to anything of the kind that English literature has hitherto produced.'—*Athenæum.*

'These ballads are as wonderful in their descriptive power as they are vigorous in their dramatic force. There are few ballads in the English language more stirring than "The Ballad of East and West," worthy to stand by the Border ballads of Scott.'—*Spectator.*

'The ballads teem with imagination, they palpitate with emotion. We read them with laughter and tears; the metres throb in our pulses, the cunningly ordered words tingle with life; and if this be not poetry, what is?'—*Pall Mall Gazette.*

Ibsen. BRAND. A Drama by HENRIK IBSEN. Translated by WILLIAM WILSON. *Crown 8vo. 5s.*

'The greatest world-poem of the nineteenth century next to "Faust." "Brand" will have an astonishing interest for Englishmen. It is in the same set with "Agamemnon," with " Lear," with the literature that we now instinctively regard as high and holy.'—*Daily Chronicle.*

Henley. LYRA HEROICA: An Anthology selected from the best English Verse of the 16th, 17th, 18th, and 19th Centuries. By WILLIAM ERNEST HENLEY, Author of 'A Book of Verse,' 'Views and Reviews,' etc. *Crown 8vo. Stamped gilt buckram, gilt top, edges uncut. 6s.*

'Mr. Henley has brought to the task of selection an instinct alike for poetry and for chivalry which seems to us quite wonderfully, and even unerringly, right.'—*Guardian.*

Tomson. A SUMMER NIGHT, AND OTHER POEMS. By GRAHAM R. TOMSON. With Frontispiece by A. TOMSON. *Fcap. 8vo. 3s. 6d.*

Also an edition on handmade paper, limited to 50 copies. *Large crown 8vo. 10s. 6d. net.*

'Mrs. Tomson holds perhaps the very highest rank among poetesses of English birth. This selection will help her reputation.'—*Black and White.*

Langbridge. A CRACKED FIDDLE. Being Selections from the Poems of FREDERIC LANGBRIDGE. With Portrait. *Crown 8vo. 5s.*

Langbridge. BALLADS OF THE BRAVE: Poems of Chivalry, Enterprise, Courage, and Constancy, from the Earliest Times to the Present Day. Edited, with Notes, by Rev. F. LANGBRIDGE. *Crown 8vo.*

Presentation Edition, 3s. 6d. School Edition, 2s. 6d.

'A very happy conception happily carried out. These "Ballads of the Brave" are intended to suit the real tastes of boys, and will suit the taste of the great majority. —*Spectator.* 'The book is full of splendid things.'—*World.*

History and Biography

Gladstone. THE SPEECHES AND PUBLIC ADDRESSES OF THE RT. HON. W. E. GLADSTONE, M.P. With Notes and Introductions. Edited by A. W. HUTTON, M.A. (Librarian of the Gladstone Library), and H. J. COHEN, M.A. With Portraits. *8vo. Vol. X. 12s. 6d.*

Russell. THE LIFE OF ADMIRAL LORD COLLING-WOOD. By W. CLARK RUSSELL, Author of 'The Wreck of the Grosvenor.' With Illustrations by F. BRANGWYN. *8vo. 10s. 6d.*

'A really good book.'—*Saturday Review.*
'A most excellent and wholesome book, which we should like to see in the hands of every boy in the country.'—*St. James's Gazette.*

Clark. THE COLLEGES OF OXFORD: Their History and their Traditions. By Members of the University. Edited by A. CLARK, M.A., Fellow and Tutor of Lincoln College. *8vo. 12s. 6d.*

'Whether the reader approaches the book as a patriotic member of a college, as an antiquary, or as a student of the organic growth of college foundation, it will amply reward his attention.'—*Times.*
'A delightful book, learned and lively.'—*Academy.*
'A work which will certainly be appealed to for many years as the standard book on the Colleges of Oxford.'—*Athenæum.*

Hulton. RIXAE OXONIENSES: An Account of the Battles of the Nations, The Struggle between Town and Gown, etc. By S. F. HULTON, M.A. *Crown 8vo. 5s.*

James. CURIOSITIES OF CHRISTIAN HISTORY PRIOR TO THE REFORMATION. By CROAKE JAMES, Author of 'Curiosities of Law and Lawyers.' *Crown 8vo. 7s. 6d.*

Clifford. THE DESCENT OF CHARLOTTE COMPTON (BARONESS FERRERS DE CHARTLEY). By her Great-Granddaughter, ISABELLA G. C. CLIFFORD. *Small 4to.* 10s. 6d. *net.*

General Literature

Bowden. THE IMITATION OF BUDDHA : Being Quotations from Buddhist Literature for each Day in the Year. Compiled by E. M. BOWDEN. With Preface by Sir EDWIN ARNOLD. *Second Edition.* 16mo. 2s. 6d.

Ditchfield. OUR ENGLISH VILLAGES : Their Story and their Antiquities. By P. H. DITCHFIELD, M.A., F.R.H.S., Rector of Barkham, Berks. *Post 8vo.* 2s. 6d. Illustrated.

'An extremely amusing and interesting little book, which should find a place in every parochial library.'—*Guardian.*

Ditchfield. OLD ENGLISH SPORTS. By P. H. DITCH-FIELD, M.A. *Crown 8vo.* 2s. 6d. Illustrated.

'A charming account of old English Sports.'—*Morning Post.*

Burne. PARSON AND PEASANT : Chapters of their Natural History. By J. B. BURNE, M.A., Rector of Wasing. *Crown 8vo.* 5s.

'"Parson and Peasant" is a book not only to be interested in, but to learn something from—a book which may prove a help to many a clergyman, and broaden the hearts and ripen the charity of laymen."'—*Derby Mercury.*

Massee. A MONOGRAPH OF THE MYXOGASTRES. By G. MASSEE. *8vo.* 18s. *net.*

Cunningham. THE PATH TOWARDS KNOWLEDGE : Essays on Questions of the Day. By W. CUNNINGHAM, D.D., Fellow of Trinity College, Cambridge, Professor of Economics at King's College, London. *Crown 8vo.* 4s. 6d.

Essays on Marriage and Population, Socialism, Money, Education, Positivism, etc.

Anderson Graham. NATURE IN BOOKS : Studies in Literary Biography. By P. ANDERSON GRAHAM. *Crown 8vo.* 6s.

The chapters are entitled : I. 'The Magic of the Fields' (Jefferies). II. 'Art and Nature' (Tennyson). III. 'The Doctrine of Idleness' (Thoreau). IV. 'The Romance of Life' (Scott). V. 'The Poetry of Toil' (Burns). VI. 'The Divinity of Nature' (Wordsworth).

Works by S. Baring Gould.

Author of ' Mehalah,' etc.

OLD COUNTRY LIFE.   With Sixty-seven Illustrations by
W. PARKINSON, F. D. BEDFORD, and F. MASEY. *Large Crown
8vo, cloth super extra, top edge gilt, 10s. 6d. Fourth and Cheaper
Edition.   6s.*   *[Ready.*

' " Old Country Life," as healthy wholesome reading, full of breezy life and movement, full of quaint stories vigorously told, will not be excelled by any book
to be published throughout the year.   Sound, hearty, and English to the core.'—
World.

HISTORIC ODDITIES AND STRANGE EVENTS.   *Third
Edition, Crown 8vo.   6s.*

' A collection of exciting and entertaining chapters.   The whole volume is delightful
reading.'—*Times.*

FREAKS OF FANATICISM.   (First published as Historic
Oddities, Second Series.)   *Third Edition.   Crown 8vo.   6s.*

' Mr. Baring Gould has a keen eye for colour and effect, and the subjects he has
chosen give ample scope to his descriptive and analytic faculties.   A perfectly
fascinating book.—*Scottish Leader.*

SONGS OF THE WEST: Traditional Ballads and Songs of
the West of England, with their Traditional Melodies.   Collected
by S. BARING GOULD, M.A., and H. FLEETWOOD SHEPPARD,
M.A.   Arranged for Voice and Piano.   In 4 Parts (containing 25
Songs each), *Parts I., II., III., 3s. each.   Part IV., 5s.   In one
Vol., roan, 15s.*

' A rich and varied collection of humour, pathos, grace, and poetic fancy.'—*Saturday
Review.*

YORKSHIRE ODDITIES AND STRANGE EVENTS.
Fourth Edition.   Crown 8vo.   6s.

SURVIVALS AND SUPERSTITIONS. *Crown 8vo.* Illustrated.
                                           [In the press.

JACQUETTA, and other Stories. *Crown 8vo.   3s. 6d.   Boards, 2s.*

ARMINELL : A Social Romance.   *New Edition.   Crown 8vo.
3s. 6d.   Boards, 2s.*

' To say that a book is by the author of " Mehalah " is to imply that it contains a
story cast on strong lines, containing dramatic possibilities, vivid and sympathetic
descriptions of Nature, and a wealth of ingenious imagery.   All these expectations are justified by " Arminell." '—*Speaker.*

URITH : A Story of Dartmoor. *Third Edition. Crown 8vo.* 3s. 6d.
'The author is at his best.'—*Times.*
'He has nearly reached the high water-mark of " Mehalah." '—*National Observer.*

MARGERY OF QUETHER, and other Stories. *Crown 8vo.* 3s. 6d.

IN THE ROAR OF THE SEA : A Tale of the Cornish Coast. *New Edition.* 6s.

Fiction

Author of 'Indian Idylls.' IN TENT AND BUNGALOW : Stories of Indian Sport and Society. By the Author of 'Indian Idylls.' *Crown 8vo.* 3s. 6d.

Fenn. A DOUBLE KNOT. By G. MANVILLE FENN, Author of 'The Vicar's People,' etc. *Crown 8vo.* 3s. 6d.

Pryce. THE QUIET MRS. FLEMING. By RICHARD PRYCE, Author of 'Miss Maxwell's Affections,' etc. *Crown 8vo.* 3s. 6d. *Picture Boards,* 2s.

Gray. ELSA. A Novel. By E. M'QUEEN GRAY. *Crown 8vo.* 6s.
'A charming novel. The characters are not only powerful sketches, but minutely and carefully finished portraits.'—*Guardian.*

Gray. MY STEWARDSHIP. By E. M'QUEEN GRAY. *Crown 8vo.* 3s. 6d.

Cobban. A REVEREND GENTLEMAN. By J. MACLAREN COBBAN, Author of 'Master of his Fate,' etc. *Crown 8vo.* 4s. 6d.
'The best work Mr. Cobban has yet achieved. The Rev. W. Merrydew is a brilliant creation.'—*National Observer.*
'One of the subtlest studies of character outside Meredith.'—*Star.*

Lyall. DERRICK VAUGHAN, NOVELIST. By EDNA LYALL, Author of 'Donovan.' *Crown 8vo.* 31st *Thousand.* 3s. 6d. ; *paper,* 1s.

Linton. THE TRUE HISTORY OF JOSHUA DAVIDSON, Christian and Communist. By E. LYNN LINTON. Eleventh and Cheaper Edition. *Post 8vo.* 1s.

Grey. THE STORY OF CHRIS. By ROWLAND GREY, Author of 'Lindenblumen,' etc. *Crown 8vo.* 5s.

Dicker. A CAVALIER'S LADYE. By CONSTANCE DICKER. *With Illustrations. Crown 8vo.* 3s. 6d.

Dickinson. A VICAR'S 'WIFE. By EVELYN DICKINSON. *Crown 8vo.* 6s.

Prowse. THE POISON OF ASPS. By R. ORTON PROWSE. *Crown 8vo.* 6s.

Taylor. THE KING'S FAVOURITE. By UNA TAYLOR. *Crown 8vo.* 6s.

Novel Series

3/6

MESSRS. METHUEN will issue from time to time a Series of copyright Novels, by well-known Authors, handsomely bound, at the above popular price of three shillings and sixpence. The first volumes (ready) are :—

1. THE PLAN OF CAMPAIGN. By F. MABEL ROBINSON.

2. JACQUETTA. By S. BARING GOULD, Author of ' Mehalah,' etc.

3. MY LAND OF BEULAH. By Mrs. LEITH ADAMS (Mrs. De Courcy Laffan).

4. ELI'S CHILDREN. By G. MANVILLE FENN.

5. ARMINELL : A Social Romance. By S. BARING GOULD, Author of ' Mehalah,' etc.

6. DERRICK VAUGHAN, NOVELIST. With Portrait of Author. By EDNA LYALL, Author of ' Donovan,' etc.

7. DISENCHANTMENT. By F. MABEL ROBINSON.

8. DISARMED. By M. BETHAM EDWARDS.

9. JACK'S FATHER. By W. E. NORRIS.

10. MARGERY OF QUETHER. By S. BARING GOULD.

11. A LOST ILLUSION. By LESLIE KEITH.

12. A MARRIAGE AT SEA. By W. CLARK RUSSELL.

13. MR. BUTLER'S WARD. By F. MABEL ROBINSON.

14. URITH. By S. BARING GOULD.

15. HOVENDEN, V.C. By F. MABEL ROBINSON.

Other Volumes will be announced in due course.

NEW TWO-SHILLING EDITIONS
Crown 8vo, Ornamental Boards.   **2/-**

ARMINELL. By the Author of 'Mehalah.'

ELI'S CHILDREN. By G. MANVILLE FENN.

DISENCHANTMENT. By F. MABEL ROBINSON.

THE PLAN OF CAMPAIGN. By F. MABEL ROBINSON.

JACQUETTA. By the Author of 'Mehalah.'

Picture Boards.

A DOUBLE KNOT. By G. MANVILLE FENN.

THE QUIET MRS. FLEMING. By RICHARD PRYCE.

JACK'S FATHER. By W. E. NORRIS.

A LOST ILLUSION. By LESLIE KEITH.

Books for Boys and Girls

Walford. A PINCH OF EXPERIENCE. By L. B. WAL-
FORD, Author of 'Mr. Smith.' With Illustrations by GORDON
BROWNE. *Crown 8vo. 6s.*

'The clever authoress steers clear of namby-pamby, and invests her moral with a
fresh and striking dress. There is terseness and vivacity of style, and the illustrations are admirable.'—*Anti-Jacobin.*

Molesworth. THE RED GRANGE. By Mrs. MOLESWORTH,
Author of 'Carrots.' With Illustrations by GORDON BROWNE.
Crown 8vo. 6s.

'A volume in which girls will delight, and beautifully illustrated.'—*Pall Mall
Gazette.*

Clark Russell. MASTER ROCKAFELLAR'S VOYAGE. By
W. CLARK RUSSELL, Author of 'The Wreck of the Grosvenor,' etc.
Illustrated by GORDON BROWNE. *Crown 8vo. 3s. 6d.*

'Mr. Clark Russell's story of "Master Rockafellar's Voyage" will be among the
favourites of the Christmas books. There is a rattle and "go" all through it, and
its illustrations are charming in themselves, and very much above the average in
the way in which they are produced.—*Guardian.*

Author of 'Mdle. Mori.' THE SECRET OF MADAME DE
Monluc. By the Author of 'The Atelier du Lys,' 'Mdle. Mori.'
Crown 8vo. 3s. 6d.

'An exquisite literary cameo.'—*World.*

Manville Fenn. SYD BELTON : Or, The Boy who would not go to Sea. By G. MANVILLE FENN, Author of 'In the King's Name,' etc. Illustrated by GORDON BROWNE. *Crown 8vo.* 3*s.* 6*d.*
'Who among the young story-reading public will not rejoice at the sight of the old combination, so often proved admirable—a story by Manville Fenn, illustrated by Gordon Browne! The story, too, is one of the good old sort, full of life and vigour, breeziness and fun. —*Journal of Education.*

Parr. DUMPS. By Mrs. PARR, Author of 'Adam and Eve,' 'Dorothy Fox,' etc. Illustrated by W. PARKINSON. *Crown 8vo.* 3*s.* 6*d.*
'One of the prettiest stories which even this clever writer has given the world for a long time.'—*World.*

Meade. A GIRL OF THE PEOPLE. By L. T. MEADE, Author of 'Scamp and I,' etc. Illustrated by R. BARNES. *Crown 8vo.* 3*s.* 6*d.*
'An excellent story. Vivid portraiture of character, and broad and wholesome lessons about life.'—*Spectator.*
'One of Mrs. Meade's most fascinating books.'—*Daily News.*

Meade. HEPSY GIPSY. By L. T. MEADE. Illustrated by EVERARD HOPKINS. *Crown 8vo,* 2*s.* 6*d.*
'Mrs. Meade has not often done better work than this.'—*Spectator.*

Meade. THE HONOURABLE MISS : A Tale of a Country Town. By L. T. MEADE, Author of 'Scamp and I,' 'A Girl of the People,' etc. With Illustrations by EVERARD HOPKINS. *Crown 8vo,* 3*s.* 6*d.*

Adams. MY LAND OF BEULAH. By MRS. LEITH ADAMS. With a Frontispiece by GORDON BROWNE. *Crown 8vo,* 3*s.* 6*d.*

English Leaders of Religion

Edited by A. M. M. STEDMAN, M.A. *With Portrait, crown 8vo,* 2*s.* 6*d.*

A series of short biographies, free from party bias, of the most prominent leaders of religious life and thought in this and the last century.

2/6

The following are already arranged—

CARDINAL NEWMAN. By R. H. HUTTON. [*Ready.*
'Few who read this book will fail to be struck by the wonderful insight it displays into the nature of the Cardinal's genius and the spirit of his life.'—WILFRID WARD, in the *Tablet.*
'Full of knowledge, excellent in method, and intelligent in criticism. We regard it as wholly admirable.'—*Academy.*

JOHN WESLEY. By J. H. OVERTON, M.A. [*Ready.*

'It is well done : the story is clearly told, proportion is duly observed, and there is no lack either of discrimination or of sympathy.'—*Manchester Guardian.*

BISHOP WILBERFORCE. By G. W. DANIEL, M.A. [*Ready.*

CHARLES SIMEON. By H. C. G. MOULE, M.A. [*Ready.*

JOHN KEBLE. By W. LOCK, M.A. [*Nov.*

F. D. MAURICE. By COLONEL F. MAURICE, R.E.

THOMAS CHALMERS. By Mrs. OLIPHANT.

CARDINAL MANNING. By A. W. HUTTON, M.A. [*Ready.*

Other volumes will be announced in due course.

University Extension Series

A series of books on historical, literary, and scientific subjects, suitable for extension students and home reading circles. Each volume will be complete in itself, and the subjects will be treated by competent writers in a broad and philosophic spirit.

Edited by J. E. SYMES, M.A.,
Principal of University College, Nottingham.

Crown 8vo. 2s. 6d.

2|6

The following volumes are ready :—

THE INDUSTRIAL HISTORY OF ENGLAND. By H. DE B. GIBBINS, M.A., late Scholar of Wadham College, Oxon., Cobden Prizeman. *Second Edition.* With Maps and Plans. [*Ready.*

'A compact and clear story of our industrial development. A study of this concise but luminous book cannot fail to give the reader a clear insight into the principal phenomena of our industrial history. The editor and publishers are to be congratulated on this first volume of their venture, and we shall look with expectant interest for the succeeding volumes of the series.'—*University Extension Journal.*

A HISTORY OF ENGLISH POLITICAL ECONOMY. By L. L. PRICE, M.A., Fellow of Oriel College, Oxon.

PROBLEMS OF POVERTY : An Inquiry into the Industrial Conditions of the Poor. By J. A. HOBSON, M.A.

VICTORIAN POETS. By A. SHARP.

THE FRENCH REVOLUTION. By J. E. SYMES, M.A.

PSYCHOLOGY. By F. S. GRANGER, M.A., Lecturer in Philosophy at University College, Nottingham.

THE EVOLUTION OF PLANT LIFE : Lower Forms. By
G. MASSEE, Kew Gardens.   With Illustrations.

AIR AND WATER. Professor V. B. LEWES, M.A. Illustrated.

THE CHEMISTRY OF LIFE AND HEALTH. By C. W.
KIMMINS, M.A. Camb.   Illustrated.

THE MECHANICS OF DAILY LIFE. By V. P. SELLS, M.A.
Illustrated.

ENGLISH SOCIAL REFORMERS. H. DE B. GIBBINS, M.A.

ENGLISH TRADE AND FINANCE IN THE SEVEN-
TEENTH CENTURY. By W. A. S. HEWINS, B.A.

The following volumes are in preparation :—

NAPOLEON. By E. L. S. HORSBURGH, M.A. Camb., U. E.
Lecturer in History.

ENGLISH POLITICAL HISTORY. By T. J. LAWRENCE,
M.A., late Fellow and Tutor of Downing College, Cambridge, U. E.
Lecturer in History.

AN INTRODUCTION TO PHILOSOPHY. By J. SOLOMON,
M.A. Oxon., late Lecturer in Philosophy at University College,
Nottingham.

THE EARTH : An Introduction to Physiography. By E. W.
SMALL, M.A.

Social Questions of To-day

Edited by H. DE B. GIBBINS, M.A.

Crown 8vo, 2s. 6d.

2|6

A series of volumes upon those topics of social, economic,
and industrial interest that are at the present moment fore-
most in the public mind.   Each volume of the series will be written
by an author who is an acknowledged authority upon the subject
with which he deals.

The following Volumes of the Series are ready :—

TRADE UNIONISM—NEW AND OLD. By G. HOWELL,
M.P., Author of ' The Conflicts of Capital and Labour.

THE CO-OPERATIVE MOVEMENT. TO-DAY. By G. J HOLYOAKE, Author of ' The History of Co-operation.'

MUTUAL THRIFT. By Rev. J. FROME WILKINSON, M.A., Author of ' The Friendly Society Movement.'

PROBLEMS OF POVERTY : An Inquiry into the Industrial Conditions of the Poor. By J. A. HOBSON, M.A.

THE COMMERCE OF NATIONS. By C. F. BASTABLE, M.A., Professor of Economics at Trinity College, Dublin.

THE ALIEN INVASION. By W. H. WILKINS, B.A., Secretary to the Society for Preventing the Immigration of Destitute Aliens.

THE RURAL EXODUS. By P. ANDERSON GRAHAM.

LAND NATIONALIZATION. By HAROLD COX, B.A.

A SHORTER WORKING DAY. By H. DE B. GIBBINS (Editor), and R. A. HADFIELD, of the Hecla Works, Sheffield.

The following Volumes are in preparation :—

ENGLISH SOCIALISM OF TO-DAY. By HUBERT BLAND one of the Authors of ' Fabian Essays.'

POVERTY AND PAUPERISM. By Rev. L. R. PHELPS, M.A., Fellow of Oriel College, Oxford.

ENGLISH LAND AND ENGLISH MEN. By Rev. C. W. STUBBS, M.A., Author of ' The Labourers and the Land.'

CHRISTIAN SOCIALISM IN ENGLAND. By Rev. J CARTER, M.A., of Pusey House, Oxford.

THE EDUCATION OF THE PEOPLE. By J. R. DIGGLE, M.A., Chairman of the London School Board.

WOMEN'S WORK. By LADY DILKE, MISS BEILLEY, and MISS ABRAHAM.

RAILWAY PROBLEMS PRESENT AND FUTURE. By R. W. BARNETT, M.A., Editor of the ' Railway Times.'

www.ingramcontent.com/pod-product-compliance
Lightning Source LLC
Chambersburg PA
CBHW030635030726
47497CB00006B/1797